DAVID SCOTT

The Eden Initiative

An Isaac Northe Thriller

First published by David Scott Books 2023

Copyright © 2023 by David Scott

All rights reserved. No part of this publication may be reproduced, stored or transmitted in any form or by any means, electronic, mechanical, photocopying, recording, scanning, or otherwise without written permission from the publisher. It is illegal to copy this book, post it to a website, or distribute it by any other means without permission.

This novel is entirely a work of fiction. The names, characters and incidents portrayed in it are the work of the author's imagination. Any resemblance to actual persons, living or dead, events or localities is entirely coincidental.

David Scott asserts the moral right to be identified as the author of this work.

David Scott has no responsibility for the persistence or accuracy of URLs for external or third-party Internet Websites referred to in this publication and does not guarantee that any content on such Websites is, or will remain, accurate or appropriate.

Designations used by companies to distinguish their products are often claimed as trademarks. All brand names and product names used in this book and on its cover are trade names, service marks, trademarks and registered trademarks of their respective owners. The publishers and the book are not associated with any product or vendor mentioned in this book. None of the companies referenced within the book have endorsed the book.

First edition

*This book was professionally typeset on Reedsy.
Find out more at reedsy.com*

To all the professionals who work tirelessly to bring every soldier home.

"The world is a dangerous place to live; not because of the people who are evil, but because of the people who don't do anything about it."

- Albert Einstein

Contents

Acknowledgement		iii
Prologue		iv
1	Alexander	1
2	Marissa	7
3	Isaac	15
4	Jimmy	25
5	Marissa	34
6	Naomi	45
7	Alexander	52
8	Isaac	61
9	Naomi	68
10	Isaac	75
11	Jimmy	81
12	Naomi	86
13	Isaac	92
14	Marissa	99
15	Naomi	110
16	Isaac	115
17	Jimmy	126
18	Naomi	133
19	Isaac	142
20	Naomi	153
21	Marissa	160
22	Alexander	171
23	Isaac	177
24	Naomi	184

25 Marissa	191
26 Isaac	196
27 Jimmy	203
28 Isaac	210
29 Marissa	216
30 Isaac	226
31 Jimmy	231
32 Isaac	238
33 Isaac	251
Epilogue	258
About the Author	259
Also by David Scott	260

Acknowledgement

While it is my name on the cover of the book, there are so many incredible people who contributed to making this story possible. I am truly overwhelmed and forever grateful.

To my wife Jessica. Babe, you're amazing and make me sound like a much better writer than I actually am. Without you, most of the women in my stories would be walking around in conservative gray pantsuits. Everyone who reads and enjoys this book is indebted to you.

A very special thank you to Dr. Renee Jordan. No matter how crazy or off the wall my 'what if' questions were, you took the time to answer them, even if it meant asking one of your colleagues. Thank you for being my go-to medical expert.

To my editor Joanna Niederer your attention to detail and dedication to researching the correct way to write things is incredible. Thank you for your patience and for taking the time to explain the reason for edits instead of just marking through them with the red pen of death. You have been hugely instrumental in my development and progression as an author.

Finally, to all those who have been a part of my getting there: Dr. David Pinion, Alexander von Ness, Anthony Gates, Bodo Pfündl, and John Stamp

Prologue

Boko Haram Stronghold, Sambisa Forest, Nigeria

Marine Gunnery Sergeant Jimmy Taylor lay shackled in the corner of a mud-brick building. To say he had slept required a liberal definition of the word. He was exhausted beyond measure. It was more than mere sleep could cure. He was weary in his soul, as his mother would say. Jimmy was lucid enough to know he was suffering from chronic fatigue, on top of the myriad cuts and bruises he'd sustained from the near-daily abuse.

"How was your nap?" The raspy voice came from the dark corner across the room.

Pushing himself to a sitting position, Jimmy peered through the murky darkness until his eyes made out the shape of the room's other occupant.

The Lebanese CIA agent, Matt Hassan, sat with his back against the wall. Matt's beard, which had always been well-groomed, was turning ragged. Jimmy's facial hair had also grown longer than it ever had in his life. Even though having a beard was a status symbol in the special operations community, Jimmy preferred to remain clean-shaven.

"Could have been worse," he replied, his voice scratchy.

"Worse than being chained to a concrete floor?"

Jimmy shrugged.

The five-gallon bucket which served as their toilet sat between them. It wasn't emptied on a regular basis. Jimmy was confident the room stank to high heaven, but after what he guessed to be weeks or maybe months, he'd gone nose-blind to the smell. He had lost track of time and had no idea how long they'd been here. Not noticing the smell was a small mercy, but the swarms of flies that gathered around the bucket were harder to ignore.

"Looks like it's about time for dinner," Matt said.

While the room had no windows, they could see a little during the day by the light which peeked through the space below the door. The setting sun now caused the light to wane. Soon they'd be left in complete darkness. On the days when their captors fed them, the meager meals had come around sunset—almost always with a side of abuse. Usually punches and kicks, though one sadistic guy liked to put his cigarettes out on their arms and chests.

"We skipped yesterday, so yeah, probably getting fed today," Jimmy agreed.

"What do you think they'll give us?" Matt asked. The question had become part of their routine. They didn't need to guess since they'd only ever been fed rice, with the occasional vegetables or chunks of meat. Jimmy was sure he had never eaten whatever the meat was, and it didn't taste like chicken at all.

"I'd be ok with a steak, baked potato, and steamed broccoli."

"Covered with mushrooms and crispy onions," Matt added, smiling to himself.

Jimmy could feel his mouth starting to water. It wasn't just the idea of steak or any of the hundreds of other things they'd imagined eating. His mouth watered in anticipation of the food he hoped to get tonight; food he wouldn't have looked at before his capture.

Capture. He still couldn't wrap his head around how they'd been taken prisoner.

Their last mission, an attack on a weapons cache in northern Nigeria, had begun smoothly. The raid would have gone down as an unqualified success, with a single member wounded. But during the site exploitation, Mr. Murphy of Murphy's Law decided to visit them. Five gun trucks loaded with Boko Haram fighters had shown up to crash the party.

Neither he nor Matt remembered bombs detonating or being dragged from the rubble and thrown into the back of a truck. As far as Jimmy recalled, one moment he'd been moving in to reinforce Matt's assault and the next he'd woken up hog-tied with a hood over his head. The rough fabric had smelled of vomit, and it had required every bit of self-control not to add to the smell. The ride had lasted for hours, their bodies bouncing and jostling against the rusted truck bed with every rut of the unpaved road.

Jimmy had spent the entire time hoping to hear the whir of helicopter blades that heralded an imminent rescue operation. For the first few days in this dank room, he'd had vivid dreams of being rescued, only to wake up and find himself still chained to the floor. Now he was starting to lose faith that he would live to see anything beyond these mud-brick walls.

"Here come the jackals," Matt muttered.

They heard what must have been a dozen men heading toward their prison. There was glee and bravado in the voices that transcended the language barrier. Matt's description was apt. They really did sound like wild dogs or jackals yipping as they moved in on their wounded prey.

The door to their cell swung open and ten dirty men dressed in a mixed assortment of camouflage uniforms piled into the room. Jimmy and Matt had just enough time to raise their arms to try and defend their heads before feet and fists rained down. It had been a while since the last mob beating, and Jimmy gritted his teeth as pain flashed across his body. He was close to passing out when a pistol cracked twice just outside the door, and the violence stopped as abruptly as it had begun.

A tall, wiry man with ebony skin and cold eyes entered. The press of men backed against the wall like mice confronted by a snake. Jimmy had not encountered this man before, but he reminded him of a black mamba he'd seen once at the zoo. When Jimmy stepped in front of its case, the deadly reptile had turned its head to look at him before raising itself to eye level. It had remained there a few moments before lowering itself back into a coil.

Jimmy had no way of knowing this was the Boko Haram leader. Still, he sensed instinctively this man was dangerous and everyone needed to tread carefully.

"You think you are big men? Very tough beating two chained prisoners who can't fight back," Black Mamba said. His voice was calm, but violence lurked just below the surface, like an alligator waiting for its prey to take one more step. Fear oozed from Jimmy and Matt's tormentors, but they remained silent.

"I told you to go get them and bring them to me," he continued.

One of the men to Jimmy's right muttered in a language he didn't recognize. Black Mamba's head snapped toward the man who had spoken. Those on either side of him moved away, trying to distance themselves from that glare. The leader raised his pistol, an old Russian Makarov, and fired a single shot into the man's chest.

"Move the Americans," he snapped, holstering his weapon and gesturing out the door.

The remaining men hurried to comply. As they removed his shackles, Jimmy saw the fallen man coughing up bright red, frothy blood onto the floor. He recognized it immediately. Blood in the lungs. The shot hadn't killed him straight away, but it would still be fatal.

The guards hustled Jimmy and Matt from their cell into a cluster of bunkers and bombed-out buildings. Fear drove them, and they didn't bother to blindfold the prisoners. Jimmy knew Matt would also be using this brief opportunity to scan their surroundings for any scrap of information they could glean. From the look of the landscape, both men guessed they were in the Sambisa Forest, the main stronghold of the terror group. Jimmy took the last moments of fresh air to turn his face upward, looking straight into the darkening sky. Maybe there was a satellite somewhere above them snapping his picture this very second, and then facial recognition would notify someone of his whereabouts.

They were shoved into a bunker that clearly belonged to the leadership, but luxury was a sliding scale in these parts. Ok, you had a TV, a nice couch, and a desk, but you lived in a bunker in the center of a war-torn region. Jimmy and Matt were placed on a pair of wooden chairs doubtless stolen from the local kindergarten, their hands cuffed tightly behind their backs.

One of their guards produced a camcorder, and Jimmy tensed, sure they were ready to record his execution. If they thought he'd just sit still while someone cut his head off, well, they had another think coming. He felt the tension in the air ease as Black Mamba set a copy of the Wall Street Journal on his lap. This video would serve as proof of life. There would be no execution today.

Jimmy suppressed a grin brought on by sudden relief, as well as a reflexive bout of gallows humor. At the sight of the newspaper, the sardonic face and dry tone of his buddy Isaac Northe popped into his head, cracking a joke about the Journal having an impressive distribution network to end up all the way out here.

The recording light from the camera blinked on, and Jimmy glowered into the lens, letting whoever watched the video know he wasn't broken.

From behind the camera the Boko Haram leader spoke, "What's your name?"

Jimmy spat a glob of blood. He was grateful not to have lost any teeth from the most recent blows to the face. Despite his discomfort, he did his best to inject as much steel as he could into his voice.

"My name is Gunnery Sergeant James Taylor, United States Marine Corps."

The process was repeated for Matt, who glared at the camcorder in silence, refusing to speak even when prompted.

Minutes later they were back in their cell, again chained to the floor, with bowls of food tossed in almost as an afterthought. The dead body was gone. However, the cleaning staff must have taken the day off because the blood stains on the concrete remained.

"You think the Agency is negotiating with these clowns to get us back?" Matt asked as Jimmy shoveled the cold rice from the bowl into his mouth with his fingers. The sun had set, so instead of a shrug, Jimmy grunted.

"Does that sound like something they'd do?" Jimmy asked when he'd finished the sparse meal.

"Maybe. I hope that's the case, anyway. We both know the official party line is zero negotiations with terrorists, but…"

"But if someone like Switzerland does it on behalf of the United States, then it's fine," Jimmy finished.

Matt grunted in agreement.

Jimmy settled himself back against the wall. "Someone has to know we're alive. We've gotta keep the faith until they come through for us."

'Keep the faith' was the mantra drilled into them during the SERE course. The Survival, Evasion, Resistance, and Escape school was the military's premier training ground for survival scenarios. Most of the attendees were those with a higher risk of separation and capture, such as Special Forces and aircrews. The survival course had been the best training Jimmy never wanted to repeat.

He didn't know when he fell asleep, but he startled awake to a series of explosions, followed by the thumping of several large caliber guns.

"Sounds like Apache cannons," Jimmy yelled to Matt.

The AH-64 Apache was a formidable weapons platform whose arrival on the battlefield often ended fights without either side firing a single shot. There were two on station, based on the rotor noise and the sounds of the guns. Small arms fire weakly answered the gunships. Moments later, several more machine guns opened up. It sounded sweeter to Jimmy than any church choir. Engines and rotor blades roared just outside the building, blowing dust underneath the door.

Jimmy would know that noise anywhere. Black Hawks landing. More AK-47s opened fire near the helicopters. Odd. He'd expected to hear American weapons. The Special Operations team must be opting to use Russian weapons. Jimmy didn't get hung up on the detail, after all he'd used non-American weapons for missions in the past.

Seconds later, the door flew open courtesy of a well-placed battering ram. Black-clad men in balaclavas flooded the room. A pair of large bolt cutters severed the chain holding the two prisoners to the I-bolts. However, their hands remained shackled. This wasn't particularly surprising. Both men knew the extraction team would want to move fast and not waste time freeing their hands.

Strong hands pulled them to their feet and shoved them toward the door. As they ran to the large helicopter, Jimmy saw two missiles leave the rails of an attack aircraft and impact the bunker from which the Boko Haram fighters had been firing moments before. After the detonations, the smoking structure remained silent.

Jimmy looked into the sky, reciting a silent prayer of thanks.

Their rescuers boosted Jimmy and Matt into their seats as the aircraft lifted off. Jimmy's heart raced with adrenaline and relief as they rose high above the Boko Haram camp.

He'd begun to settle in his seat, and was about to ask for his shackles to be removed, when the blue cabin light glinted off a flag on the uniformed shoulder beside him.

Jimmy's heart plummeted through the floor. It wasn't Old Glory, the Union Jack, or the flag of any other ally. It was a large star, and an arc comprised of four smaller stars.

His blood ran cold.

They'd just been rescued by the Chinese.

1

Alexander

Fort Worth, Texas

Alexander gritted his teeth as the Bell 407's skids impacted the helipad on top of Mallick Tower. Even the helicopter pilots were cowboys in Texas. No sense of class or finesse. He wasn't accustomed to such rough handling—ordinarily, it was the pilot who announced they'd landed, not a high-five with terra firma.

"Hey, sir," the pilot bellowed. "we'll be back in about 30 minutes to take you back to your plane."

Unbuckling his seat belt, Alexander masked his annoyance with a smile, threw the pilot a thumbs-up and opened his door to climb out of the aircraft. Another rarity in his travels these days. It wasn't that he needed someone to open the door for him. It was just nice to be able to move without the door being in the way.

The United States was a cesspool of egotistical, entitled children, but Texans took it to the next level. Incredibly arrogant, not only believing in their superiority but branding and marketing it to the world. Texas's love of God, guns, and giant pickup trucks was in effect a celebration of the primary sources of the problems in the world today.

Despite Alexander's dislike for the state, they did make it incredibly easy to run a nonprofit. The charity enabled him to accomplish work he was genuinely passionate about—making the planet a better place for future generations. A half dozen people hovered around the rooftop door, all appearing uncomfortable with not being the most important person in the group.

The welcoming committee. More's the pity.

Sometimes Alexander wished he could go places without this dog and pony show, like he had earlier in life. As a spy, he'd been concealed in obscurity. A shadow, with few people even knowing he existed. That part of his history felt like a lifetime ago, another life belonging to someone else. He still moved in the shadows, but the stakes were higher, and he now hid in plain sight. It was a fantasy he allowed himself to entertain at times, wondering what things could have been like if he'd remained as he was and not evolved into the person he was now. Intellectually, he knew espionage was a young man's game and that he was now positioned to make a far more lasting impact.

But still, it was enjoyable to reminisce.

He was pulled from his reverie by the extended hand of a man in his mid-sixties.

"Good afternoon, Mr...."

The rest of the greeting was lost to the whine of the helicopter increasing power to take off. Alexander shook the offered hand and went through the motions of being introduced to the group, all the while concealing his disgust with a smile.

Three of the group wore cowboy boots as though they'd been out on the ranch before this meeting, but he was well aware they were a status costume at best. He knew all of their names and backgrounds, and held little genuine respect for any of them.

Life was a chess board, yet you had to know the location of the pieces as well as their capabilities. Even though these pieces were pawns, it would be an amateur move to dismiss someone based on their individual importance. Threats came from a combination of proximity and capability. Many games had been lost, and empires had fallen because an enemy pawn had ended up somewhere it shouldn't have been.

"We appreciate your support and are delighted you could make it," a woman in a conservative pencil skirt and fitted suit jacket drawled as she ushered him toward a conference room on kitten heels. Sandra was the mother of twins. One studying medicine at Harvard, and the other living in California as an amateur surfer. Sandra was a deacon at her local church, but she didn't let that stop her from enjoying the occasional weekend tryst with her high school boyfriend when her husband was away on business.

Alexander recoiled inside at the meeting space, but his face revealed nothing. The office building had been built in 1968 and the space showed its age despite having undergone extensive renovations after a tornado hit in 2000. The current occupants were doing nothing to improve the situation, though. Smells of old coffee and Chinese takeout combined to lend the cheap, dark wooden furniture a greasy feel.

Alexander waved his hand dismissively as though the hundreds of millions he'd contributed were inconsequential.

"HERMES is a huge step forward. I'm happy to be able to play a part."

The High-Efficiency Relay and Multipurpose Earth Satellite was a plan to launch 200 high-bandwidth satellites. Each satellite weighed 14 tons, twice that of other communication units on the market. The computing and broadcasting power of the rigs was staggering, with each one capable of handling all the internet traffic of a mid-sized town without any noticeable lag. The people in this room believed these 25 were proof of concept. They planned on launching the remaining 175 over the next two years. The reality of what HERMES brought to the proverbial table was destined to have a far greater impact than these small-minded philanthropists could possibly imagine.

Alexander still had to find a new company to put the remaining satellites in orbit. Their current service provider was a bit too curious about the payload. Hopefully, the new space venture in California on his to-visit schedule would be willing to take the money and launch the platforms without asking too many questions.

This project was just one of the levers he was pulling in an effort to secure the future, but it was always better to let people think you were just a bit player in the drama rather than revealing too soon that you were, in fact, the director.

The meeting room was small, with two dozen chairs crammed around an oval table sized for half that number. A large, wall-mounted TV showed a video conference that hadn't started yet. Floor-to-ceiling windows offered a view of downtown Fort Worth. The skyline had all the flair of a concrete wall, lacking the history and artistic appeal of major European cities.

Alexander glanced at his Rolex before taking his seat at the head of the table facing the TV. A large man seated to his right raised his white Stetson to wipe the perspiration from his brow. His thick, graying beard was likely an attempt to hide a double chin and jowls. Sam owned a large oil company and a dozen Dallas/Fort Worth car dealerships. A lifelong bachelor and outspoken conservative, he secretly donated to his local NPR station. He looked like Porky Pig, although there were still glimpses of the hard oilfield roughneck he'd once been.

"It's almost time to make the call," Sam said. The statement was a request for permission to proceed.

Alexander pulled the sleeves of his suit jacket back over his wrists before nodding his assent. Waving a meaty hand, Porky signaled the computer guy in the corner of the room to begin.

"HERMES has a good link. Connecting," the man said in acknowledgment.

Six participants were now connected to the virtual meeting. A cheer exploded from the assembled crowd, and even Alexander smiled. They'd done it. After years of planning and close to a billion dollars, it was here.

"Greetings from Texas. Can y'all hear me?" Sam asked in a booming voice.

On-screen, six men immediately gave a thumbs-up and the room erupted into applause again.

This web call was anything but ordinary. The participants had joined the call from some of the most remote spots on the globe.

The top row showed a video from Easter Island in the middle of the Atlantic, an Antarctic research station, and the heart of the Sahara desert. The bottom row featured locations of the Kwajalein Atoll in the middle of the Pacific, Ellesmere Island, the northernmost human settlement, and

Nauru, a small Pacific Island with the honor of being the least visited country in the world.

"Congratulations on being the first call of HERMES. This groundbreaking technology will provide cost-effective internet and data connections to the most remote areas of the planet, making it possible for every human to connect with the global community," Alexander said.

This was not the first call HERMES had made, but Alexander couldn't admit that. The HERMES constellation had been used to make secure satellite phone calls by a former employee selling weapons to Nigerians. Those calls had been a lapse in judgment and a threat to his ongoing operation.

The people around the table applauded as though he were a political candidate stoking ideological fires.

When all 200 satellites were in the sky, HERMES, like the Greek god after which it was named, would be able to relay messages from anywhere worldwide without delay. No longer would a scientist trying to solve the climate crisis in the middle of the Amazon have to worry about transmitting critical data. Soon hikers on wilderness trips would no longer need to pray to God that someone would find them after they broke their leg. There were hundreds of communications satellites already in the sky, but none of them possessed the capabilities of HERMES. This project would literally change the course of humanity and the global power balance.

Alexander wasn't interested in power for its own sake, but rather in the ability to correct the deficiencies of modern society. Most of the problems plaguing the world were due to expansionist agendas. HERMES represented one step toward rectifying that.

Before Alexander could continue speaking, his phone rang. It was never on silent due to the rather short list of people who knew the number.

"Excuse me. I need to take this phone call," Alexander said, rising from his seat and pulling the device from his pocket. Once he was far enough away from curious ears, he answered the call from the other side of the world.

"Hello, friend," Alexander greeted the caller in Mandarin. The simple phrase was the extent of his knowledge of the language.

"Your information was accurate. Pickup was 10 minutes ago."

"Complications?"

"Our pilots spotted other helicopters in the area, but we managed to avoid them."

"Other helicopters?"

"Most likely American Special Operations. There has been a lot of activity in that area lately."

"You're sure you got in and out without any issues?" Alexander asked.

"They are still in the process of exfiltration, but yes, they are cleanly out of the immediate area."

"Good. Keep me updated." Recently he'd authorized an in extremis cauterization of a security leak. The current operation would show if that action had been successful.

Alexander disconnected the call. He checked the time before returning the phone to his pocket, disgusted to find he still had 15 minutes before the helicopter arrived to take him back to Arlington Municipal Airport.

2

Marissa

Andorra la Vella, Principality of Andorra

The door in front of Marissa stood slightly ajar. Murky beams of light slid around its edges, throwing a slash of brightness across the darkness of the floor. A faint sickly-sweet smell turned her stomach.

She didn't want to go through that door.

Turning around, she stared at the long Victorian-style hallway extending into a black void. In the distance, a figure stood, its features shrouded in darkness.

The figure advanced, seeming to carry the darkness with it. Instinctively Marissa backed up, reaching for a weapon only to discover she wasn't carrying one. Her back brushed against the door. The noxious, sweet smell grew stronger. The silhouette flickered forward, stopping just short of the edge of the finger of light emanating from the door. A soft buzzing issued from the figure, high-pitched and difficult to hear.

Gripping the knob, she swung the door open. The light advanced down the hall. With a hiss, the figure retreated into the darkness. Marissa could feel its malice rolling over her like waves on a beach.

Stepping through the doorway with care, she spotted a lone, gnarled, leafless tree atop a hill. A raven perched on one of its twisted branches. The large, black bird raised its head at the click of the door closing behind her. She could still hear the buzzing, as though the figure was just on the other side of the door. The raven studied her, then with an angry cry, it lifted off its perch and flew straight for her. She knew she should run, but she was frozen in place. Time seemed to slow, each flap of the raven's massive wings lasting minutes, its razor-sharp talons dripping with blood. Then abruptly, everything sped up and the bird rocketed toward her, its claws aimed at her face.

Marissa flailed awake, sweat-soaked and panting in a dark, cramped corner. After she'd taken the job with Banque Suisse, she'd thought these days were long gone. But here she was again, ignoring a comfortable bed to sleep on the floor of a closet.

She'd discovered a team hunting her in Toulouse, France. That little run-in had resulted in two dead operatives and confirmation that she wasn't paranoid. Neither man possessed a scrap of information on his person to offer clues as to her hunter's identity. If she'd still been with Project Olympus, there would have been an analysis of dental work, stomach contents, and hair samples to determine probable identities. Alone and on the run, none of those capabilities had been available to her. Still, the lack of information was helpful in itself. Their hand-to-hand fighting styles might have revealed more, but she'd opted to shoot them in the face instead of engaging in an information-gathering fistfight.

Under the pillow in the closet was the reassuring shape of a pistol. Easing herself into a sitting position, she realized she still heard buzzing. She knew that sound. Through the slats of the closet, she could just make out a small, dark shape on the other side of the curtains in her room. A drone. It would have been invisible if the Moon hadn't been so bright.

Marissa's phone vibrated in her pocket. The cameras she'd placed around the house had gone offline.

How had they found her?

She didn't have time to worry about the 'how' right now. The more important question was 'who.' It would also tell her about the capabilities of the men being sent and their goals.

The CIA and Interpol were both hunting her. Capture by either group would result in arrest and interrogation. The CIA would be less gentle, and their hospitality would end with her permanent retirement to a black site without a trial or hope of freedom. Interpol would at least have a public trial, but pressure would be applied several weeks after her conviction. A quiet transfer would occur, moving her to CIA custody and the same ultimate end.

Her old employer, Banque Suisse, also had a vested interest in finding her. They would want to give her a severance package, paid in full with hot lead. They were the wildcard. They certainly had the funding for an operation like this, but that was a single variable in their decision matrix. Her employment had been proof. She had provided a costly, but value-adding service. The bank's ultimate concern was profitability. Was spending massive amounts of money on a manhunt profitable? While she couldn't rule them out, they were lower on the probability chart.

And there were still others. Marissa had made plenty of enemies in her time with the CIA. Becoming the bank's in-house assassin had only added to that list.

Not for the first time, she thought about how all these problems could have been avoided if she'd completed that last job for Banque Suisse as contracted. The intriguing Isaac Northe and his GQ model friend had been minor inconveniences. She could have killed them both with little difficulty before jumping out of the plane with Greggor, collecting her payment for his extraction, and returning to her little Zurich apartment in peace.

But, in her heart, she knew that was only partly true. Maybe she could have gone home, but there would be no peace. She'd still be a hunted woman, but Sarah Powers wouldn't be looking to interrogate her. Her old teammate would make sure Marissa knew who killed her.

No, if she'd killed Sarah's employees, she would have had to kill Sarah and Naomi as well. How do you kill a force of nature? Especially when…

No. Marissa slammed the door on that line of thought. There was no time for it either. She knew she'd made the right choice, but there were still consequences. The disbanding of Project Olympus had been one of them.

She looked back at her phone. No cell service or Wi-Fi. That was bad. Taking out the Wi-Fi was a simple denial of service operation. Jamming the cell towers took more juice. She had to admit, it was clever of them to come at this time of night. There wouldn't be enough people awake to notice or be upset about the loss of cell service.

She mentally ticked through the information she had on her visitors. They had drones, cell jammers, and a reasonably stealthy entry. That made a containment perimeter a foregone conclusion. She wasn't going to bet her life to a sniper's bullet trying to prove otherwise.

Dozens of spies, assassins, and commandos had been killed quietly without offering up a fight. That wouldn't be her. The team in France had learned the hard way that this petite Puerto Rican was a serious threat. She wondered if the current team had gotten the memo.

A soft creak told her the front door had opened. They were inside the house now. Marissa was out of time. She opened the closet door and moved through the bedroom like a wraith, leading with her pistol.

Pivoting to her right, she fired a single shot through the window, taking out the hovering drone. It was a calculated risk. The shot had been unsuppressed, and now the invaders knew she was aware of their presence. But at least they didn't have eyes on her.

Shouts from downstairs and the thud of boots confirmed her suspicion. They would attempt to flood and secure the space before she could change locations.

She crept into the hallway. Speed was the essence in both sides' playbook. She dropped to one knee, flattening herself against the wall corner next to the stairs. The risk was too high that the team would be wearing body armor, and headshots were impractical when they were swarming her. Instead, Marissa stuck her pistol around the corner at waist level and began to shoot down the stairs. Her goal was a leg or groin shot that would trip up the first man and pile up the stack.

Suppressed rounds began tearing into the top of the stairs and the corner she huddled behind. Bits of wood and drywall peppered her face. They sounded very close to the top of the stairs.

Man, those guys are fast, and the suppressors aren't a good sign.

On her fourth or fifth shot, she heard a grunt and a thud. The firing stopped as men swore, trying to clear the bottleneck. The voices were speaking English. That might mean the CIA, Delta, or DEVGRU. They also might be an international mercenary unit whose common language was English. The American government had a solid lineup when it came to elite tactical hit teams, but there were more than a couple of outfits capable of putting together a unit like this. She would know; she'd trained with them during her tenure with Project Olympus. Chancing a glance, she saw that she'd hit the first and second man, while the third tried to disentangle himself from his predecessors.

Marissa popped up like an Olympic sprinter off the block, came around the corner and jumped, landing on the point man's chest. Continuing the movement forward, she bounded toward the available free space, landing hard on the banister.

That's going to leave a bruise.

As she slid past the second man, she grabbed the third man's rifle just as he leveled it at her. Flipping her legs to the outside of the banister, she pulled the commando's weapon with all her strength.

Nine times out of ten, she wouldn't have had a prayer of winning a tug-of-war match against a man his size, except she had momentum and gravity on her team. Still connected to his weapon by the sling, the man was yanked backward onto the fourth man, collapsing the entire stack that ascended the stairs. She considered shooting them in the face but decided she might need the ammo elsewhere.

Strong hands ripped her off the staircase, throwing her into the hallway wall. The starburst in her vision looked like the New York City fireworks she used to watch on the Fourth of July. The impact took her breath away and sent her gun flying. A second four-man team entered the front door, all pretense of stealth gone.

"GET DOWN ON THE GROUND. PUT YOUR HANDS ON YOUR HEAD," voices thundered at her. She was familiar with the tactics, but that didn't make them any less effective. Still, she wasn't going down quietly.

Her heartbeat could have been the kick drum at a rock concert. There were no good options. Marissa had known for years things would probably end like this, but it didn't mean she had to go without a fight.

Suddenly, her brain registered a critical detail. They were trying to take her alive. The tactical center in her brain processed that fact and understood it for the opportunity it was. They would in all likelihood succeed, but Marissa would make them work for it. She now knew the rounds on the staircase had been fired to keep her head down, not kill her. These men would be trained to shoot through walls to eliminate enemies.

She stretched herself across the width of the hallway inch by inch. They had a weakness, and she could use it. She doubted they would avoid killing her at all costs, but she might be able to use a split-second hesitation to escape. A metallic snick told her a steel baton had been snapped open. Alive didn't mean undamaged. After all, if she resisted, like everyone in the room expected, what other choice did they have? Marissa decided to give them a legitimate reason to beat her.

Kicking out with her legs, she caught the lead man behind the knee and dropped him to the ground. Frantically she patted the floor, looking for the fallen firearm. The baton came whistling in, and she had to roll to prevent it from catching her in the face. She saw three others in the room before the lead man flipped on his weapon-mounted tactical light, blinding her. She grabbed the barrel of the rifle, pulling herself to her feet as the man tried to free his weapon.

Vaguely she registered the others screaming at her to let go of the weapon and put her hands in the air. They had all turned their flashlights on, bathing the hallway in blinding white light. The second man was on his feet again and moving in with a taser.

The commando was so busy trying to wrestle his rifle back from her that he was unprepared for it to be shoved back at him. She drove the buttstock of the weapon into his throat before releasing it and grabbing a knife from his tactical gear.

Lashing out against the taser-wielding operator, her new knife's razor-sharp blade bit into his forearm and severed his hand's gripping tendons instantly. The taser fell to the ground. Marissa grabbed the now bloody arm, pulling him toward her as she mule-kicked the first man in the groin.

Despite being shorter than her prisoner, she wrapped her arm around his neck and held the blade against his throat while grabbing his sidearm. Now she had a human shield. The first guy still lay curled on the ground groaning in pain. Huddling behind her hostage, she opened fire on the advancing flashlights. She heard a grunt as one of the weapon lights spun up in the air, its owner hit. The other two winked out. She knew they had night vision, and she was blind. She attempted to turn her shield to shoot the guy she'd kicked when she felt a stinging pain in her neck from the prongs of a taser. Someone else had managed to get a shot off. Her legs turned to jelly. The gun in her hand clattered to the floor along with the knife.

The guy she'd been holding delivered a vicious elbow to her side. The blow sent her into the side of the staircase. Slumping to the floor, she watched as a hulking figure advanced toward her. One massive hand clamped around her throat while the other gripped her left knee. He picked her up like she was a toy, carried her into the small kitchen, and dropped her in a chair. He glanced at the knife block, then scooted it well out of reach.

"Best not to tempt fate," he said to her. His tone clinical and professional.

"They weren't wrong. She is feisty," a gruff voice said. Several other voices mumbled things she couldn't make out.

"What do you want?" Marissa managed to croak. She was still conscious but unable to move.

"Just delivering a message," the voice said, tossing a brown folder on the counter next to her.

"You could've just mailed it," she said, finding it difficult to believe they hadn't given her a severe beating just out of spite. The man barked a laugh before walking out of the room. His team melted out after him.

The violence, noise, and blinding light of the past few moments gave way to darkness in seconds. Silence swallowed her whole, its presence more unsettling than the assault, or even death, which she'd been expecting.

Marissa was alone, without an organization to provide her with backup or support. All she had were her skills and they'd proved insufficient tonight.

Several minutes passed before she rose and retrieved the folder.

Her late-night visitors had come to relay a message. Her particular skill set was required. Message received, loud and clear.

She sighed. No sense feeling sorry for herself. At least she now knew what she faced, and she could formulate a new plan.

There were no lone wolves in this world, at least not ones that lived long. Marissa was in this situation because she'd chosen to avoid a conflict with Athena. Sarah Powers had built her own pack and Marissa had information that members of Sarah's company would find valuable. If she played her cards right, she might be able to get this new monkey off her back at the same time.

3

Isaac

Miami, Florida

I leaned back in the wrought iron chair at the bistro table outside Analog Brew, tilted my face toward the sunshine, and inhaled the scent of saltwater. The warm temps and sea breezes were high on the list of reasons why I loved living in Miami.

I shifted the straw in my cup to draw out the last drops of iced coffee hiding under the cubes at the bottom. I'd resisted the temptation to turn it Irish. Temptation had not been in short supply since we got back from Switzerland.

That one had been quite the eventful affair, beginning with the biggest security testing contract my employer, Peregrine, had ever landed. It ended with my colleague Derek and I infiltrating a private jet to recover the stolen source code for a state-of-the-art Artificial Intelligence entity called Titan. The code had been swiped by the head of security for Omniburton, the world's largest defense contractor, which also happened to be our client at the time.

Our secondary objective had been to ensure Greggor was taken into custody by a CIA agent waiting for us in Zurich. He'd been running an international arms operation for years and had been labeled a threat to national security.

After boarding the plane to intercept Greggor, I learned he'd activated the Titan Protocol instructing the AI to eliminate a Marine assault team who was closing in on his operation. That team included Jimmy Taylor, my best friend. He'd been minding his own business, raiding a Nigerian weapons cache, and then BOOM, bombs dropped by an AI-controlled drone obliterated him.

I had long since come to terms with battlefield losses, even those of close friends. But it was the news that Jimmy's death had been cold-blooded murder, and not a casualty taken in the line of duty, that had hit me hard and almost sent me spiraling back into the bottle.

It would be very easy to lie to myself and pretend I could control it. It would start off small. A beer here, a whiskey there. I wouldn't get blackout drunk or go picking fights with anyone who looked at me wrong. At least not at first. It wasn't that I went out looking for trouble when I drank. It was more I just didn't care.

For this reason I'd made a point of checking in with my sponsor and attending several AA meetings. I needed my support community now more than ever.

My phone buzzed on the table, and I picked it up, expecting to see a social media notification from one of my favorite authors about their latest novel. Instead, there was a message from my boss, checking on a detail about an upcoming job. After helping the CIA capture Greggor and stopping a weaponized AI from falling into the wrong hands, Peregrine's stock rose. Our security consulting expertise was now in high demand by those in the know, and as a result we were planning our best job yet: robbing a bank. Or, at the very least, evaluating whether or not it could be done.

I remembered sitting on a beach in Okinawa as a Marine, talking about robbing banks with Derek and Jimmy. I'd put at least a dollar on the fact that most young military members, tactically trained and underpaid, had thought about knocking over a bank. Because, as famed robber Willie Sutton said best, "That's where the money is."

Now I got paid to plan bank robberies. And not just any bank, but the Federal Reserve. I would be flying to Denver for the initial reconnaissance in a couple of weeks. We still had some sites to test for Omniburton, but this new gig felt like Christmas had come early.

Lost in thought about knocking over the Federal Reserve, I was startled by a woman's voice close behind me.

"Do you mind if I sit down?"

It was apparently a rhetorical question as she took the seat before the words were out of her mouth.

I turned my head to respond that I was just leaving, when I found myself staring into the brown eyes of Interpol Agent Angelica Garcia.

Snapshots flashed through my mind like an old-time newsreel.

Angelica in a flight attendant's uniform, pulling a weapon from behind her back.

Her whispered comments to Greggor as she'd zip-tied him to a leather armchair.

Flirtatious banter that momentarily distracted me from the video proving Greggor had ordered the deaths of 14 Americans, including Jimmy.

A cup of coffee.

The blast of the door blowing off and the gust of air as she'd stepped to the edge.

"Tell Athena, Hestia says hello."

No, she's not an agent. I reminded myself. *Her name isn't even Angelica; it's Marissa. And according to Sarah, she's a serious threat. What's she doing here?*

I couldn't have been more surprised if the President of the United States himself had come striding up to my table to tell me I was needed for a top secret mission to save the world. A job that only I could do.

For that scenario, at least I had a plan. I'd look him in the eye and tell him I was going to do it my way—with my own crew. A diverse cast of criminals, several of whom were the best in the world at their specialty, but yet had somehow managed to land in prison.

This scenario was less predictable.

I sat up a little straighter. I couldn't fathom what her agenda might be, but her presence here told me she had one. If she wanted to hurt me, she could have. So I decided to take her cue, keep things casual, and try to figure out what was going on.

"The last time I saw you, you'd drugged my coffee and were jumping out of an airplane." I kept my tone conversational.

A faint smile crossed her face.

"It was either that or shoot you."

"I'll take being drugged over shot every time."

She smirked, but I could see she was less than thrilled to be here. From where I sat, she looked like a rabbit coming out of the briar patch after the hawk had disappeared from view. But an audacious one at that. She had been moments away from killing me, and now she was here, behaving as if the entire thing had been a simple misunderstanding.

Sitting at a table, attempting to make casual conversation with someone who'd been ready to murder me in cold blood was a first for me. It wasn't how I'd seen my day going when I woke up that morning.

The reason I was listening and not punching her in the face was my conversation with Sarah on the flight back from Switzerland.

When I'd relayed the cryptic message, Sarah had seemed unsurprised.

"Her name is Marissa Diaz," she'd told me. "Naomi and I worked with her in the CIA. She is unbelievably skilled. But you can't take anything she says or does personally."

When I raised an eyebrow at this, Sarah continued, "She's the closest thing to amoral that I've ever seen. She would perform any job she was assigned, with the highest level of precision and professionalism. But she never asked questions. She had zero qualms about anything she was told to do. Emotions never entered the calculation. Right and wrong were all relative. Her driving motivation was survival. If she'd killed you, it would have just been part of the job. But the fact you're still alive isn't personal, either. First and foremost, she looks out for herself."

The insight into her mindset was helpful, but I still found myself growing annoyed.

"I appreciate your restraint," I said before continuing. "Sarah told me your name is Marissa, and you two used to work together."

Marissa stiffened at the mention of Sarah before relaxing and offering a shrug.

That's interesting. She had to know I would've talked to Sarah. She almost looks afraid.

I watched her carefully, trying to find any traces of the Angelica I'd bantered with on the plane. Had any of it been real? I really enjoyed our conversation. I'm a pretty good judge of people. My time with her had felt genuine and I had liked her. That made her betrayal even harder to swallow.

"So...we had such a good chat on the plane, you thought you'd come to Miami for a catch-up? Or maybe you decided you couldn't leave any loose ends?" I asked, not quite sure why I was poking the proverbial bear. "Here to finish the job?"

Am I trying to pick a fight?

Marissa started to stand, but I grabbed her wrist. "Sit down." She glared at me, her eyes dark pools.

She's thinking about killing me right now. That's fine. Let her try.

She lifted her left hand, starting to pull something from her pocket.

I prepared myself for a fight. The first thing I needed to do was to get Marissa off balance. A shove would do nicely. My brain began to branch through various fight sequences, taking into account the weapons I had at hand. The purse hanging on the chair next to me would be a good standoff weapon if she pulled a knife. On the other hand, if she had a gun, I'd need to close the distance. I knew she was right-handed, but Sarah had described Marissa as 'very dangerous,' which gave her a lot of credit in my book. It also meant she'd be able to shoot with her left if required. I had my knife, but didn't want to go to the police station for stabbing someone. Besides, I was wearing a new pair of jeans. I could do without blood stains.

The object cleared her pocket. It was a phone, and all further thoughts of fighting were filed under 'I' for irrelevant. She placed the phone on the table and sat back down, shaking my hand off her wrist. "The last guy who grabbed me like that lost his hand," she said.

I don't think she's joking.

I lifted both hands and made a point of placing them on my side of the table. She'd come for a reason, and starting a fight wasn't productive. Before she'd drugged me and parachuted out of the plane, I'd invited her to Miami. The situation might not be what I'd had in mind at the time, but I could still hear her out. For sheer curiosity's sake, if nothing else. "Sorry about the unpleasantness. Seeing you reminded me of my friend's death," I said.

She grimaced. "I get that."

"So, why are you here? I imagine there must be more than a few people who want to chat with you."

Both Naomi and the Swiss interrogators had expressed more than a passing interest in bringing Marissa into custody. It was hard to imagine she wasn't on a number of terror watch lists with active arrest warrants. I was impressed she'd even managed to enter the United States undetected.

"Correct. Followed by locking me away in a small cell at some black site where I'd never see the light of day again."

Miami isn't the most incognito location if you're looking to avoid Johnny Law, and Guantanamo Bay is just 500 miles away.

"Well, we have plenty of daylight here. I might even be able to get a To-Go bag from the coffee shop so you could take a bit of it with you," I said, gesturing at the bright blue sky.

Marissa almost laughed, then, looking embarrassed, she asked, "What happened to you after the plane landed?"

I noticed how she'd ignored my question and shifted the conversation back to me. It did nothing to allay my suspicions about her motives, but I let it go. I found it amazing how humans could move past things and revert to normalcy. Besides I still had some time left on my lunch break and I figured she'd get to the point soon enough.

Adopting what I knew was a terrible British accent, I said, "Typical private jet stuff. A small welcoming party, complimentary jewelry, and luxury accommodations."

Marissa arched her eyebrows. "By welcoming party, you mean police?"

"HA! Nothing so pedestrian, my dear. My mates and I were escorted off the plane by Einsatzgruppe TIGRIS!"

Marissa gave a little whistle. "Swiss Special Forces. I'm sorry I missed that."

"No, you're not."

"No, I'm not." She didn't even hesitate. "But I'm glad you're all right. How long did they keep you in interrogation?"

"I think it was about 24 hours, but I'm guessing you didn't come here to make sure I got off the plane okay."

Marissa shook her head and took a deep breath before unlocking the phone and sliding it toward me. I noticed her hand trembled as she said, "I discovered this after I landed and…" Her voice trailed off.

And now we've arrived at the reason for the visit.

I looked down at the phone, where the play arrow of a video gleamed.

I looked back at her, but her face was unreadable.

I hit play on the video and watched in confusion. It was just a few seconds long. After it ended, I continued to stare at the device, my mind failing to register what I'd just seen.

The honk of a car horn startled me and my hand jerked, knocking my iced coffee to the ground. The lid popped open, ice cubes bouncing and scattering.

I ignored it, my eyes returning to the phone in front of me.

With a trembling finger, I touched the play button again.

I watched in shock as the shaky video centered on the one person I'd know anywhere.

Jimmy. He was dirty, too thin, and he'd clearly been tortured. But his eyes were defiant.

A Wall Street Journal sat across his lap, the date visible, but not making any sense.

How is that possible? He's dead. He was vaporized. Or so the CIA told me.

I'd been at his funeral in Arlington, where he was buried with full military honors. Stood next to his brother Mike as Taps played in the pouring rain. There had been so much rain. The thunderstorm had raged for hours as though nature itself was grieving with me.

In the video someone off camera asked his name. Jimmy spat a glob of blood before answering. The video ended, and I turned to stare at Marissa.

I still didn't fully understand what I'd just watched, but my mind was already racing ahead.

I'm going to find him and God help anyone who gets in my way.

I was ready to burn and kill. It felt like the red-eyed prehistoric wolf of my recurring nightmare was trying to claw its way out. All I had to do was let go. I'm sure if I'd looked in a mirror, I would have seen its eyes shining through my own. The way Marissa recoiled, she must have seen it, too.

"Where did you get this?" I almost didn't recognize my own voice.

I can't believe he's alive.

Was alive, I corrected myself. The newspaper on his lap was over three weeks old. The day before we'd captured Greggor, and Marissa had drugged me. The lead could be all but cold by now.

"It was sent to Greggor's phone," she replied, her voice small. "I took it from him on the plane."

He's lucky he's in CIA custody right now.

I was numb. Jimmy could still be alive.

I should be…honestly, I didn't know what I should be.

I felt lost and guilty for not being happy. But how could I be happy now that I knew my friend was possibly alive, but being held in secret and tortured?

Early in my military career, I'd been christened with the call sign Honey Badger. At the time videos of the impressive animal fighting snakes, porcupines, and bees were becoming popular on the internet. Its ability to endure pain and continue pursuing its mission objective led to the viral phrase, "Honey Badger don't care." Apparently there was something about me that had reminded my then-team leader of a honey badger.

Jimmy had saved my life in both literal and figurative terms. He'd become the brother I'd never had. I made up my mind then and there to either find and get Jimmy back or kill everyone involved in his death.

I was willing to light the world on fire and watch it burn to get him back.

"Isaac, is this the coffee shop you told me about?"

Marissa and I jumped as a feminine voice with a French lilt spoke right behind us. We both turned to see a tall brunette looking at us, one eyebrow raised in question.

"Sarah," Marissa gasped.

The look of sheer terror on her face snapped me out of my plan for apocalyptic destruction.

Seems like this wasn't part of her plan for the day.

Sarah smiled placidly. "It's so nice to see you. It's been a while. I just had lunch delivered to the office. Why don't you join us, and I can show you the place?"

Marissa looked as though she'd rather defuse a nuclear bomb with a sledgehammer and blowtorch.

I hadn't thought about what a reunion between Sarah and her old colleague would look like, but this unflappable politeness didn't surprise me. Sarah was never one to lead with her emotions.

Naomi, Sarah's friend and CIA contact, had had a different response when she'd heard about our adventure on the plane. She didn't have Sarah's live-and-let-live attitude.

Marissa nodded, seeming to compose herself. I stood, debating whether I should tell Sarah about the video then and there, but it seemed like a conversation best held in private. Peregrine was like a family and while she wasn't as close to Jimmy as I was, she was close to his brother. Mike was Peregrine's resident hacker and the fact he was on the autism spectrum made her even more protective of him.

I wasn't sure how Sarah would respond upon seeing the video, but I was confident she'd help me get the resources I needed to bring Jimmy home.

I pocketed the phone instead of giving it back. If Marissa changed her mind and decided not to join us for lunch, I'd still have the device for Mike to work on. My mind kept replaying the video. Was I dreaming?

No, I'm not dreaming. I only ever have the one dream.

How had Jimmy survived? The bombs Titan dropped on his location had leveled the compound, and one of the survivors had last seen Jimmy near the center of the blast. There were no answers here. But I was going to find them.

As Marissa stood, Sarah offered her a rather awkward hug. I glanced at the ground, seeing the ice cubes had melted for the most part. I considered going to order a new drink, but then dismissed the notion. There was plenty of coffee, better quality too, back at the office.

4

Jimmy

Undisclosed Location

"I brought you a coffee."

Jimmy looked up from his book as Colonel Zhao entered his cell.

The word 'cell' was somewhat of a misnomer. The room was small, but the bed was comfortable, and there was an adjoining bathroom. There were no bars or chains. On the other hand, there were also no windows.

The colonel placed a disposable paper cup on the small table next to Jimmy's bed. The man appeared old enough to be his father. Jimmy wasn't the best at judging people's ages, but he'd wager Zhao was in his late 60s to early 70s. He doubted a man as old as Zhao was still in the military.

"Thank you," Jimmy said as he reached for the cup. While he wasn't a coffee enthusiast like his friend Isaac, he did enjoy a cup in the morning.

What he wouldn't give right now for a good cup of Isaac's latest rare blend, which he would grossly underappreciate, while he and Isaac listened to Mike explain the latest bit of software he'd built.

Jimmy's brother was a next-level genius who had earned his Ph.D. in Computer Science, despite a rocky beginning at their underserved public school with its outdated technology and overworked staff who hadn't known how to handle Mike's incredible intellect. Jimmy remembered getting suspended from school for punching a racist teacher who had called Mike a "retard" and then said he'd grow up to live on welfare for the rest of his life if he didn't end up in jail first. The racial slur he'd used at the time had been so offensive that Jimmy had lost all self-control and had to be dragged off him.

Validation for Jimmy's actions had come when Mike was accepted into MIT. Tech companies began throwing 6-figure job offers at Mike before he'd even completed his sophomore year. By the time he'd graduated, the only tech companies that hadn't contacted him were those who knew they couldn't afford him. Yet, he'd turned down all those offers to join Peregrine, simply because Isaac had asked him.

Jimmy hated being so far away, unable to speak to his brother. How was Mike coping with his disappearance? It was reassuring to know there were friends like Isaac and Sarah Powers watching his back in Jimmy's absence.

Taking a sip of the lukewarm beverage, Jimmy knew the strong brew would blow through him. It was the first coffee he'd had since being captured in Nigeria.

"Of course. I'm sorry it got cold. I had a lot of paperwork to do," Zhao grimaced, turning his palms up in a helpless gesture.

Both men knew this was a charade. In the hands of someone like Jimmy, hot coffee was a weapon.

Zhao straightened the jacket of his military uniform before taking a seat in a chair that had been brought in for him.

"I prefer to let my coffee cool before I drink it anyway," Jimmy said, not calling the Chinese officer on his lie. There was no reason to create unnecessary hostility.

"How did you sleep last night?" Zhao asked. This was the beginning of their daily routine. Jimmy knew his captor was aware of everything that took place in his rooms. Several dark domes occupied the ceiling, and he would have been surprised if there had been no audio monitoring.

"Pretty well, but I was wondering if I could see Mr. Hassan today?" Jimmy answered. He and Matt had been separated after arriving…wherever he now was. Jimmy had been drugged for portions of the trip. He assumed they were in China, although realistically, they could be anywhere.

JIMMY

Zhao affected a look of mild embarrassment.

"I'm sorry, that's not possible. Mr. Hassan was rather uncooperative and has been relocated to another facility more capable of accommodating him."

Jimmy was unsurprised by this news. He hadn't worked with the CIA paramilitary officer long, but he seemed like a guy with an axe to grind. Hassan had been indignant over the fact that a woman had led the last operation. So, getting along with someone like Zhao wasn't going to be high on his list of priorities.

"That's unfortunate. When will I be able to speak with an embassy representative?" Jimmy asked.

"Gunnery Sergeant Taylor. Honestly, if it were up to me, I would've turned you over to the American government as soon as we had you out of hostile territory. But, as you Americans say, those decisions are above my pay grade."

Jimmy found it oddly formal that his captor always addressed him by his military rank. But then, the entire phase of his captivity had been odd. Jimmy had expected to be subjected to unspeakable horrors, but the Chinese had been almost indifferent to him. Colonel Zhao, if that was even his real name, was the only person he'd spoken with the entire time. Their conversations had been friendly, like colleagues chatting at the water cooler.

Every day Jimmy asked about Matt and requested to speak with an embassy representative. Every day brought a new politely worded rejection to both requests. It all coalesced to leave him confused as to why he was even here.

"I'm grateful, but also curious why you rescued us," Jimmy said.

Since his transfer to Zhao's custody, he'd wracked his brain a million more times trying to remember what had happened in Nigeria. But there was still no recollection after the point he moved to assist Hassan during that firefight. It was just...gone. He suspected the United States didn't know either of them was alive. Two American servicemen presumed dead might make a tempting intelligence target, but two from the Special Forces and CIA would be irresistible.

If the United States didn't know he and Matt were still alive, Jimmy couldn't see an incentive for the Chinese to ever let him go. The thought of seeing his brother Mike was a bright spot in these gray days, but he was no longer sure he'd ever get the chance.

"Isn't it obvious?" the Colonel asked.

It was obvious he was a potential intelligence source, but he had no idea why he'd been here for so long. He estimated it was around three weeks. During that entire time, he hadn't been asked a single question regarding sensitive or classified information. What was their game?

Jimmy's silence prompted Zhao to continue. "No soldier deserves to be left in the hands of savage terrorists. We serve different countries that don't always see eye to eye. But we're both soldiers. Wouldn't the United States do the same?"

"Of course," Jimmy said. The trap was subtle, like turning up the temperature on a frog in the frying pan degree by degree. It was a gradual change that wouldn't be detected until it was too late. Colonel Zhao had expertly placed them on the same team against the savage terrorist.

"Since you were a prisoner of Boko Haram, I'd imagine you were working with the Nigerians to root out that scourge on civilization. I applaud those efforts."

There was no question. Nothing for Jimmy to deny. Zhao picked up his cup of tea and took a sip before continuing. "Did you know we're also working with the government to improve living conditions?"

Jimmy had heard of the Belt and Road Initiative. A global infrastructure development strategy designed to grow China's political and economic power. Honestly though, he didn't know much. Some of the more politically-minded guys in his unit used to rant about it, but Jimmy didn't pay much attention to politics. His job was to be the pointy end of the spear.

"I wasn't aware of anything specific that your country did in Nigeria," Jimmy said, uncomfortable about his limited knowledge of world events.

"What unit were you working with?" Zhao asked.

"What do you mean?"

"You said you were there working with the Nigerian army. I was wondering which unit you were working with," the Chinese Colonel clarified.

JIMMY

"I'm not sure. It was a training assignment. We train so many units it's hard to keep track of them all," Jimmy said. Zhao nodded, smiling and making no comment about the obvious attempt at deception.

"This was just a training assignment where you were teaching them some of your Special Forces tactics?"

"I don't know what you mean by Special Forces tactics. I just teach the classes I'm asked to teach," Jimmy said, trying to downplay any significance of his time in Nigeria.

"Pardon my ignorance of your military rank structure, but I was under the impression that a Gunnery Sergeant was a fairly senior non-commissioned officer."

"No, not senior. More like middle management," Jimmy said with a chuckle.

"My mistake. What sort of classes were you teaching?" Zhao asked.

There wasn't anything special about the training the Marines had been conducting with the Nigerian Special Forces. Standard marksmanship, room clearing, and urban warfare, but he wasn't supposed to be talking about his mission. Especially not with a foreign power.

"Basic soldier stuff," Jimmy replied.

Zhao looked incredulous. "Come now, Gunnery Sergeant Taylor. You can't expect me to believe that one of the premier militaries in the world traveled to a country like Nigeria to teach basic soldiering." Jimmy just shrugged, offering what he hoped was a disarming smile.

"Who does Matthew Hassan work for?" The subject change surprised Jimmy, but he had an answer prepared for this question. "He was part of the training team. He was in Nigeria when I arrived." Those facts were true. From a technical perspective.

"Why would the CIA be teaching basic soldier stuff?" Colonel Zhao inquired. The conversation was becoming more pointed. Jimmy had been waiting for it, and he believed he was prepared.

"The CIA? I told you I was in the Marine Corps," Jimmy protested.

"Not you. Mr. Hassan. He's already told us he works for the CIA."

"He told you that? He told me he worked for the Queen of England."

Zhao smiled at this deflection but continued his questions. "So, you were just there teaching?"

"Yes," Jimmy confirmed.

"Then why were you on a raid against Boko Haram?"

"Hands-on training is the best kind," Jimmy said, discomfort growing in his gut from the coffee.

"That makes sense," the Chinese officer said. For several minutes, he sat there in silence, appearing to be considering the answer given. Jimmy's urge to use the bathroom was overwhelming. He was now making a conscious effort not to poop his pants.

"I would agree that hands-on training is superior. It makes me wonder why none of the Nigerians accompanied you on the raid. According to a news interview with their commanders, they had no idea what you were doing that night. So, what were Marine Special Forces and the CIA doing in the middle of Nigeria without Nigerians?"

* * *

Zhao sat down in his office chair with a weary sigh, feeling every year of his age. He could already tell it wasn't going to be easy to break the Americans. His initial interrogation had yielded nothing of value. They had been a target of opportunity, essentially low-hanging fruit that could be acquired at minimal risk. They were more of a curiosity to the Chinese government than anything.

Alexander, on the other hand, thought Taylor and Hassan were of critical importance. There was a chance the failed American raid had stumbled across evidence that could unravel their plan. Or more accurately, Alexander's plan. The one he had been plotting since they'd been kids at Swiss boarding school all those years ago.

The bureaucracy of Chinese intelligence had taken weeks to decide what they were going to do with Gunnery Sergeant Taylor and Mr. Hassan. At one point in time, his superiors had considered turning them over as a goodwill gesture. There had also been several days of debate about using them as leverage to get certain Chinese spies out of American custody.

Despite needing to pump them for information about the operation in Nigeria, he was forced to wait. Ultimately, they had been deemed more valuable as intelligence sources than pawns for trade, and Zhao was finally given the green light to extract their secrets. He could have started out by pulling fingernails or teeth, but those methods didn't yield the best results.

Finishing his notes, he opened the top desk drawer and pulled a phone from underneath a stack of papers. Alexander would want an update.

"Hello," Alexander said. His voice soft-spoken with a confident self-assurance. That was something Zhao liked about his old friend. He'd never heard him sound anything but in total control. Alexander always had a plan and was five steps ahead of everyone else. In school he'd been a talented chess player. He'd convinced Zhao years ago that there were bigger things at stake than the mere fate of nations. Together they would make the world a better place for future generations. That began what they now called The Eden Initiative.

"I have received approval to begin questioning the Americans," Zhao said.

The interest in Alexander's voice was unmistakable. "What have you learned?"

"Not much. I suspect the Middle Eastern one works for the Central Intelligence Agency; he has refused to answer anything other than his name. The Black man is Special Forces and—"

Alexander cut him off. "I'm less concerned with who they are and more so with what they were doing in Nigeria. Did they find anything at the site? If so, were they able to transmit it to anyone?

The Swiss banker was keeping something from him, but that wasn't surprising. He never told anyone everything.

Zhao took a deep breath before letting it out slowly. "The conversation with Taylor was unproductive. He claims they were there on a training assignment."

"Then I guess you need to turn up the heat and be a bit more persuasive. I don't think these Americans are what they seem."

"Of course." Zhao didn't appreciate being told how to do his job, and he disagreed with Alexander. Taylor and Hassan were just what they seemed to be. Hassan was CIA and Taylor was the Spec Ops muscle. Whether or not they had found anything potentially dangerous to The Eden Initiative, a different story.

"Excellent. The pieces are in place. HERMES is launched and the North Koreans are getting closer, but these Americans are complicating the situation."

Zhao knew the ineptitude of giving a Boko Haram gangster a satellite phone was the real complication. However, he kept his thoughts to himself.

"Should I just kill them?" he asked. The pause on the other end was long enough that Zhao pulled the phone away from his ear to check whether they'd become disconnected.

"No. We need to find out if the American government knows about that phone. Besides, Boko Haram recorded proof of life videos. That's how we became aware of their location. They were using a Nigerian information broker. We assume the end goal was to ransom them back to the United States," Alexander answered.

Zhao snorted. "The United States would have paid that ransom with several Black Hawk helicopters full of Navy SEALs. Not my preferred currency." Left unspoken was the fact the US didn't get the chance because Chinese Special Forces had beaten them to it.

The bigger question was why had the Chinese forces gotten there first? It wasn't like the United States lacked special mission units in that part of the world. The logical conclusion for them not being rescued was the Americans believed both men were dead.

"The videos appear to have been sent, but we don't yet know to whom," Alexander said. Things would get complicated if America knew two of its men were still alive. Without a doubt.

Once again Zhao found himself being asked to solve a problem that someone else had created. The last time had been when Sergej Aksyonov, the Russian businessman turned playboy, got into an embarrassing situation at a Macau casino. Zhao was infuriated that he risked so much to protect someone whose only job was to help them move money.

It must have been great to inherit millions. Zhao was now rich by any reasonable standard, but he was a self-made man. He'd worked his way up the ranks in the Chinese Army. Sergej was in a different league and as much as Zhao was loath to admit it, he was a savvy entrepreneur. Therefore, Zhao would do his job as he had every time before. He'd clean up this latest mess and ensure mission success.

5

Marissa

Miami, Florida

Marissa was well acquainted with the maxim that a plan never survives first contact. It was the core tenant in her mission planning. However, this operation was going better than expected and that was part of what made her apprehensive. Sarah was not one to be coerced. Athena needed to believe she was the one bringing Marissa in from the cold. Sarah's weakness was her compassion and empathy. On one occasion, Marissa had seen her leave a witness alive so a small child wouldn't be orphaned, despite Marissa's protestations about the need to 'maintain mission security.' Yes, an indirect emotional appeal was her best way into Peregrine.

Marissa's new masters had given her an assignment in Turks and Caicos. The job wasn't strictly target elimination, but it wasn't outside her wheelhouse. Before Banque Suisse, a large part of her job had been retrieval and intelligence collection, which also involved targeted killings. This stopover in Miami to deliver the video needed to be quick, but if she played her cards right, she'd be back.

When she'd approached Isaac in the coffee shop, she'd really wanted to walk up and say, *"Oh hey, fancy meeting you here. How am I? Well, just great, aside from being a wanted fugitive. Ya know, I was just thinking about that time we were riding a private jet together, and I drugged you, blew the door off, and jumped out without regard for anyone except myself. Crazy times, huh? Soooo...anyway, I received this video on the phone I stole, and well, this is awkward, but you know that friend you thought was dead? He's not. Surprise! Here's the video, looks like he's being tortured. Just thought you might want to know. Catch ya later."*

Marissa wasn't sure why she'd inter-dialogued like Malibu Barbie, and if she was honest, she didn't have time to think about it right now. In any case, Isaac's reaction to seeing her, and to the video, had made the conversation anything but nonchalant.

Sarah showing up had been a surprising complication and the offered hug a shock. It made Marissa uncomfortable, but Sarah wouldn't have done it if she had plans of shooting her in the face. That was the nice thing about Sarah. You always knew where you stood with her. At least, that was the case the last time they worked together. The danger was conflicting with one of Sarah's interests or loyalties.

Marissa, on the other hand, didn't get bogged down by the moral implications of her actions. Despite having worked against the interests of the United States and the CIA in particular, she didn't hold any animosity toward her country or former employer. To her, there wasn't a big difference between a country or a corporation having someone killed to protect their interests.

"So, what brings you to Miami?" Sarah asked, as they walked across the parking lot.

"Just passing through. I have a job offer in the Caribbean."

It was accurate enough. Marissa's training had taught her that the best deceptions were mostly based in truth. Sarah raised her eyebrows but said nothing. They both knew the kind of work she did. Work they used to do together.

"Your office is around here?" Marissa asked as though she didn't already know. Sarah's bemused smile told her that her former colleague knew the score.

"We've rented some space in the Sabadell Financial Center," Isaac said, pointing to a tall concrete and glass building facing the waterfront.

"Our office is on the 30th floor," Sarah added as they walked into a large marble lobby.

Marissa would have preferred to take the stairs, but knew it wasn't practical. Elevators were the worst. Total death traps. She'd realized the folly of riding in one after a target termination. It had been so easy to disable the safety mechanisms and cause the elevator to free fall.

She gritted her teeth and held her breath the entire ascent. Isaac gave her an odd look when she breathed an audible sigh of relief upon exiting the elevator, but she didn't care. Tempting fate once today was enough; she'd be leaving via the stairs.

"She's scared of elevators," Sarah said in response to his look. Isaac took the information in stride as though learning someone had elevatophobia was an everyday occurrence. The comment served as a reminder of how well Sarah knew her.

Marissa had envisioned a sleek glass door like the legal and accounting offices in the rest of the building. Instead, Peregrine's door was solid steel and magnetically locked.

Several cameras monitored the space. Marissa correctly assumed they were linked to facial recognition software. Isaac placed his hand on a biometric palm scanner and entered a code on the PIN pad. There was a brief pause before the lock clicked, and Isaac swung the door open to step inside.

"Welcome to Peregrine," Sarah said, leading her into an office that looked like it belonged to a hedge fund or venture capital group.

Marissa felt like she was entering a lion's den. No other offices were listed on the 30th floor, according to the directory she'd walked by in the lobby. She was no real estate expert, but she was confident office space in downtown Miami was expensive.

"You own the whole floor?" Marissa asked.

"We don't own it; we lease it. But yes, Peregrine occupies the entire floor," Sarah said, her eyes twinkling. She was clearly proud of the company she'd built. The two women had similar qualifications, but even if she were so inclined, Marissa doubted she could have leveraged her skills in the corporate world.

"I think we should talk in the conference room," Isaac said, pulling Greggor's phone out of his pocket. Sarah eyed the device but motioned for him to lead the way without comment.

Despite the air conditioning, Marissa felt beads of sweat forming on her back, and her throat suddenly felt parched. Sarah's reaction to the video was an unknown variable. Marissa hoped she would take it in stride like she used to in the past.

The tactical center of her brain was now in overdrive, and she felt naked without a weapon. She could always depend on the environment to provide something, but she missed the comfort of a good knife and a pistol. At that moment, she'd rather be back in that remote Afghan village assassinating a Taliban leader in the middle of a Special Forces raid. The more she thought about it, the more this felt like a trap.

With great effort, Marissa forced herself to stop this line of thought. She knew she was spiraling and needed to reassess the facts, not her fears. Isaac led them into a sizable windowless meeting room that smelt like coffee. The well-furnished area looked comfortable yet professional.

The room was in the heart of the thirtieth floor, with airy, open-concept workstations forming a square around the perimeter. The walls were solid concrete and covered with soundproofing panels.

"Can I get you anything to drink? Coffee, tea, or water?" Sarah asked. Marissa could see the energy and soft drinks through the clear refrigerator door, but she didn't drink that stuff, and Sarah hadn't offered.

"Water's fine."

"Chilled or room temperature?"

"Bottled water, please," Marissa said, pointing to the fridge.

"Marissa showed me a video I think you should see," Isaac said.

"What is it?" Sarah asked.

This was the moment of truth. Marissa felt her muscles relax as she prepared for a fight. The rational part of her brain said there was no reason to worry. But she hadn't stayed alive this long by being rational.

Isaac flexed his jaw muscles several times before answering. "A proof of life video for Jimmy." Sarah's poker face was incredible. She didn't even blink. Had she known or suspected what was on the video?

Turning to Marissa, Sarah asked, "Where did you get it?"

There's the Athena I was banking on!

"It was a video message sent to a phone I took from Greggor before I…," Marissa paused, feeling embarrassed.

"Disembarked the plane?" Isaac offered.

"Yeah," Marissa agreed. She allowed herself to come down from DEFCON 1. There was still reason for vigilance, but she didn't have the proverbial finger on the trigger right now. This was so weird. She hadn't seen Sarah in over five years, and it was as though no time had passed and they were discussing operational details for their next mission.

Sarah seemed to be taking events well, but Isaac had an emotional investment in the situation.

"Can I see it?" Sarah asked, extending her hand. Isaac pulled the phone from his pocket and handed it to Marissa so she could unlock it. Marissa gave the unlocked device to Sarah, the video set and ready to play. Sarah watched it in silence. They'd all seen graphic footage, but a personal connection had a way of changing things. The last time Marissa faced this very same issue, her actions resulted in the disbandment of the most effective covert tool since World War Two.

Sarah pursed her lips. "It looks real, but we won't know until we have the metadata examined."

"I'm not sure showing it to Mike is a good idea. It'll be pretty traumatic seeing his brother like this," Isaac said.

"I know, but it needs to be verified before we do anything."

His brother works here?

The pieces of the puzzle were starting to fall into place. Isaac's reaction to the video started making more sense. It left Marissa wondering what Sarah planned on doing.

"Could you go get the rest of the team?" Sarah asked. Isaac grunted in response as he headed out the door.

"What have you been up to?" Sarah asked once they were alone. Marissa debated not telling her, but decided it didn't matter. Sarah was one of the few people in the world who wouldn't judge her.

"I've been working for a bank for the past few years."

"What kind of a bank requires your skill set?"

"The kind that caters to the uber-wealthy and augments their returns through illegal activities."

"I see. Which bank was it?"

"Banque Suisse," Marissa said.

"I'm sure they didn't have that occupation listed on the internet job board."

Marissa offered a small smile. She didn't feel like talking about the introduction that had resulted in her working for Banque Suisse.

To her relief, Sarah didn't press, instead asking, "Why were you on the plane?"

"To extract Greggor."

"Why did you decide to leave him?"

That was another topic Marissa didn't want to discuss. It was complicated, and she was still processing how she felt about the whole situation. She shrugged.

"Well, no matter your reasons, I appreciate you not killing Derek and Isaac," Sarah said.

Wanting to change the subject, Marissa asked a question that had been on her mind for a while now.

"Why did you name your company Peregrine?" The name was unique. She'd read everything she could find online about the company but had never seen an answer.

"The company name was Powers Solutions for the first few months. One day during a random conversation about military history, Isaac mentioned something Captain Williams, one of his former commanders, told him. Roman legionnaires born in conquered lands were called Peregrines. They were kind of like hired guns, working for the Romans but not true citizens of Rome. That history, combined with the characteristics of their namesake, the Peregrine falcon, led to me changing the name to Peregrine," Sarah explained.

Marissa loved that answer. It was trademark Sarah. Looking around the space, she asked, "They didn't have conference rooms with a view?"

Sarah smiled. "There was one, but we had this custom-built. It's our SCIF. We would be terrible at our jobs if we discussed sensitive information in an insecure location."

Marissa remembered the Sensitive Compartmented Information Facility at Project Olympus. That place was drab and functional, very government.

"It would send a *'do as I say, but not as I do'* message to our clients," Isaac said, walking back into the room trailed by the other guy she'd seen on the plane.

Marissa searched her memory. Sarah's boy toy. He was ridiculously handsome. She thought further before remembering his name was Derek. Derek scowled when he saw her.

"Looks like the team's all here. Isaac shut the door," Sarah said as a small Indian woman and a Black man walked into the room.

Marissa deduced the latter was Jimmy's brother, Mike. The family resemblance was unmistakable. Mike held a Rubik's cube, which he solved, scrambled, and solved again on his way to sit down next to Derek. Marissa had never seen anyone do that before. The fidgeting combined with his speed at solving the cube spoke of an incredible intellect.

As Isaac swung the door closed, Sarah moved to the front of the room, where she could address the seated group.

"Since there is no better way to say this, I'm just going to rip off the bandage. An old associate of mine has brought a proof of life video for Jimmy. "

The Rubik's cube spun at blinding speed. The rest of the room sat in hushed silence. While they were overjoyed to hear Jimmy had survived, the deliberate use of the phrase 'proof of life' conveyed the grim reality. He was alive, but in captivity.

"We're working on the assumption the video is legitimate?" Selma asked. The slight Indian woman had slid in beside Mike. Despite her diminutive frame, her posture was that of a protective big sister.

"That has yet to be verified. Selma, could you look at it?" Sarah asked.

Selma shifted, appearing to consider the question. "Yes, probably, but if we want to be 100%, Mike should really be the one to do it. He can pull things from the data I wouldn't even know to look for."

"There's also the issue that the video is over 3 weeks old. A lot can happen in that time, especially to a captive," Isaac said. His voice was now clinical and devoid of the emotions he'd displayed when first seeing the video.

Derek leaned on the table, his handsome features twisted. Looking at Marissa, he made no attempt to disguise the disgust in his voice. "Three weeks? When did you get this video? Last time we saw you, you were blowing the cabin door off a jet and jumping out." Technically speaking, Derek had been unconscious when Marissa had made her exit, but it wasn't a point worth debating.

"The video was sent to a phone I took off Greggor. It didn't arrive until after I'd left. I saw it right after I landed," Marissa said.

Isaac set his coffee mug down. "So, you received the video soon after it was recorded. Why did it take so long to bring it here?" Marissa felt her face flush and she bit back the instinctive response. She recognized this was a critical moment. She couldn't tell them about her new overlords, not yet anyway. Her primary objective was to be viewed as a valuable asset. Sarah knew her well enough to know if she lied. Marissa also suspected Isaac and Derek would be trained to read body language and micro-expressions. She could tell the truth without giving all the details.

"Aside from being on every no-fly list known to man, being wanted by a dozen countries, and being actively hunted by a half dozen intelligence and law enforcement agencies? Honestly, when I saw the video, I wasn't sure what to do about it. I sat on it for a while before deciding to bring it here," Marissa said.

Isaac leaned back in his chair, seeming to contemplate her answer. However, Derek had already made up his mind. The guilty verdict had been passed. His voice dripped with sarcasm. "The big secret to not being an international fugitive is don't do illegal stuff. Obey the law and you'll be fine."

Mike's Rubik's cube clicked through its sequences as he said, "Why doesn't that work for Black people? We try to obey the law, but still get pulled over and arrested at a disproportionately high rate." Derek glared at the hacker and Marissa fought hard to hide the smirk on her face. Mike stared at the cube and didn't see either expression.

Sarah cleared her throat. "While every society on Earth has vast room for improvement, that's a bit off-topic at the moment. Regardless of travel arrangements or circumstances, we have the video now. Our primary focus should be on seeing if we can get Jimmy back." Nods all-round confirmed the group consensus.

"Mike. Mike, I need you to look at me," Sarah said. Mike slowly raised his head. Marissa couldn't imagine what he thought right now. The conversation about his brother swirling around him.

The sincerity in Sarah's voice was like a warm hug. "Mike, I need to play this video. Jimmy looks healthy but he's pretty beat up."

"I've seen the video. It's going to be rough, bro. But I'm going to get him back," Isaac said as though Jimmy's return was a preordained destiny. Marissa noted the singular shouldering of responsibility like he was Superman showing up to fight Steppenwolf after the Justice League had been thoroughly manhandled.

The cube stopped for the first time since Mike had entered the room. "Ok."

The big screen on the wall came to life as Sarah cast the video from the phone. The clip wasn't long. Marissa had seen it so many times she knew it by heart. The shaky video focused on a wooden chair occupied by a large Black man. His face was bloody. His bare chest and arms bore numerous cuts and what Marissa recognized as cigarette burns.

A voice with a heavy accent said, "What's your name?" The prisoner glared at the camera, beaten but unbroken. The answer was hoarse. "My name is Gunnery Sergeant James Taylor, United States Marine Corps."

Marissa observed that everyone focused on Mike's well-being. Putting their own feelings on the back burner, just like a family might. This was a special pack of individuals who looked after their own.

Mike stood up, his movements jerky like a puppet with an unskilled marionette. Holding out his hand, he said, "Give me the phone."

Sarah stared at him for a moment. "Are you sure?" Mike nodded. She walked over to him and gently placed it in his hand. "Whatever you need. Just let me know."

Marissa watched as Isaac moved to stand in front of Mike. Isaac placed his hands on Mike's shoulders. "We're going to bring Jimmy home, no matter what."

Selma's grip was gentle as she took Mike by the arm, pulling him toward the door. "Come on, we've got work to do."

Marissa wanted nothing more than to disappear. With her objective of delivering the video now complete, it was time to move on to her next assignment. "Well, I'm off," she said. It sounded awkward and lame even to her.

Sarah reached out and touched her on the forearm as she passed. "Thanks for bringing the video. You didn't have to do it. This is my family, and you just gave us a sliver of hope. I owe you one."

"Of course. I've got a thing to do, but once it's done, I'd like to help if I can." Marissa said. Her head swam. This was what she'd been hoping for, but much more than she'd dared to expect.

Sarah cocked her head, studying Marissa. Seeming to reach a decision, she clasped both of Marissa's hands. Fighting the urge to pull away, Marissa looked at her former teammate searching for signs of deception.

Sarah's face showed nothing but sincerity. "I'll talk to Naomi. She's still with The Company; she might be able to help turn down your heat state. I'd imagine you're radioactive right now."

Marissa hoped her smile didn't look as forced as it felt. She wasn't sure how inclined Naomi would be to help. Artemis had a serious anger management problem as well as a tendency to take things to heart and hold grudges. Still, if she could make amends, Naomi might be the best-placed person to help her with her current predicament.

"Thanks. I'd appreciate that," Marissa said. She was in a daze, not noticing Isaac until he joined her in the stairwell.

"It's a long way down. Care for some company? Maybe a bite to eat or that cup of coffee we talked about on the plane?" Marissa nodded. That sounded amazing right now.

6

Naomi

The Bat Cave - Baltimore, Maryland

"Have you seen this?" Naomi asked, glancing over at her partner's workstation. Unsurprisingly, the desk was empty. Looking toward the kitchenette, she saw Clark making himself a snack. The man never stopped eating.

"Seen what?" he asked, walking back with a sandwich and bag of chips.

"Do you remember the bank where we suspect our Russian billionaire is hiding money?" Naomi asked.

"Yeah, did we get access to those financial records?"

"No, not yet. But, I set a Google alert to notify me if the bank was mentioned in any news articles," Naomi explained.

"And it was?"

"Yes, the President of the Turks and Caicos branch was killed last night," Naomi said, pointing to her screen. Clark bent over to read the article, dropping several chips on her keyboard in the process. Naomi rolled her eyes, picked up the chips, and tossed them in the trash.

"It says here they think it was a targeted killing. Several other employees were working after hours, and no one reported any gunshots. They found him when his secretary came in to ask him a question," Clark said.

"The plot thickens. He was killed with what was likely a suppressed weapon, and no one saw the killer enter or leave," Naomi whispered conspiratorially.

Her computer dinged, signaling a message had just arrived in her secure CIA inbox.

"I'll send you the link to the article," she said as she navigated to the inbox. She was surprised by the contents of the message.

"So, a VIP at a small private bank is killed, and several hours later, we get access to the account info from that particular bank. What are the chances those two events are not related?" Clark asked from behind his computer, apparently having read the message Naomi was still staring at.

"The same as you not eating again within the hour," Naomi muttered.

"I'm sorry. What was that?" Clark called.

"Nothing. I just said it's not very likely."

Naomi and Clark's capture of Greggor almost a month ago had put them back into HQ's good graces. Making the 7th floor look good was always a solid career move.

Their current assignment was looking into the money and technology flowing into the North Korean missile program. The Hermit Kingdom's ballistic capabilities had accelerated by orders of magnitude. The past two months had seen a sharp rise in tests with rates of failure on an exponential decline. At the current rate of progression, the North Koreans would rival Space X's capabilities within the next six months. The United States government was understandably concerned.

Their current focus was on a Russian billionaire, Sergej Aksyonov. Naomi and Clark had established the link, but they believed he was just a front. A mechanism for funneling money. There was an unknown party with a vested interest in improving the DPRK's missile program.

The effort was well-coordinated and most effective in circumventing sanctions and helping North Korea obtain the latest technology. The endeavor was too well organized not to have been set up for this express purpose. The DPRK wasn't dumb, but it didn't have the resources to engineer something like this. With the kind of money being moved and logistical complexities, there had to be another nation-state behind it.

The obvious suspects were China and Russia, but there was no clear motive. It would be like giving a shotgun to the crazy neighbor who thinks the squirrels are spying on them. Although, to be fair, it was Iran and not North Korea that had arrested 14 squirrels and accused them of espionage.

Sergej Aksyonov was, to Naomi's thinking, a typical Russian billionaire. His family fortunes had begun soon after the Bolshevik Revolution. Excelling in the production of ammunition helped them through the Second World War. The prudent management of their political ambitions enabled them to survive communism as well. However, they made their true fortune in the late 1990s when Sergej invested large sums of money in Russian oil production.

He then transferred that windfall into several technology startups, which blossomed into Big-Tech juggernauts. He even owned an English Premier League soccer team. At present, Mr. Aksyonov's primary occupation was being rich, enjoying his super yachts, and apparently funneling money to North Korea. Naomi and Clark believed Sergej was just a stop in the monetary pipeline. Nothing in his profile would suggest a connection with North Korea. They were convinced he was just a front man.

Over the past three weeks, they had traced the movement of funds through numerous shell companies and accounts until they dead-ended in a small private bank in Singapore. The sheer volume of money the man had was mind-boggling. Naomi couldn't imagine what it was like to have so much personal income that you had your own firm to manage it.

"I bet they contracted the job out," Naomi said.

"I wonder how you apply to become a contract killer for the CIA," Clark pondered.

"The killing was doubtless a diversion to cover the network compromise," Naomi said, thinking that's what she would have done if it was her assignment. None of that mattered because all she cared about was getting access to the information they needed. The email to her and Clark stated the agency now had a persistent backdoor into the network.

"It seems like nowadays we're contracting out most of our work," Clark said. It was true, many of the positions and jobs that used to be performed by federal employees were now filled by the private sector. There was big money in federal contracts. Companies like Microsoft, Amazon, and Google aggressively recruited service members with top secret security clearances to fill their ranks.

"It would have been a lot easier if we could have just remotely accessed the files," Naomi mused.

"Physical site infiltration was the sole remaining option. The computer geeks over at Fort Meade told us the entire bank network was on some super-secure intranet with encryption that would have taken years to break. We also couldn't use diplomatic pressure due to the risk of tipping off Aksyonov," Clark explained.

Naomi already knew all this, but it didn't make it any less frustrating that they had to resort to breaking into places to gain access. She'd watched enough movies to know the US government was supposed to be all-powerful, with access to every scrap of info on the planet.

"Do we know if the bank president's death is related to our case?" she asked.

"Does it matter?"

"No, I suppose not. But if I'd known breaking into a branch in Turks and Caicos was on the table, I would have volunteered for the job," she said.

"Do you have the skill set to infiltrate a bank? Is that what you used to do before we became partners?" Clark asked, steepling his fingers.

Trying to figure out what Naomi did before becoming his partner was one of his favorite pastimes. His curiosity made him both superb at his job and most annoying when it came to her past.

Naomi had never told Clark about that part of her career with the CIA. One reason was he didn't have the necessary clearance or need-to-know for information about Project Olympus. The second and more important reason was a lack of desire to relive that part of her life. If he ever found out she'd been an assassin in a disbanded unit, the sun would be a cold chunk of charcoal before the questions ended.

Instead, she gave her standard, well-rehearsed response, "Ask me about it again in five years." Clark rolled his eyes. She had no idea what he imagined she'd done. For all she knew, he thought she used to be a starship captain working out of Area 51. They had been in enough bad situations for him to draw conclusions, but it wasn't her job to validate them.

Several hours later, the rest of the team arrived back from lunch. They were adding to the relationship map built for Aksyonov.

"How does anyone have this much money? I'd be satisfied making as much as Boris spends on cars," Clark said.

"You know his name isn't Boris. It's actually—," Shane, one of the Bat Cave's analysts, started saying before Clark interrupted him.

"It doesn't matter what his name is. I know it's not Boris, but Sergej is boring. It sounds like he was named after the butler or something."

"Wouldn't the butler be named Winston or Jeeves?" Shane countered.

"Does any of this help us," Naomi said, massaging her temples. This part of the job was never included in the recruitment brochure or the movies. The US Intelligence Services were staffed by children. Technically skilled and extremely intelligent, but children, nonetheless. Maybe it was time to start hunting for employment in the private sector—such as with Peregrine.

"Yes, kind of," Shane said, pushing his glasses back onto the bridge of his nose.

"How…does…it…help…us?" Naomi said, dragging out the words after the analyst failed to elaborate.

"We have all bank transaction records for the past eighteen months. That equates to millions of data points. A veritable gold mine. We've already managed to identify half a dozen accounts that belong to 'Boris,' Shane said, placing air quotes around the name.

Shane still hadn't answered her question. "We have more data than before, but have we learned anything?" Naomi asked.

"We know more, but not anything that will give us a specific direction. Each account has between five to twenty-four companies depositing money. Many of the transactions are in the millions of dollars. He's hiding the movement in plain sight. To further complicate matters, several accounts have crypto wallets they've deposited and withdrawn money from," Shane said.

"Aren't crypto wallets untraceable?" Clark asked.

"Most people, including many criminals, think so, but no. They're difficult but not impossible. It would be a lot easier if we could gain access to the wallet and monitor it while funds were transferred," Shane said.

"Do you believe the crypto wallets should be our area of focus?" Naomi asked.

"Yes."

"Why, Shane? I'm not saying I disagree with you, but I'm curious about your rationale," Clark said.

"The psychology of it. Most people believe them to be untraceable, and we haven't encountered crypto until this point. Someone like Aksyonov is smart. He knows that cryptocurrencies are a red flag, so he'd likely only use them near the beginning of the chain to obfuscate the true origin."

"So, the crypto is a handoff from whomever we believe is feeding the money to Aksyonov?" Naomi asked.

"Basically, yes."

Naomi had a growing headache. A shooting pain behind her eyes. "Ok, Shane. You can have a few days to try and run that down. Let me know if you need anything."

This was not the part of her job she enjoyed. Running down leads would be tedious. They'd have to check each company; most would be legitimate transactions. 'Needle in the haystack' didn't even begin to describe the problem. Thankfully they had powerful computers that would apply machine learning and pattern analysis to find the next target. They might get to an answer by the time North Korea put a man on the Moon.

The Signal app on Naomi's phone chimed, and she jumped at the opportunity to excuse herself from what was shaping up to be a nerdy tech talk. She saw the text was from her old colleague, Sarah. The message asked if she could talk. Naomi tapped out a response.

"Hey, I need to go topside and make a call. I shouldn't be too long."

The Bat Cave, where the CIA team worked, was hidden below an operational warehouse. MerchWork was a logistics front doing legitimate business to facilitate the movements of its assets. The cover of being cargo expediters allowed Naomi and Clark to operate in many countries that would otherwise pose a problem. After all, even warlords and dictators needed to have their supercars transported.

Settling into a chair in her topside office, Naomi looked around. She had hosted many business meetings with companies looking to hire MerchWork to move cargo in this office. She wondered what the companies would think if they knew there was a secret CIA facility directly below. Pulling out her phone, she called Sarah.

Sarah answered on the second ring, "Hey, thanks for calling so quick."

"Of course. No problem. I figured it was important. What's up?"

There was a long pause followed by, "Are you sitting down?"

Naomi knew that Sarah wasn't one for theatrics.

"Yes," she answered.

"I have just received and authenticated a proof of life video for Jimmy Taylor."

Naomi felt the dark angel raise her head. The mere possibility was enough for the entity of rage and violence to stir.

Sarah continued, "I wanted to get it to you so we could start the process of locating him and bringing him home."

"Where did you get this video?"

"I'd rather not disclose my source, but I have the original device the video was sent to."

Naomi nodded to herself. The team in Nigeria had gone in on her orders, and she bore the responsibility for their deaths. She would champion this rescue and bring Gunny Taylor home. The video and device could be scrubbed for metadata and provide leads to locate the sender.

"That's fine. Let's meet so I can get things moving and get him back."

"Isaac and I are already in the air headed your way. We'll see you in a couple hours."

7

Alexander

Mojave Air and Space Port, California

When he stepped through the cabin door, it felt like he was walking into an oven. The dry heat was overwhelming and suffocating with a burnt smell that is unique to the desert. Alexander had seen the commercial airliner storage where dozens of planes were parked. Most would be stripped for parts before being turned to scrap. The meeting in Texas had lasted far longer than desired, but one wore the requisite disguise to complete the mission.

Change wasn't something that the great powers found easy, but it was the pruning that allowed the rose to realize the greatest version of itself. If the rose could, it would likely resist the shears, not understanding the beauty and growth that would come after the pain. The rose would try to fight back, to send its thorns after him. That was fine. They could have him after he'd accomplished what he needed to do. The pruning shears were almost ready. The philanthropists in the Lone Star state unknowingly provided shielding for his real agenda. It was protection against the rose discovering the true plan until it was too late. The Texans believed the HERMES satellites would make the world smaller and better. They were right; HERMES would do that, just not in the way they expected.

The path he'd taken to get here was a long and dirty one. He'd been forced to work with unsavory people, some of them genuine monsters, criminals, and terrorists who had no thought for anyone other than themselves or those like them.

It was all a means to an end.

Alexander reflected on his actions, contemplating the monster he'd had to become. He wasn't a psychopath. He didn't enjoy the pain he'd caused. His consolation was that most of it had been against evil people. Still, there had been, and doubtless still would be, innocents caught up in the proverbial net.

Labor pains were the price one paid to bring new life into the world. And generations of those new lives to come would be the ones to benefit from his actions.

A golf cart waited to meet him as he descended the stairs. The driver was none other than the CEO of the space industry startup Alexander was here to see. He was a former SpaceX engineer who'd realized he could create an improved delivery system while lowering operating costs.

SpaceX had demonstrated that with funding and ingenuity, there were huge profits to be made. The company, founded by tech visionary Elon Musk, had revolutionized the industry by creating better rockets that could be reused by landing themselves. It was a technological marvel, the inner workings of which Alexander could not even begin to understand.

He remembered the awe he'd felt when man had first walked on the Moon. The surge of creativity and hope at the idea of the boundless potential of humanity when people worked together toward what seemed like an unattainable goal. The cell phone now in his pocket held greater computing power than all the technology which had safely guided those brave pioneers. Mankind had extended the limits of possibility by risking everything and venturing into the unknown, fueled by a common purpose.

Common purpose. That's what the world lacked now. And Alexander would provide it.

This small company needed a sizable contract to show investors they were a risk worth taking. Alexander was in the market to have more satellites launched. The CEO was eager to secure the contract as it would signal to the venture capitalists that his operation was a legitimate player and worth additional investment.

Alexander was given a running tour as they drove toward the hangar from which the company worked.

"Did you know that Mojave Airport was the first facility in the United States to be licensed for the horizontal launch of reusable spacecraft? It was certified in the early 2000s as a spaceport."

"I had no idea," Alexander said. "That's why you chose to locate your company here?"

"Yes, exactly. This place has become a Mecca of sorts for those trying to enter the Space industry. A lot of flight testing takes place here. Mojave is home to the National Test Pilot School. The supersonic corridor is helpful, and due to the airfield's proximity to Edwards Air Force Base, the airspace is restricted from ground level to an unlimited height. It's kinda funny because it means when the Moon is passing overhead, it's actually entering restricted airspace."

Alexander smiled like an indulgent father. "You must see some pretty interesting things here."

"That's for sure. Do you see that plane over there?" the CEO said. Alexander looked in the indicated direction at the specified aircraft. He was familiar with the Lockheed L-1011 TriStar, having ridden on them many times during their tenure in commercial aviation. The design was visually unique, with engines on the wings and one on the tail.

Declining to elaborate on his experiences, Alexander nodded. "Yes, it's interesting. You don't see many like that anymore."

The CEO laughed. "I should say not. That's the last one of its kind still flying. It's called *Stargazer*, and Northrop Grumman uses it to launch Pegasus rockets. They even played around with some anti-satellite capabilities. Interesting concept, but not the route you need to worry about considering the satellite size you're putting into orbit. Speaking of which, my team has some issues which need your input."

"I will do my best, but to be honest, I'm just the finance department. I'm not well-versed in the technical aspects of the equipment. I can connect you with the right people if you need more details than I can provide. Also, is there any possibility I could get a tour of *Stargazer*? My father was an airline pilot. The first flight I ever took was on that model."

It was true in part. Alexander's father had been a pilot, but not for an airline. As a member of the Royal Norwegian Air Force, he'd flown with the No. 331 squadron that helped defend London during World War 2. His father's military accomplishments had secured him a job as the chief pilot for King Olav V after the war. That position opened the door for Alexander to attend a prestigious boarding school in Switzerland.

"Absolutely. I'm pretty good friends with the guys over at Northrop Grumman. I could even see if they have any pilots around to take you on a short flight if that would be something you're interested in," the CEO said, delighted to be able to win extra points with a big client.

"That would be lovely," Alexander said.

* * *

The Grand Coulee Dam, Washington

The meeting in California with Alexander's new partners was most productive. They agreed to facilitate the launch of 15 satellites over the next four months, with an option for 100 more if everything went according to plan. Their state-of-the-art standalone launch system was one of the reasons the startup had appealed to Alexander in the first place, but he found himself even more pleased with their strict security protocols. The CEO was concerned to the point of near paranoia about rival companies hacking his servers for proprietary data. This suited Alexander rather well, as it meant their current setup was seemingly impenetrable, and the CEO was in contract negotiations to hire a company to provide even further evaluation.

During the meeting, the company made some massive claims. He was familiar with a few already and was impressed by the solid data they'd used to back those assertions. The most notable boast was one of the engineers saying they'd be able to launch the satellites no matter what. Even in the middle of an apocalypse if needed. It was rather brash, but Alexander liked the man's confidence.

Now he was here in Washington. The final stop in what he hoped would be his last visit to the United States for a long time. If he was fortunate, he'd never have to return.

The bureaucrat from the Department of Reclamation waiting for Alexander at the start of the road spanning the Grand Coulee Dam preened like a peacock. From the look of him, he'd bought into whatever self-congratulatory rhetoric his department used for ego-boosting propaganda. Undoubtedly they claimed something like the security of the universe depended on them to keep the sunlit and Earth spinning.

As he approached, Alexander surveyed the massive structure. It was the largest hydroelectric dam in the United States, standing 500 feet tall with a length that fell 57 feet short of a mile. He couldn't help but be impressed. A small part of him was sad to think about the impending destruction of this architectural marvel.

"Daniel Ivan Matthews. You can call me Danny," his guide stretched out a hand. Alexander smiled and pulled his own hand from his blue windbreaker to shake it.

"Alexander. Thank you for taking the time to show me around."

"Of course. But I gotta say I've never given a private tour. Is there anything in particular you what to see?" Danny asked.

"Why don't you proceed as you would. If I have specific questions, I'll be sure to ask."

"They said you were some kind of investor. I don't believe the dam is for sale," Danny said.

Alexander smiled. "I'm not looking to buy the dam. My firm is a big proponent of clean energy and green technology. We have a client who is interested in building several hydroelectric dams. I would like to understand the technology, environmental impact, and sustainability before giving the ok."

"Where are they wanting to build?"

"Europe, but that's all I'm at liberty to say," Alexander said, attempting to stem this flow of curiosity before he had too many lies to remember.

Seemingly satisfied, Danny turned and began his tour spiel. "Construction on the Grand Coulee Dam began in 1933 and was completed in 1941." Alexander tuned out the monologue.

"How much power does it generate?" Alexander asked, when an appropriate pause presented itself in Danny's commentary. He peered over the railing at the blue waters below. They looked so calm and peaceful. Content to remain where they were.

"Around 21 billion kilowatts per year. That's enough to power 2 million homes, and it's all clean energy," his guide assured him.

Alexander gave a low whistle, and Danny nodded proudly as though he was the one turning the huge turbines that produced this almost unbelievable amount of power.

Those power numbers and this dam were a testament to the truth about water. Like a Ring Wraith in a Tolkien story, it was always hunting, searching, and pushing for the slightest weakness against which to exercise its full might.

The water just needed a little help. Help that one of the HERMES satellites would provide. While the communication technology on board was as advertised, the platform also hid a secret. A 20-foot-long, nine-ton tungsten rod, along with a targeting and launch system. The impact would be equivalent to a tactical nuke without the radiation that would render the area uninhabitable for generations.

The idea of kinetic orbital strikes was generally thought to be the stuff of science fiction. However, the US Air Force had studied it for decades, ending the project in the early 2000s. The cost of these weapons was significant and for governments such as the United States, they held no significant advantage over the use of conventional weapons. For Alexander the option was perfect.

HERMES provided the ability to hit multiple targets around the planet at the same time. The destruction of the largest energy production facilities and oil refineries would force the world's population to take the conservation of Earth more seriously.

Presently poisonous political policies, shortsighted, self-centered systems, and countries courting cancerous corporations were formidable obstacles to be sure, but Alexander was patient. Unlike the water behind this dam, he would create the opportunity for change. The Eden Initiative had been decades in the making. Once launched, it would not only be able to stop but also reverse the systematic ecological rape of the planet.

He felt the weight of his responsibility to future generations. It seemed as though everyone around him was racing to see who could be first to destroy the planet. Fossil fuel consumption was out of control. Most studies agreed that if current trends continued, Earth would run out of oil in less than 50 years.

Alexander would not be alive to witness it, and for that he was grateful.

Change was imperative. A paradigm-shifting realignment of priorities.

"Did you know when the dam was completed in 1941, it was considered the eighth wonder of the world?" Danny asked.

Alexander shook his head, lost in his own thoughts.

This place could be a cornerstone to build on. The key to a revolution that would hopefully save Earth.

Save the planet. Now that's a rather grand and ambitious idea. It's all so simple. Just change the way everyone lives.

Most of humanity had what Alexander liked to think of as 'Burger King Syndrome.' They wanted everything fast, cheap, and their way.

The easy choice was to keep getting inexpensive electricity from coal power plants and driving gasoline-powered cars. The harder but more logical option was the sustainable choice of investing in renewable energy.

Politicians in America had somehow managed to turn protecting the planet into a divisive topic. Solar power and wind farms were the new dirty words. In fact, in an ode to convenience, most Americans couldn't be bothered to engage in even the most basic forms of recycling. It was easier to buy cheap garbage from China than to create a culture of conservation.

Alexander's phone rang, interrupting his thoughts about the world that could be. The name on the caller ID snapped him right back into the present. Placing his hand on Danny's elbow, he held up the device.

ALEXANDER

"A business associate. I must take this call," he apologized, already moving away from his tour guide.

"What have you learned?" Alexander skipped the pleasantries and got straight to the point.

"We have a problem. The Americans have the video."

"How do you know?" Alexander asked, feeling pressure starting to build in his sinuses. He didn't understand why this country couldn't keep their nose out of everyone else's business. It would feel so good to put them in their rightful place. It had been hard to resist the temptation of targeting Washington DC with one of the orbital strikes. It would be so very satisfying to see that swamp with a smoking crater in the middle of it.

"One of our people reported it was brought to his section for verification and to check for any metadata that could provide exploitation opportunities."

Alexander's mind was racing.

The American government was unparalleled at tracking targets, particularly through electronic means, though the Chinese were progressing in that field as well. Their persecution of the Uyghur people was an excellent case in point. There were bigger things to worry about than the idiocy of religion. Mankind needed to get off their knees and realize they were responsible for their destiny. There was no supreme being who would save them when they succeeded in destroying the planet.

Very soon Alexander would take all the sticks away from the bickering children and force them to work together. The initial loss of life would be terrible. Hundreds of thousands would die and he regretted it had to be that way. However, billions more still would be saved and the survival of humanity would be ensured. As long as this crack in his plan wasn't allowed to develop into a cavern.

A lapse in judgment by one of his employees had placed him in this situation. One couldn't provide advanced technology to monkeys and expect no one to ask questions when it was discovered. The betrayal had been so personal he'd wanted to handle the termination himself. He'd been robbed of that opportunity for now.

Alexander clenched his jaw. The pain moved from his sinuses to his temples. He wanted to scream but instead modulated his voice to a soothing, reassuring tone. "I have complete faith in you. Handle this."

Unlike Sergej, who got into trouble when left to his own devices, Zhao was resourceful and operated best with direction and room to maneuver. Alexander had spent decades creating his networks and developing contacts. All with a single-minded purpose of protecting the planet. Humanity was like a small child who needed a rational adult to care for her. Fortunately for them, he was a competent manager willing to take on the job.

8

Isaac

Miami, Florida

I wasn't sure I'd slept at all. Jimmy's beaten and bloody face had taken up permanent residence in my mind. I felt the grinding frustration of needing to act but having nowhere to go. I knew it was foolish to rush off to Nigeria in search of my friend without more information, but it didn't make waiting any easier.

The flight to Maryland had been a distraction, at least. It had been nice to get in the air and cruise. Sarah and I had met Naomi, grabbed some lunch, and handed over the phone. She had assured us she'd make sure it was a priority. Now that the CIA had proof he was alive, they would be able to point their vast resources toward getting him back. That was a win.

On the other hand, there was nothing for me to do. I was supposed to be planning the Federal Reserve job, but I struggled to focus. Sarah seemed to understand. Yesterday when she came into my office, where I was staring into space, plotting a Ramboesque solo infiltration of a terrorist encampment, she'd sent me home to relax. I grabbed Derek and we decided to go diving instead. He had needed to let off steam anyway. Something was up between him and Sarah, but I hadn't asked for details. I had enough on my mind.

It turned out to be a memorable dive.

THE EDEN INITIATIVE

* * *

I dove off the back of the *Grace O'Malley* into the dark blue of the Atlantic Ocean. The cool water felt like a lover's embrace. A welcome home I could get lost in forever. As I swam deeper, the water pressure embedded the goggles into my face.

I was about one hundred feet below the *Grace O'Malley* when I stopped, rotating myself so that I hung motionless. I didn't have a depth gauge; it was just a general feeling based on experience. It was deep enough to afford solitude without going so far it would rob me of my relaxation time.

The water around me was empty save for the boat and the anchor chain that descended into the darkness below.

The video of Jimmy had replayed over and over in my mind for the entire boat ride. He sat in that wooden chair, hands tied behind his back. He'd been tortured but was unbroken. Unbroken and alive.

A feeling. A primal sense more than a conscious thought caused me to look to my left. A blue-gray shape moved against the navy blue of the water beyond. As the form solidified and loomed closer, my heart stopped.

A Mako shark was headed right for me. Despite being an extremely aggressive species, very few Mako attacks are reported, because the animals themselves tend to stay miles offshore. It's also likely most people who are attacked offshore don't survive to report the encounter.

Even if I'd started swimming the moment I saw it, there would have been no chance of making it to the safety of the boat. The creature's dead black eyes were locked on me as it approached, mouth slightly open, displaying a terrifying array of jagged teeth. Its eyes seemed to drill into my soul. It wasn't swimming at top speed, but the almost lazy flick of its tail propelled it at a rate faster than any Olympic swimmer. I felt my right hand slowly curling into a fist.

So, now you're going to punch a shark? How do you see that playing out?

The Mako was no more than 10 feet long, but in that moment it was like standing on a runway watching a C5 Globemaster about to land on me. Its mouth looked as huge as the caves I'd seen in Afghanistan.

ISAAC

The massive predator banked in a half circle around me. The creature was close enough that I could have reached out and touched it. I wished I could say I was brave enough to do it.

I'll turn in my man card later.

Frozen in terror, I watched it descend into the darkness below. Then came the rush of adrenaline, and my heart raced the kicking of my legs as they launched me through the water faster than I'd ever moved in my life. During the entire ascent, my mind screamed at me that the Mako was right behind me, its jaws closing.

I was up the ladder before I had time to register that I'd reached the safety of the boat.

I pulled myself up onto the dive platform, turned, and vomited back into the ocean in relief.

* * *

I blinked my eyes and shook my head as the sound of eggs sizzling in the frying pan pulled me back to the present. That huge, toothy grin was seared into my mind. It was the stuff of nightmares. A sip of coffee helped me settle back into the reality that I was on dry land with all my limbs intact.

Between the encounter with the shark and memories of Jimmy, I'd found myself at the liquor store for one of the first times since getting sober. Then I'd sat on the couch staring into the bottle of Jim Beam I'd purchased for what seemed like hours—fighting the overwhelming urge to open it and drown the guilt.

I looked over my shoulder into the living room. The bottle sat, unopened, on the coffee table.

Did I refuse to drink it because not being able to escape is the bigger torment?

I couldn't stop thinking about Jimmy. As of a few weeks ago, he'd been alive. Was he still? If so, where was he? Why hadn't there been a ransom demand or even, God forbid, an execution video? What possible benefit could it serve some second-rate terrorist group to hold him in secret? If I was honest, it didn't matter. Boko Haram was going to experience the full wrath of the United States military when they came for Jimmy.

I smiled, imagining Special Forces infiltrating the camp like silent, creeping death. Once they had Jimmy secured, they would call for an evacuation. Hearing the sound of the Black Hawks approaching, the base would stir like a hornets' nest mistaken for a piñata. That's when the camp would get lit up like the Fourth of July. Hellfire missiles fired from drones that had quietly watched the infiltration would race in, destroying machine gun installations. It would be a waste of time to radio for reinforcements because the NSA would have disabled all their communications equipment.

I wished I could be on the team who went to bring Jimmy home. That would be worth staying sober for. But instead I was left with the only thing I could do right now: wait for the powers-that-be to find him and execute the rescue.

Maybe I should take a couple of days to relax and go diving before heading to Denver to case the Federal Reserve. This time though, I'd be sticking a bit closer to shore. No sense in tempting fate. It would be a shame to get myself eaten by a shark. Then I'd have no story to tell Jimmy when he came home about how I'd infiltrated the most secure bank in America.

I still couldn't believe I was getting paid to break into a bank.

A knock on the apartment door interrupted my reverie. In a move borne more of habit than any perceived necessity, I snatched my pistol off the coffee table as I headed toward the door. If I didn't, it would be the one time I'd actually need it.

Looking through the peephole, I saw Marissa standing in my hallway.

At least she knocked. That's likely more than she does for most people she visits. I wonder if she took the stairs all the way up here.

When we'd left the office to go to lunch the other day, Marissa had insisted on taking the stairs. When I asked her why, she offered some explanation about needing to get her steps in. As far as excuses went it was second-rate, but I hadn't pushed. We'd gone out for fish tacos and it had turned out to be a rather enjoyable lunch. I did make a point of never letting my food or drink out of sight. As they say, "Drug me once shame on you, drug me twice, it's kinda my own fault."

ISAAC

I still didn't know what sort of work Marissa, Sarah, or Naomi had done when they worked together at the CIA, but it had to be a job for which they didn't list vacancies on their website. Well, I say I didn't know, but that was only because none of them had ever said, "Hey Isaac, I used to kill people for Uncle Sam." When I took what I knew of working with Sarah, added my own line of employment, and combined those with Marissa's theatrics on the plane and dozens of other bits of information I'd gleaned from all three women… I might not have all the puzzle pieces, but I didn't need them to gain a clear picture.

I clicked the deadbolt aside and swung the door open.

"I won't bother asking how you found my apartment."

"And yet you went through the trouble of saying you weren't going to ask."

Marissa pushed past me toward the kitchen.

First point goes to Lady Shoot' Em-in-the-Face. That nickname is weak. Maybe Princess. Nah. I'm gonna need something better.

"Why don't you come on in? I'm making breakfast," I said to her back, having no clue what was going on. Why was she in my house? When we had coffee a few days ago, she'd mentioned she was going out of town for a job. It seemed unlikely her new job was as a traveling Bible saleswoman, but I hadn't asked.

She didn't respond, instead helping herself to a cup of coffee. She then turned the stove heat off and dumped the eggs on a plate.

"I thought you were supposed to be a good cook," Marissa said, looking mischievous.

"Have you ever eaten anything I've made?"

Picking up a fork, she took a small bite of egg. Tapping the ends of the fork against her lower lip, looking as though she was a cooking show judge. "I mean, it's ok."

Pretending to be offended, I grabbed the plate from her and said, "If you know someone who makes better eggs, you should go barge in on them. Besides, what if I hadn't been dressed?"

Marissa took a sip of her coffee, giving me a salacious look. "Do you normally answer the door undressed, or did I just have the misfortune of picking a time you had clothes on?"

I felt my cheeks redden. "No, but I can't say it's never happened."

"That's disappointing. My chances might have been better though if that had been opened," she said, waving her hand to indicate the bottle on the coffee table.

I decided to ignore that witticism.

"Why are you here? I thought you had a job."

"I did, but it's done. For now. It's kinda like an ongoing freelance assignment."

"Welcome back."

"Thanks. So, you going to put the gun down or shoot me?" Marissa asked, acknowledging the firearm for the first time.

"I haven't decided yet," I said as I placed the gun on the counter.

I took a moment to consider the paradox now occurring in my kitchen. Less than a month ago, this woman, by her own admission, had been planning to kill me and then jump out of an airplane with the guy I was there to capture. Instead, she had drugged me, disappeared, and then reappeared with video evidence that my best friend, who had been declared dead, was in fact alive and being tortured. Oh, and she had waited three whole weeks to let me know. And now, I was flirting with her.

I wasn't sure where things were headed with Marissa, if anywhere. For my part, I had no expectations. At this moment in time, she was a Pumpkin Spice Latte. A seasonal treat that should be enjoyed while here and remembered fondly when gone.

They said cocaine was a good drug, but human rationale. Now, that will take you on some crazy trips.

"Where was your job?"

"Turks and Caicos."

A straight answer. That was a surprise. I had expected a redirect or a sudden feigned interest in some picture in my living room.

"That sounds terrible. Having to work in one of the most beautiful places in the world. It must have been murder." I made a mental note to do a search engine check for recent events in that part of the world.

Taking another sip of coffee, she offered a knowing smile, ignoring the insinuation. "This coffee, on the other hand, is delicious. Where did you get it?"

"It's from a local shop that does small-batch roasts. Maybe I'll take you there sometime. If you're around. And if you tell me why you're here."

She sighed. "I was wondering if I could catch a ride with you. I need to talk to Sarah. I don't want to just show up at her house."

"Good choice. Arriving unannounced here is one thing. Doing that at Sarah's wouldn't be a healthy life decision." I left her to interpret that however she wanted, but I was thinking about Sarah's two huge Dobermans.

Fifteen minutes later, we were driving toward Peregrine's office.

"This is a pretty nice car," Marissa said in a loud voice to make herself heard over the engine's roar and wind whipping through the open windows.

"This old thing? Just a hobby car."

The truth was when I found Shelly, she was a beat-up rust bucket sitting in the yard along with three other vehicles. The owner had no idea it was a 1969 Mustang Boss 429 and an absolute jewel of American muscle.

I bought her, along with the family of squirrels living in her trunk, for $1,000. I'd worked on the car for the better part of two years in between frequent deployments. Shelly was now in mint condition, and I'd had several people make cash offers for $400K. I loved my car. She reminded me of simpler times.

9

Naomi

Miami, Florida

Naomi exited the Uber four blocks from her target building. A habit developed over years of covert intelligence operations. The distance would allow her to stretch her legs while also assessing her environmental situation. She couldn't remember a point in her life when she hadn't tactically assessed her surroundings. Ever since her grandfather had joined the OSS after fleeing Nazi Germany, espionage had been the family business. The training started at a young age. She hadn't realized until she was much older that the fun games with Daddy were in fact lessons grooming her to pay attention to the world around her.

As far as the day went, the blue morning sky and tang of the salt from the sea air felt refreshing. There was something therapeutic about a sunny beach and an ocean breeze. But therapy would have to wait. She was here for work.

Stretching her arms out as though to embrace the beautiful day, Naomi yawned. The morning meeting with Peregrine had necessitated an earlier flight than she would have preferred, and she was in need of coffee. There had been a significant development with the video Sarah and Isaac had brought her. Due to the nature and sensitivity of the information, she'd felt an in-person meeting was best.

NAOMI

Twenty minutes later, Naomi ascended the front steps of the Sabadell Financial Center coffee in hand. It was incredible what Sarah had been able to accomplish since leaving the CIA. She'd walked out with nothing but her name and somehow managed to build a multimillion dollar business with a corporate office in the high-powered section of Miami. Naomi was proud of her friend's success. There was no doubt in her mind that if Sarah had chosen to set up shop in New York City, she'd have an address in downtown Manhattan.

The dark angel grumbled deep within the pit that held her. It was an irritation Naomi did her best to ignore. She and Sarah had served The United States of America for years. Project Olympus eliminated more threats and saved more lives than the world would ever know.

Even though Naomi had understood the decision to disband their unit on an intellectual level, it had torn her apart. They'd been a family, even if a slightly dysfunctional one. Sarah and Marissa had abandoned her and their country, leaving Naomi to toil alone in meaningful service to her country. It wasn't like there was a Former Assassins Anonymous support group she could attend. Sarah and Marissa were, quite literally, the only two people in the world who understood what it was like to work sub rosa, terminating threats to the US. And then they were gone.

Marissa had disappeared soon after exiting CIA employment. That hadn't been a huge shock. Despite the best efforts of the other two, she'd always held herself apart. Any feelings of loyalty Naomi might have attributed to her while they were working together had obviously been her imagination. When it became clear Marissa didn't want to be found, Naomi and Sarah assumed they'd never see her again.

The mention of the call sign Hestia after Isaac and Derek had landed in Zurich had shocked her to her core. It was clear Marissa had been attempting to extract Greggor from that plane. He must have been a high priority if she was contracted. However, the who and the why remained a mystery.

While Marissa's behavior had stung, Sarah's betrayal had almost been worse. She'd taken the skill set her country had given her and leveraged it for personal gain and built an empire. She remained the same warm, caring friend Naomi had always known, but now talking to Sarah sometimes made her feel like a middle-aged man wearing a letterman jacket, pining for the glory days when their high school football team had gone to the state championship.

It would have been one thing if she'd turned into just another contractor supporting the military-industrial complex, but Sarah had become something more. That was the unspoken fear Naomi barely acknowledged. A fear that Sarah had achieved heights she herself could never reach.

She did her best to take a machete to the vines of jealousy that grew out of the dark chasm where Artemis was chained. And not a moment too soon. Seeing Sarah waving in the marble atrium brought Naomi back from the abyss. She raised her coffee in acknowledgment and tamped down all the conflicting emotions.

"Hey, friend. Thanks so much for coming down to see us," Sarah said, opening her arms for a hug that Naomi accepted.

"Of course. I'm glad to do what I can. How have you been?"

Sarah gave a soft laugh, hooking her arm in Naomi's and guiding her toward the elevator bank. "There have been some interesting developments we need to talk about in private."

Naomi's interest was piqued. She wondered how her information would affect the current circumstances. Did Peregrine already know? She didn't see how, but the team had recently proved they were just as adept at gathering intelligence as anyone Naomi had worked with to date.

The entry security to the Peregrine office reminded her of the Bat Cave's setup. The secure facility located below the MerchWork warehouse in the middle of the Baltimore Harbor complex was Naomi's base of operation. The Peregrine office offered more of a high-tech-security-consultant feel, as opposed to the secret lair vibe The Bat Cave gave off.

Peregrine might have biometrics, fancy cameras and magnetic locks, but she doubted this office had the hidden, remote-operated machine guns hers did.

The lobby interior reminded her of the visit she and Clark had made to BlackRock corporate headquarters in New York City. The massive hedge fund had required the logistical expertise for which MerchWork was so renowned.

"That view of the harbor always gets me. I don't think I'd ever go home if I worked here," Naomi said.

"That's because you're a workaholic," Sarah smiled. Naomi couldn't argue the truth of the assertion. Still, was it a bad thing that she was dedicated to the defense of her country?

Sarah's personal office was small and spartan. A testament to the fact that she did most of her work with the team.

"Where's everyone else?" Naomi asked.

"Mike's in his office. He spends more time here than anyone. Everyone else will start arriving in another 15 minutes or so. I'm glad you got here a bit early. I have a rather delicate matter I need to discuss with you."

This is getting more ominous by the second.

Naomi folded her hands and rested them on her lap. A slight nod of her head conveyed her agreement. "Sure, what's up?"

"Ok, there's no easy way to say this, so I'm just going to rip the bandage off. Our source for the video is Hestia. She delivered it to us shortly before we brought it to you."

Naomi's nostrils flared, but she remained silent. There would be time for questions later.

How did she make it into Miami? There have to be at least a dozen agencies hunting her right now. That doesn't count the bounty hunters looking to cash in on that huge reward.

There might be a significant reward for Marissa's capture, but Naomi pitied the fools who attempted it with anything short of a SWAT team. Marissa had been a predator unmatched by anyone other than the woman sitting across from her. Based on the operation to extract Greggor, Naomi had to conclude that Marissa's skills were just as sharp as ever.

"She's offered to help with the hunt for Gunnery Sergeant Taylor. Between that and the fact that I owe her a favor, I hoped you could help her with her current situation." Unspoken was Naomi owed Sarah. A chip Sarah had never looked to cash in until now.

The thought of seeing Marissa after all this time tied Naomi's stomach in knots, bringing up unwelcome feelings. So, she did what came naturally to her. She shoved them into the dark place with all the other things she didn't want to confront.

Naomi bit the side of her lip and scratched her head before smoothing down her ponytail. "You know I'll do what I can, but I don't have a lot of pull over who the Agency is hunting. Can you explain why she was on that plane? Aside from the terroristic actions of blowing a door off an airplane in flight, the only thing the CIA is interested in is her connection to Greggor. I'd need something to counterbalance her actions."

Sarah steepled her fingers, drumming the tips in contemplation. "Marissa worked for a company called Banque Suisse."

Naomi leaned forward, massaging the bridge of her nose with thumb and pointer finger as she groaned.

"You're familiar with them?" Sarah asked.

"You could say that. I can't share much, other than they provide assistance to The Company, which makes them close to untouchable."

"That has to be frustrating."

"Usually, yes. But for our purposes, it could help," Naomi mused. "I'm not surprised they have someone with Marissa's skill set on the payroll…" her voice trailed off.

Unbidden she recalled the video from a Special Forces helmet cam in an Afghan raid where a Taliban commander had been killed. Based on the photos she'd seen, it seemed likely an assassin had terminated the commander in the middle of the assault and disappeared without a trace.

Naomi's mind jumped next to the crime scene photos of the Player One club in Tokyo, Japan. Two dead-end leads in a hunt that eventually led to Banque Suisse. At the time, she'd suspected a professional hitter, but had had no definitive leads. Those kills had been well within the scope of Marissa's skill set. Was it possible her former colleague had been her shadow adversary?

Sarah raised her eyebrows and pretended to look through some papers on her desk. "I'll have to recheck, but I don't think an in-house assassin is included in my bank's services."

Naomi laughed. "I'm just a government employee. I'm happy with direct deposit and free checking."

"I remember those days. You should come to the dark side. It pays better."

"There was this drug cartel leader's house I…ummm visited once. It was a fancy place. A fountain in the courtyard and everything."

"And they say crime doesn't pay," Sarah replied with a twinkle in her eye.

Naomi grunted in response.

Sarah checked the time on her phone. "Most of the team should be here by now. Do you want to come with me to the conference room to tell us what you've learned about the footage we gave you?"

Nodding she rose and followed Sarah, wondering again what the other woman knew. It seemed odd that Sarah hadn't asked about the analysis and intelligence data the CIA had gleaned. Athena had always been looking to collect that one extra bit of information that could prove decisive.

Naomi's scan of the room was short-circuited by the sight of Derek Russo. She allowed herself a second to admire the view, but remembered not to stare. Looking back at Sarah, she was surprised to see pursed lips and a glare aimed in Derek's direction. Trouble in paradise? Naomi wondered if the situation was personal or professional. The idea of dating a subordinate was strange, and felt like it crossed a few ethical lines.

"Boy drama?" Naomi whispered.

"A difference of opinions," Sarah said, not bothering to lower her voice. As Sarah moved to talk to Selma, Naomi noticed Marissa sitting at the end of the table. The smaller woman stared at her. Naomi scolded herself for not doing a better scan of the room when she'd entered. Failing to notice people was the kind of mistake that got people killed.

It was the first time she'd seen Marissa in person since she'd walked out of the Project Olympus facility. Naomi felt numb… unsure what she should say or do. In Sarah's office, the idea had been theoretical. Now it was real.

"How have you been?" Naomi asked, suddenly aware of the fact she didn't know what to do with her hands. She resorted to sticking them in her pockets. Naomi was also startled to find she'd crossed the room to stand in front of Marissa.

Marissa's smile was small and looked forced. "I'm ok."

In the intervening silence, Naomi became aware that the other occupants of the room had gone quiet and were watching their reunion intently.

What else is there to say? Now perhaps isn't the best time to confirm my suspicions about Afghanistan and Japan.

"I'm going to grab a water. Want anything?" Naomi asked, desperate to extricate herself from the awkward situation. Marissa raised a water bottle in response. Naomi pivoted on her heel and walked to the mini-fridge at the other end of the room.

Sarah was talking to Selma when she arrived.

"Have you seen Mike or Isaac? I assume Isaac is here, since Marissa is here."

Why would she assume that?

"I just saw them both in Mike's office," Selma said.

"Would you mind going to get them?"

"No problem. I'll be right back."

Sarah turned to Naomi. "How about you? Are you ready? We're excited to hear what you have."

"Yeah," Naomi said, remembering to grab a bottle of water before she turned to a nearby seat.

Her head swam with all the new information she'd just received, the probable puzzle pieces that had fallen into place. And she still had to get to the reason she'd come all the way down here.

The situation was overwhelming. She was in serious need of some gym time or cordite and gun smoke aromatherapy after this. Perhaps both.

10

Isaac

Peregrine Office - Miami, Florida

"Let's see if Sarah is in her office." I led Marissa through the lobby, glancing back to make sure she wasn't lagging too far behind. I couldn't allow her to walk around our workspace unescorted, and I needed to speak to Mike. He had mentioned some new tech toys he wanted to try on the Federal Reserve recon and I was anxious to see what he had.

Sarah's office door was closed, which was unusual. I assumed she was with Naomi since we'd been expecting her at the meeting today.

"We'll go to the conference room. You can grab a seat until Sarah comes out. I have a few things I need to do and…"

"And you don't need me wandering into a sensitive area. I get it." Marissa gave me a reassuring pat on the arm.

Fortunately Selma was in the meeting room and she took over chaperone duties, directing Marissa to the mini-fridge. I ducked out to touch base with Mike.

To call the space where Mike worked at Peregrine an 'office' was like referring to a water park as a bathtub. At least a dozen drones of varying sizes hovered overhead. Two had mechanical arms and were tossing a golf ball back and forth in a game of drone catch. There was a literal buzz in the air from an open server rack. Mike leaned back in a chair, fidgeting with his Rubik's cube, staring blankly at six massive computer screens.

The Rubik's cube had been a Christmas gift from Jimmy. Mike had mastered it in minutes and then it had taken up residence on his desk and I'd never seen him touch it again. Until after I got back from Switzerland. Now he was never without it. Before I could start asking Mike about new tech toys, Selma Wade entered the room.

"Who's with Marissa?" I asked.

"Derek."

"What a gentleman. That's taking service to the next level," I grinned.

Selma didn't answer, but her facial expression conveyed her doubts.

"You and Mike are needed in the conference room; the meeting is about to start."

If I were into understating things, I'd say the tension in the room was palpable. Derek's eyes were shooting daggers at Sarah, who ignored him. Elsa's ice palace was a warmer atmosphere than the awkward unease between Marissa and Naomi. The two were sitting at opposite ends of the table and looking anywhere but at each other.

Next to me, Mike appeared oblivious to the atmosphere in the room, as he fiddled with his Rubik's cube. It had become his new coping mechanism over the past few weeks. Selma and I glanced at each other before looking back at Mike. I cracked a smile that she returned. It seemed we were both thinking the same thing. At least some things were still normal.

Sarah stood up as soon as we'd taken our seats. "We all know the primary focus of this meeting is for Ms. Kaufman to provide an intelligence update for the proof of life video we received from Ms. Diaz. I'm going to turn the floor over to Ms. Kaufman.

Okaay...we're using last names and being professional now.

Naomi stood as Sarah took her seat. "Thanks so much. I have a couple of quick questions before I continue." Naomi turned to look right at Marissa. "Ms. Diaz, where did you get the video?"

Marissa cleared her throat before speaking. "It came to the phone I took from Charles Greggor."

Naomi nodded as though she'd suspected as much. "Were you aware Mr.

Greggor was responsible for the deaths of more than a dozen Americans?"

What does any of this have to do with the video of Jimmy?

Marissa's features turned hard and her eyes showed a defiance that hadn't been there just a moment earlier.

"No," Marissa said.

Namoi had clearly been practicing these lines in her head. "If you actively worked against the interests of the United States of America, that makes you a traitor."

Are we in court? What's the deal with the cross-examination?

"It was just a job," Marissa said, rolling her eyes.

"Just a job!? Just a job!? That was my team. THOSE WERE AMERICAN SOLDIERS! You're a traitor, and I should put a bullet in you right now!!" Naomi roared.

"You're lucky it was just a job. Otherwise, I would have killed you in Tokyo. I watched you and your partner go into the Yakuza enforcer's apartment. I could have walked in behind you and shot all three of you. It would have saved me a lot of trouble. Instead, I only eliminated him," Marissa countered.

And now we've arrived at the Confessing to Murder to Defend Other Actions portion of the show.

Naomi's anger faltered. For a moment, she stood there in silence, before addressing Sarah. "Be that as it may, keep in mind she may have an ulterior motive for giving you that device, especially in light of what I've learned."

"More than likely, Naomi. But don't you think I wouldn't have verified the video first?" Sarah asked.

"I'm sure you did the best you could," Naomi replied.

"The best I could? What does that mean?" It was Sarah's voice that now dropped to glacial range.

"Unfortunately, the video is a deception. The NSA and CIA each confirmed it. Their analysts determined it has the markers of a deep fake." Naomi's bravado was gone and her disappointment at being the bearer of such disheartening news was clear.

The mood in the room felt like someone had deflated the bouncy house while everyone was still playing inside. I had recently read about deep fake technology. It was a by-product of deep learning algorithms and artificial intelligence, things far beyond my understanding. Simply put, if you had enough images of a person, this technology enabled you to make them appear to say or do anything you wanted. Technology had progressed to a point where you couldn't determine what was real or false without skilled computer experts on your side.

"No! No! No! No!" Mike said, shaking his head. He had put his cube down and was now laser-focused on Naomi.

"Mike, would you be able to verify if it's a deep fake?" Sarah asked.

"I already did. It was the first thing I checked. It's an obvious candidate for it, so yes, it's literally the first thing I checked for. The equipment they recorded it on. The camera must have been old. Some of the file got corrupted in the transfer. But no, it's one hundred percent real," Mike insisted.

"If Mike says it's real, I believe him," Sarah said. I knew for a fact that Mike's skills were legendary. Still, I hadn't known how far Sarah's faith in him extended until that moment. Apparently far enough that she'd put him up against the combined brainpower of the NSA and CIA.

If Sarah believed him, so did I.

Naomi stared at Sarah, evidently nonplussed—doubt written on her face; no matter how talented Mike was, he couldn't have found something all those brilliant people with their university degrees had missed.

"Sarah, it's not just the video. It's also bomb damage analysis and an eyewitness account of Gunnery Sergeant Taylor's location just before the detonations. There is no plausible way he could have survived. The event has been simulated hundreds of times, and he dies every time. That video was also traced back to the HUMINT source we used to locate the weapons in Nigeria." The frustration was evident in Naomi's voice. It was obvious she wanted the video to be real so they could send in the cavalry and get him back. However, the human intelligence source in Nigeria seemed to be the final nail in Jimmy's coffin as far as Naomi was concerned.

It's fake? How is that possible?

My heart was in my throat. I felt like I was watching game seven of the

World Series, bottom of the ninth, and my team trailing by two runs, down to their last strike. Comebacks like that had happened, but I didn't know whether my team had enough magic left to pull it off this time.

"Why don't you believe it's real if it's from the same source who gave you the weapons caches?" Marissa asked.

Naomi whipped her head around to glare at the smaller woman. "We have very strong evidence he's the one who sold us out. I guess it was just a *job* to him, too!"

"What's the name of the informant?" Sarah asked, before Marissa could fire off a retort.

I agreed with Sarah's line of thinking. It would be nice to talk to him. Chances were he wouldn't enjoy our conversation, but in the end, we'd find out why he'd sent the video. Or, at least, where he'd gotten it. Real or not, the video had been created and sent for a purpose.

"I can't tell you that," Naomi at least had the decency to look apologetic.

"You've got to be kidding me. You didn't hesitate to share information before." Derek had been quiet up to this point, taking everything in, but now he joined the fray.

"That was different," Naomi said.

"It sure was, wasn't it?" Derek was on his feet. I recognized the look on his face. He was fired up. "You had a problem. A problem that the big, bad CIA with all its vast resources couldn't solve. So, where did you come? Here to little ol' Peregrine, just out here doing the 'best we could.' We risked a multimillion dollar contract to help you, but you know what? It's not even about the money. The best we could. Well, it seems like our best is better than yours."

It was decent, as far as rants go. But Derek had certainly done better. I'd give it a 7.5. Higher scores would have required him to draw on an old standby military reference, maybe something about the Spartans at Thermopylae being more skilled despite having fewer soldiers. Any reference to George Washington, Chesty Puller, or the Marines from WW2 would have put it in the 9 point range. Furniture throwing was required for that last point conversion, and Derek had yet to show that level of dedication.

The veins in Naomi's neck were bulging and it looked like she was winding up with a comeback when Sarah took control of the room. "Fighting with each other won't help us solve anything. Naomi, I understand you can't disclose classified information. But Derek has a point. This is a business. We're not just here for the convenience of the CIA."

Derek returned to his seat as Naomi nodded. She still looked tense, but less likely to jump across the table and strangle someone now.

"What about the phone? Can we have it back?" Sarah inquired.

"Property of the US Government now. You know how it goes," Naomi said.

That's awkward. We give you a phone asking for help, and now you tell us the video is a hoax, and we can't have the device back.

"We appreciate you coming down here in person to give us the news. I understand your restrictions, and I don't want to ask you to do something out of line." Sarah's tone was cordial, but her intention was clear. The meeting was over, at least for Naomi. She took the hint, and followed Sarah toward the door. Before she left, she turned and addressed the room, making eye contact with me before looking at the floor. "I'm sorry things turned out this way."

Yeah, well, you and me both.

11

Jimmy

Undisclosed Location

Jimmy's fingers locked onto the arm of the wooden chair. Every muscle in his body had contracted at once. His brain felt like it was on fire, and he was unable even to scream.

As suddenly as it had come, the pain was gone. Jimmy's chin fell to his chest. He could see the electrical cables connected to the shackles around his ankles. Blackness crept in at the periphery of his vision.

"Did you find a satellite phone on your last raid?" Colonel Zhao asked.

Gone was the grandfather figure Jimmy had met at the start of his captivity. The Chinese officer had morphed into a monster that made the beatings by the Boko Haram thugs look like amateur hour. Where the Nigerian terrorists had used fists, feet, and cigarettes, Zhao employed electricity, stress positions, and drugs.

For days Jimmy had lain bound and naked in this room on the razor's edge of hypothermia. The technique known as environmental manipulation served to break prisoners without doing any permanent or physical damage. Jimmy had first become aware of this approach when he brought several high-value prisoners to a CIA black site. Now he was experiencing it firsthand.

Jimmy's eyelids were leaden, and he longed for unconsciousness. He barely felt the needle's prick but was aware of its effects within seconds. The lights seemed to brighten, and he could hear the hum of the fluorescent bulbs in the ceiling. A cold hand lifted his chin, the tips of manicured nails digging into his skin.

"You're not done answering my questions," Zhao said. Jimmy's gaze moved from Zhao's wrist, down his forearm and then stopped, transfixed. On the colonel's shoulder crouched a massive, brown hairy spider.

Clenching his jaw, Jimmy willed the creature to disappear. He'd hallucinated spiders several times from the drugs they'd given him. Instead of disappearing, the spider began to advance down Zhao's outstretched arm, its beady eyes fixed on him.

Jimmy's arachnophobia was like leg day at the gym, intense to the point of defying comprehension.

How did Zhao know he hated spiders? What else had he revealed?

"What electronic devices did your team discover during their on-site exploitation," Zhao asked again. The huge spider had reached his forearm, and Jimmy could've sworn he heard the giant pincers click. He wrenched his head free from Zhao's grip, trying to distance himself from the arachnid.

"Is The Chairman distracting you?" The colonel asked, seeming to notice the spider for the first time. Scooping the creature off his arm, Zhao held it out in his open hand, inches from Jimmy's face. Jimmy thrashed, pushing against the back of the chair, trying to create distance. The logical part of his brain would've told him this animal was a Goliath birdeater. Despite being the world's largest spider, it wasn't a threat to humans. However, right now, the logical portion of Jimmy's brain was being suppressed. Big time.

Pulling his hand back, Colonel Zhao deposited The Chairman in a glass terrarium sitting on the table a few feet away.

Jimmy hadn't noticed it there before and felt like he would have seen that giant abomination otherwise. The shock of the spider being real had rocked his confidence in his perception of reality. Had the other spiders been there? Was this real? Jimmy had experienced this sensation at times when he hung from a pull-up bar. When he was exhausted, and the sweat from his hands made it hard to maintain his grip. But now it was his mind struggling to

JIMMY

hold on.

"Gunnery Sergeant Taylor, I'm just asking about the electronics you saw. I know elite units like yours wear cameras so that your superiors can watch the action in real time. Our own units do the same. I also know there are frequent burst transmissions of high value data that might have immediate follow-on potential. Did you locate any satellite phones?" There was that question again. He kept asking it. Jimmy knew he was on the verge of breaking. Everyone broke.

"You're lying to me. Do you remember what happens when you lie?" The Chinese officer continued, sounding almost regretful, like a parent forced to discipline a rebellious child.

Jimmy remembered. He'd been on the other side of this interrogation routine and while he never enjoyed it, he had always done what was necessary to get the desired information. He also knew that everyone broke at some point, except Rambo and James Bond.

"I don't think you're really a Marine. You're actually a CIA paramilitary thug pretending to be a United States Marine. I know about the Marines. They are honorable and you are not."

That accusation hit deep and enraged Jimmy to his core. Earning his Eagle, Globe, and Anchor at Parris Island had been one of the greatest days of his life. He remembered crying when the Drill Instructor had placed it in his hand, bestowing on him the title of Marine.

"I'm a Marine, not CIA," Jimmy spat, knowing the pain that would come even before Zhao flicked the switch. Familiarity didn't make it any less terrible. The burning and instant seizure of all his muscles weren't something a person could ever get used to.

"Mr. Hassan's statement doesn't agree with that."

Jimmy's head sagged, but he managed to nod as he spoke with care, "Ok, ok, I admit it. I am part of an elite unit."

"Now that we've established you work for the CIA—," Zhao began, before Jimmy interrupted him with a mighty roar of defiance.

"I'm a United States Marine, and we are the greatest fighting force in history." His grip on reality slipped, and he had enough self-awareness to know it. Colonel Zhao looked annoyed as he casually flicked the switch and turned a knob, increasing the voltage coursing through Jimmy's body.

Jimmy was so tired. He had no concept of time and didn't want to fight anymore. The torment would stop if he just answered the questions. He stood at a crossroads with no good decisions. Survival or Death. Survival meant betraying his country. Resistance meant certain death, but there was no telling how long and painful the road to that destination would be. He thought about what Isaac would do. The notion of Northe's undoubtedly belligerent response produced the idea of a smile. Anything more was impossible for him right now.

"There is no reason for all this pain. Let's just have a conversation like two men."

Jimmy began to sing, "From the Halls of Montezuma to the shores of Tripoli."

The clinical mask broke, and Zhao stared at Jimmy as though he'd lost his mind. Maybe he had. It didn't matter anymore. He wished Zhao would just kill him and be done with it. However, Zhao wouldn't kill him; Jimmy would either break or go insane. Maybe even both.

"We fight our country's battles in the air, on land, and sea."

"Just answer the questions I ask," Colonel Zhao said, having regained his composure.

"First to fight for right and freedom and to keep our honor clean."

Zhao sighed as he turned the dial to increase the voltage. Jimmy gave him a defiant look as his voice swelled, "We are proud to claim the title of United States Marines." Before he could continue the next verse of *The Marine's Hymn*, he was hit by a jolt of electricity that caused his muscles to spasm so hard they felt like they were about to be torn off his body.

Jimmy's scream was ragged and primal.

"Gunnery Sergeant Taylor, I think we are done. For now. I will get the answers to my questions," Zhao rose from his chair and walked calmly toward the door. He turned with his hand on the knob to look back at Jimmy.

"But before I go, I'll tell you something. You are never going back to the

United States. You've been abandoned by your own government. Your Central Intelligence Agency received the video Boko Haram made. But they will not act on it. You've been declared dead. I want to help you and stop all this nonsense. Life could be so much easier for you if you would just cooperate."

The feeling was like walking backward and stepping off the edge of a cliff you didn't know was there. The panic was almost heart-stopping. Jimmy didn't want to believe it, but one thing Zhao had yet to do was lie to him.

"How do you know?" Jimmy whispered.

A wicked smile spread across his captor's face, and his next words chilled Jimmy more than a thousand blasts of cold water.

"Because our spies in the NSA declared it to be fake."

12

Naomi

Miami, Florida

Naomi wanted to punch something. Or better yet, someone. She knew better than to bring it up in her debriefings or annual psych evaluations, but when she was angry, it felt good to inflict pain. There had been a time during her days with Project Olympus when she would have gone looking for a fight on a day like this. Back then her rage had consumed her. But it was under control now.

Her dark angel could goad her all she wanted. She wasn't going to pick a fight with some random Joe Citizen just to make herself feel better. Still, she wouldn't turn down the opportunity if it presented itself. There were times when it was useful to unleash her violent side, but right now, Artemis would remain chained in that deep, dark hole.

Naomi stood on the sidewalk outside Sarah's fancy office building, and fumed. She hadn't expected to be dismissed that way. Especially after being asked to cancel an international manhunt for a wanted fugitive who had made her life a living hell. It would be so cathartic to place an anonymous tip detailing Marissa's current whereabouts. But it wasn't feasible. If the SWAT team executed a high-risk arrest warrant on the Peregrine office, she'd be the obvious source. Marissa had an invaluable skill set. Not to mention, her work with Banque Suisse had in all likelihood made her privy to information the intelligence community would kill to get its hands on. Someone would end up cutting a deal with her. She'd be free within weeks and her first order of business would be to exact retribution on the person who'd turned on her. A death sentence so certain that Naomi might as well put the bullet in her head herself.

It wasn't ideal that she had to keep the phone, but she didn't make the rules. With the exception of Mike, they'd all worked for the government. They had to understand her hands were tied.

She was going to have to listen to Clark's gloating "I told you so." He'd urged her to deliver the news in a phone call or an email, but Naomi had insisted on coming in person. She needed to start giving Clark more credit. As annoying as he could be at times, he always had her back.

Naomi looked up and down the street, considering her next move. Like an idiot, she'd booked her return flight for two days from now. She hadn't been so naive as to think she could tell them the video was fake, dust off her hands, and just take Isaac up on the offer he'd made while they were in Switzerland for some scuba diving and great restaurants. But she'd at least expected to be able to process the disappointment with her friends.

Instead, she was out here on the sidewalk and Marissa, in her new role as trusted source, was still inside.

Naomi couldn't wrap her head around it.

You've been replaced by that amoral sociopathic traitor.

She should have known something was amiss when Sarah went all 'sources and methods' on her, refusing to divulge where the video had come from. That was always the first tip-off that something shady had happened. How had Sarah allowed herself to be fooled?

Naomi took a deep breath as her swirling thoughts slowed. She wasn't being entirely fair. Marissa Diaz was many things, yes, maybe even a sociopath. But she wasn't a liar. If Marissa had approached her with the video instead of Sarah, Naomi would have accepted it as credible, too.

She didn't know what to make of the revelation that Marissa had been in the apartment complex in Tokyo. Finding out she was the assassin working for Banque Suisse filled in so many gaps.

But why hadn't she taken out Naomi and Clark? She had to know the pair were a risk to her operation. Marissa knew firsthand the lengths the CIA would go to eliminate threats. If the tables had been turned, she and Clark would not have afforded Marissa the same courtesy. She shuddered, remembering the police report she and Clark had seen, detailing how Daichi Yamamoto had been found murdered in his apartment, still tied to the chair where they had left him. It was sobering to think the Yakuza enforcer had been dead before their elevator reached the ground floor.

I'm alive right now because it really is JUST a job for her. It must be liberating to be able to disconnect from work. It's always personal for me.

But none of this changed the facts about the video. Marissa might not have been in on the deception, but that didn't mean the video was authentic. Didn't Sarah know Naomi wanted Jimmy Taylor to be alive? She had sent him into that warehouse, to his death. She would give anything for him to be alive. But the facts didn't support that reality.

At first, the CIA team had agreed with Mike's findings and believed the video to be authentic. It had looked real to Naomi, but then, so did most of the deep fakes she'd ever seen. That was the point of deep fakes, they looked real. The CIA team lead suggested sending it over to the NSA to see if they could find anything that would help in a targeting package.

The NSA techs were the ones to discover the video was a hoax. The biggest giveaways for most deep fakes are audio flaws and awkward shadows. This footage had none of those problems. It hadn't been until they'd dug deep into the waveforms of video signals that the irregularities became apparent.

Besides, it was absurd to think a single computer guy had found something the NSA's Computer Network Operations (CNO) unit missed. Formerly known as the Tailored Access Operations the CNO was the NSA's premier exploitation unit and quite literally a group of hackers in a league of their own. She'd been told the video was dissected to the binary level.

The Sarah she knew didn't operate on hopes and wishes. Why was she so convinced the footage was authentic despite all the evidence pointing to the contrary?

As Naomi walked down the sunny streets of Miami, she considered returning to give them the informant's name. It wasn't like the CIA was using him anymore, at least for the moment. Friends and enemies tended to be seasonal in the espionage game. The Agency suspected the Nigerian informant had sold them out, but was unable to prove it. Assets were a lot like her dad's mason jar of randomly sized screws; you kept them around on the off chance you found a use for them one day.

But no, she wasn't about to go crawling back, begging to be part of their little club. They could figure it out without her, if they were that good.

It killed her to admit it, but Naomi knew Peregrine *was* that good, even if they operated in the deep gray areas of legality. She'd seen them in action while hunting for Greggor and the stolen Titan software.

The thing about the video that kept eating at her was the why. 'Why' was usually the critical question; the one that often answered the who, and then the how.

The video had been produced by Boko Haram—all the computer nerds had agreed on that. They had even determined that the vocabulary, accent, syntax, and cadence of the off-camera voice supported it being Nigerian.

Why bother going through the effort of creating a deep fake of an American Special Forces Marine who was killed in a weapons raid? What was the end game? How did the terror group have the technological ability to create those types of videos? It had been good enough to make it through several rounds of analysis. It wasn't until the NSA dug deeper that they discovered the truth. That meant it wasn't made with off-the-shelf software.

These were all questions she wished she could discuss with the Peregrine team. But it wasn't going to happen today. She might as well take herself to the beach.

Standing on the elevated platform waiting for the train, all her dreams came true, at least her most immediate. She felt someone grab her butt. The dark angel smiled, and for a fleeting moment, Naomi hoped they had enjoyed it. Turning, she saw her groper was in his mid-forties and sporting an off-the-rack suit.

Her first jab hit him in the windpipe. Then her fingers closed around his fleshy throat as she squeezed his Adam's apple. His right hand flailed toward her, trying to fend off the attack, but Naomi grabbed the hand, rotating the wrist away from his body. The joint manipulation had the desired effect of transforming him into a compliant subject. Pulling his face close to hers, she said, "You need to start paying attention to where you put your hands. Don't worry. I'm going to help you remember."

Releasing her hold on his throat and using both hands to torque his right arm, she felt the satisfying snap of his wrist breaking. He screamed. A knee strike to the groin bent Mr. Handsy over. Smashing her left elbow into the side of his head, he collapsed to his knees. Then she grabbed his good hand and began to twist, but this time more slowly. The dark angel roared in exultation. Handsy blubbered, begging her to stop.

She couldn't stop. His right wrist snapped, and he screamed and thrashed. A vicious knee to his ribs resulted in another satisfying crack as several broke. Stepping over his arm, she sat on his shoulder and trapped his arm between her legs. She was going to break every single one of his fingers.

Her momentary daydream was shattered by a surfer with long, blonde dreadlocks punching Mr. Handsy in the face. The surfer looked at the man in disgust, saying, "Bruh, it's NOT ok to touch a lady like that."

The dark angel growled in frustration. While her fantasy was enjoyable, it wasn't as therapeutic as breaking the pervert's bones. He'd never know he'd gotten off easy. Chivalry might not be dead, but it had deprived her of a golden opportunity to hurt someone.

Naomi waited, expecting the surfer to make some kind of a move to talk to her. Men always did that. They did a single decent thing, acted like a human being, and then expected a reward. If he thought she was going to fawn over him in gratitude, he was wrong.

To her surprise, he slipped his hands into the pockets of his cargo shorts without a second glance at her as he shuffled off, his sandals clicking across the red-tiled platform. She wasn't sure whether to be relieved or disappointed.

The beach was perfect. Just what she'd dreamed of, but she couldn't relax. The same questions swirled through her mind on a loop. Why would someone send a fake video to Greggor? How had the CIA guys missed the clues? Who had made it in the first place?

The blue sky and foamy surf held no answers.

Bottom line, she had two options. She could drop it and move on with her operation against the Russian billionaire. Or she could go after some answers. Option two would mean returning to Nigeria and questioning her old source. The one the CIA believed sold her out in the first place.

Naomi knew herself well enough to realize she couldn't just leave something alone. That was the whole reason she'd violated a dozen laws by partnering with Peregrine to hunt an international arms smuggler.

Maybe Derek had been right about her using them. They were a highly effective team that didn't get bogged down in bureaucracy. Sadly, that type of agile capability didn't scale well.

The Aksyonov investigation had stalled out, and while they had been exploring options for jump-starting it, their best idea was so far-fetched it would never be approved. Until a lead came up, she was at a standstill.

Naomi knew herself well enough to know she'd return to Africa. She needed answers. Clark would help her cook up a reason to be there. He was always good at coming up with official-sounding justifications.

Satisfied she had a plan, Naomi laid her head back on the blanket, and allowed the sun to soak into her bones. From the abyss, her dark angel smiled. She hadn't been able to punch anyone today, but Artemis knew she'd get a chance to come out and play once they were back in Nigeria.

13

Isaac

Peregrine Office - Miami, Florida

"What was up with kicking Naomi out of here?" I asked. I understood the basis of the disagreement, but it didn't mean she needed to be ejected like a spent weapon magazine. It wasn't like Sarah. There were a lot of questions on the table, and it would have been nice to get Naomi's input.

"We're giving her plausible deniability," Sarah explained. "She's given us the official finding. Don't worry. I intend to go hunting for Jimmy myself. To use one of Isaac's favorite activities as an analogy, I plan on cracking a lot of eggs to make a great big omelet."

I felt the beast stirring inside. I relished and feared the thought of it being set free.

"Thanks for bringing that down to my level," I said with a wink. Sarah ignored the comment.

Derek raised his hand. "Don't we have a small problem? She didn't give us the phone back."

Mike shook his head. "We don't need the device. I cloned it before we gave it to the CIA. Not only do I have everything on the phone, but if anything else is sent, we'll get that as well."

I had expected as much. Mike was an electronic hoarder with no concept of personal privacy. He likely had clones of all of our phones.

"Naomi has to know that's the first thing Mike would do," I said.

"No. I think she suspects, but she doesn't know for sure. That's why I got rid of her before we started discussing means and methods," Sarah said.

Giving her plausible deniability makes sense, but asking her to grab us some coffee with a wink might have been a better approach.

I didn't know Naomi well, but if I'd been in her shoes, I would have been ticked.

"Mike, go grab your computer. We're going to start a strategy session and see what we can come up with," Sarah said. Mike left, and I stood up, moving toward the coffee maker.

"I'll brew us a fresh pot."

"Is there any more of that stuff you made the other day? That was great," Selma said.

"The Topeca? Nope, just the one bag," I said. A friend of mine living in Tulsa, Oklahoma, had sent me a bag of locally roasted coffee. A single-origin roast from a small farm in Ethiopia, and it was terrific. They didn't need to know I expected a resupply delivery in the next day or so. I wasn't keen on sharing.

"Then it sounds like you need to order some more," Selma said.

Marissa had gotten up to get a bottle of water and was now looking awkward and undecided about what to do next.

"You know, if you want to leave, the door is right there. There's no need to blow the window out of the frame and jump," I said, trying to lighten the mood.

"You want me to leave?" she asked.

Perfect response, Northe. How has MasterClass not contacted me to teach a How to Talk to Women module?

"No, I just meant..."

Marissa stood there looking at me, eyebrows raised.

Shrugging, I said, "I don't know what I meant. I know what I didn't mean. I didn't mean to tell you to leave."

"Nice save," Derek stage-whispered. He elbowed me so that I stumbled toward Marissa. I grabbed his arm to keep from falling into her. Then he tried to shove me with his other hand, which I trapped.

Before the situation could devolve into a 3rd-grade wrestling match on the floor, Sarah intervened. "Gentlemen, as enjoyable as the two of you hunks rolling on the floor would've been to watch, there's work to do."

Mike was back and already had the big screen mirroring the one on his computer. The coffee pot hadn't finished, so I grabbed a bottle of water and joined everyone else at the table.

"Mike, do you know who sent the video or do you need some time to figure it out?" Sarah asked.

"I traced the video back to a Nigerian named Danjuma Adebayo."

Mike's fingers flew across the keyboard, sounding like a machine gun on full auto. I watched in amazement as half a dozen windows opened, displaying a location in Google Maps and several social media profiles.

Derek was the first to speak, "What's the plan for getting into Nigeria? It's not like we can just pack long guns in our suitcases and jump on the next Delta flight heading that way."

"The first question is, where does Mr. Adebayo live? That's going to have a big impact on what we need to bring," Selma said. The logistics specialist was a child chess prodigy and a strategic thinking and analysis expert.

"Mike, can you answer that?" Sarah asked. Mike looked up, clearly having become engrossed in whatever he'd been doing.

"Huh? Answer what?"

"Where does Mr. Adebayo live?" Sarah repeated her question.

"Oh. Yeah. He's in Abuja," he muttered distractedly.

"Abuja is the capital city. It's one of the fastest-growing cities in Africa. Overall, it's a wealthy city and a regional power broker," Selma said as though she was reading a Wikipedia article. For all I knew, she might have written it.

"I don't think we'll be able to just knock on his door and ask him about the video," I said.

We were going to need a place to interrogate him. In an ideal world, there'd be a location we could control, where no one would hear him scream. If I were still employed by Uncle Sam, we'd do the ol' snatch n' grab. However, we had no official backing or support. We weren't even a quasi-government organization like the ones found in Jack Ryan thrillers.

"What do we know about him?" Sarah asked. The tone of her voice told me it was a leading question. She was going somewhere and wanted the rest of us to think through the process.

"He was an informant. The CIA believes he sold them out to Boko Haram." I ticked off the facts on my fingers.

"Right, but we also know he sent this video to Greggor," Sarah added.

"He's an information broker," Marissa said.

"Exactly," Sarah said, pointing at Marissa.

"Are you thinking we can just pay him for the information?" Derek sounded incredulous.

I heard the coffee pot beep and got up to grab a cup. Over my shoulder I called, "I doubt he's an idealist. We know he was in contact with the CIA, had the info to contact Greggor, and there's enough circumstantial evidence for the Agency to believe he sold them out to Boko Haram. This is his business. He's not going to willingly give up his life to safeguard some scrap of info."

Marissa drummed her fingers on the table. "I'm not sure that's exactly true. While this may just be a job for him, he wouldn't stay in business very long if he just caved and gave information to people whenever they threatened him."

It was a good point. The Nigerian informant might be a hard nut to crack, but the sledgehammer I planned on bringing with me would be more than up to the task.

"What about guns? I don't want to be running into Boko Haram without weapons," Derek said.

"While there have been Boko Haram attacks in Abuja, it's not one of their controlled territories," Selma replied. "Your bigger concern would be private security and government forces."

Sarah made a point of catching each of our gazes before speaking. "Make no mistake, Jimmy has been abandoned by his government. We're going to get him back. Danjuma Adebayo is our new priority. We have no sanction for these actions. What we're about to do is illegal. I don't care, because on the moral side of the ledger, we're in the right."

I felt the conviction of her words. This was why I'd come to work for her in the first place. I could take my skill set and make more money in many other places. But Peregrine was about more than just money. Sarah brought a moral yardstick into every scenario against which she measured everything else. Early in my career, I learned the hard lesson that being legal didn't make an action ethical.

Heads around the table were nodding in agreement, with the exception of Marissa, who sat silent and expressionless. I couldn't imagine her having any issues with the proposed plans. This also wasn't her fight and I wasn't sure why she was still here. Sarah continued issuing marching orders. "Selma, make a logistics plan to get us and our equipment to Abuja. We're also going to need a safe house."

The logistics coordinator gave a thumbs-up, "I have some contacts in the region who I think can help."

"Isaac and Derek, get a targeting package together. We need to know his routines and the local atmospherics before we just drop in and snatch him up," Sarah said, looking at us each in turn. I glanced at Derek and we nodded in understanding. He appeared ready to put aside whatever personal issue he was having with Sarah to get the job done.

"Mike, start assembling tech kits so you can provide reach-back capabilities. See if you can get a head start into any systems in Abuja. Cameras, databases, and communications channels. You and Selma will be staying here," Sarah said.

"What about me?" Marissa asked.

Sarah turned toward her with raised eyebrows. "What about you?"

"I think I could help. Nigeria is a dangerous place, and you could use an extra gun in the fight. Plus, I'd blend in better than you three. Your white skin will be noticed, even if no one says anything," Marissa said, pointing at Sarah and me.

"I'm not white. I'm just as dark as you," Derek protested. He liked to joke that his olive skin made him ethnically ambiguous. In Hollywood, he would've been able to play anything from Hispanic to Middle Eastern.

"You are way too pretty to go unnoticed," Marissa countered. The words were complimentary but her tone made it clear they weren't.

Derek shrugged. "It's a burden I bear every day."

"Your bravery is inspiring. I'm going to recommend you for a Medal of Valor," I said. Derek winked at me, ignoring the sarcasm. However, his face turned serious at his next comment, "Not to be rude, but is she on our level in tactical terms? We're a small unit and need to move fast."

Sarah folded her hands, laughing softly. "Derek, dear, you should be more concerned about performing on HER level." There was a condescension in her voice that made me wonder if something more than a regular lovers' tiff was going on.

Ouch. That's not what any former Spec Ops guy wants to hear. Not from his boss. Or from his girlfriend.

"Isaac and I were in MARSOC for years. We were Tier 1 operators," he objected, seeming to feel that both of our credentials were in question. The belief MARSOC was Tier 1 was common among Marines. While they were an elite unit, objectively, the claim wasn't valid.

Sarah and I glanced at each other. This touched on one of Derek's nerves. While he and I had served in MARSOC, 'The Virginia Boys' had run a selection test. He, along with 200+ others who ran the test, hadn't made the cut. Jimmy and I had.

Sarah held up her hands. "All I'm trying to say is she won't slow us down. Marissa could be a useful addition to the team, but…" she said, holding up a finger to forestall comments, "we're going to collect information, not just shoot people."

"I think I can manage that," Marissa said.

"Ok, everyone has their assignments. Let's make this happen, people," Sarah said.

"I'm going to grab some lunch," I said, to no one in particular.

Marissa rose from her chair. "Hey, wait up. I'll come with."

Derek had started to get up as well, but I could see him change his mind. Probably for the best. I didn't view Derek as a threat for Marissa's attention.

But he was being particularly antagonistic toward her, and that vibe didn't lend itself to a pleasant lunch environment, or personal conversation.

14

Marissa

Miami, Florida

"So, what's good here?" Marissa asked, sitting down across the table from Isaac. The place was a little hole-in-the-wall that he claimed was his favorite lunch spot. She wasn't so sure she believed him. The health code grade posted on the door was a 'C,' but Isaac seemed unconcerned. In Marissa's experience, a place like this would either be incredible or give you food poisoning. Possibly both. She scanned the menu for a safe option.

The bell over the door chimed as a customer entered. Marissa locked onto him the moment he walked into the restaurant. He had a muscular physique and the operator beard that was so popular with the veteran community nowadays. His demeanor telegraphed that he was doubtless good with a gun, but not especially covert. The Gray Man this guy was not.

If Isaac noticed the newcomer, he gave no indication.

"I'm going to hit the little boys' room. Look that thing over, but before you order, I have a couple of recommendations you should consider." Isaac pointed to several dishes before walking off toward the kitchen area.

Marissa pretended to peruse the menu, but the contractor never left her focus. She wondered if these guys believed the polo shirts and tactical pants were fooling anyone into believing they weren't a sheepdog on the hunt for a wolf. Marissa wasn't sure what she was anymore. By any objective standard, she fell into the wolf category. Now the sheepdog was coming over to bark at her.

He might have been one of the guys who'd raided her Airbnb in Andorra to inform her of her involuntary reemployment contract with the CIA. The terms and conditions were most generous, actually. In return for her Tier One, all-inclusive target elimination package, they suspended the international manhunt and removed the flag from her passport. She could live her life as she wanted, on one condition: when they contacted her on the Signal app, they expected her to answer.

One eye on the approaching sheepdog, she thumbed her phone open and saw the notification. She must have forgotten to take the phone off 'Do Not Disturb' when they'd left Peregrine.

"Check your messages," he growled, placing both hands on the table and leaning in to glare at her. It was cute. Like a puppy menacing a squirrel from the other side of the glass door.

"Already on it," she said, dancing the phone in the air for him to see. Through the kitchen door, she saw movement. Isaac was in there, talking to one of the cooks.

"If you want to maintain your cover, you should leave before he gets back," Marissa's tone was casual as she gave a head flick at Isaac.

For a moment he didn't respond and she braced herself, unsure of what he was going to do. Finally, he leaned back.

"I don't know or care who you are. Just answer your messages." He turned and left the restaurant, the bell jangling to punctuate his departure.

The message in the app was short. A few lines of text and a JPEG. She didn't need to read the message to know the picture was her next target.

When she looked up, Isaac had sat back down. The annoyance she'd been feeling must have manifested on her face because he asked, "What's going on? Is everything alright?"

"Sorry. I've gotta go," Marissa said ruefully.

A smirk crossed his face. "Another job interview?"

"Yeah, something like that. Listen, I'm sorry. I wanted to go with you guys to Nigeria, but…"

"You've got a thing that requires your attention. I get it." His tone sincere. *How could he get it? Yet, it sounds like he does.*

"Let me know if you need anything. I haven't updated my LinkedIn account for a while, but I have a killer skill set and am open to work." He gave an exaggerated wink.

Marissa laughed. It was nice to laugh; the life she led didn't offer her many opportunities.

"I'll keep that in mind."

Isaac pulled out his own phone, and several seconds later, a connection request appeared in her Signal app. She clicked Accept, closed the app, and stuffed the phone back in her pocket. Now she might look forward to hearing the messenger chime for once.

"I'll take a rain check on lunch,"

"Can I give you a ride anywhere? The airport?" Isaac offered.

In most cases, she'd just leave. She was used to getting by on her own. But how could it hurt to have him give her a ride?

"The airport, please." As they passed under the noisy bell she felt a little sad she wouldn't be able to find out if Isaac was trying to treat her to an amazing meal or get her back for complicating his life. At least not today. She had to play nice with the CIA for now. But as soon as she figured out how to extricate herself, maybe she could come back to Miami and roll the dice.

* * *

New York City, New York

Marissa waited outside the Downtown Manhattan Heliport. Despite not having worked with one for years, she wished she had a team. This operation included a lot of variables, and she couldn't account for all of them. Of course, if the job was easy or legal, someone else would be doing it. There would be no one coming to save her when this thing went sideways.

She'd been handed a key in an airport bathroom at JFK. The locker it opened was one of hundreds available for rent around NYC. While casing out its location in the Financial District, she'd briefly considered whether the weapons pickup there could be a trap. But, the CIA had no reason to trap her and would spring her in hours if it was the FBI or NYPD.

The plan was ambitious and creative. Marissa was surprised it had been approved.

Her mission kit was now stored in the knockoff Prada mini cross-body she'd acquired after landing. A Maxim 9 integrally suppressed pistol, a pair of zip ties, and a karambit. Its small half-moon-shaped blade was perfect for close-in fighting. Hopefully, she wouldn't need it.

Marissa's best weapon was not the gun or the knife but rather her ability to blend into most populations. Today she was dressed in the travel uniform of the young, hip private jet set: a comfortable tracksuit and Nikes, huge Gucci sunglasses, designer bag, and rose gold Beats by Dre on-ear headphones. No one gave her a second glance. The lemmings saw what they expected to see. Several tour helicopters were operating here, but she wasn't concerned about them. They were further down the pier and not a factor as yet.

The wind from a Sikorsky S-76 corporate helicopter blew her ponytail off her shoulder, threatening to take the glasses off her face as well. The big chopper gently touched down, and Marissa could hear the noise of the engines slacken as they were brought back to idle.

Her target had arrived on schedule. For once the location and timeline in the intelligence briefing had been correct. Not that Marissa hadn't done her own research through open-source intel to corroborate. She'd learned her lesson long ago after receiving more than one dossier with sketchy information because some overzealous analyst wanted to make the mission happen and score points with the boss.

The intel packet had been top-tier and nothing in her own assessment conflicted with the report. A Russian billionaire like Sergej Aksyonov would arrive in New York at one of the major international airports in Queens, maybe even in Newark, but he wouldn't be traveling into Manhattan with the bridge-and-tunnel crowd. Aside from not wanting to waste the playboy's oh-so-valuable time in traffic, his security team would be happy with the prospect of not traversing the uncontrolled, notoriously congested streets of the Big Apple.

So, here she was at the heliport watching his aircraft land at the predicted time and location.

Glancing behind her, Marissa spotted a black Mercedes G Class SUV turning into the parking lot. His ride was here, bringing with it additional complications. She hated complications, especially the kind that carried guns. Time to get moving.

Pulling out her phone, she opened the camera. This way, she could appear to be absorbed in the phone while maintaining situational awareness. Marissa marched toward the aircraft with confidence, looking to all the world like a long-lost Kardashian cousin. She noted the single pilot. It wasn't surprising in a world of cost-saving measures. He exited the S-76 and opened the cabin door, allowing a no-neck-looking slab of muscle to step out on the tarmac.

This would be the bodyguard. His gaze locked on Marissa in a flash. Through the camera she saw him hold up his hand. Mouth moving in an unheard command.

You're not close enough.

Fighting the impulse to draw the Maxim 9 and start shooting, Marissa continued forward in her role of a vapid, self-absorbed heiress. No-Neck strode toward her, waving and trying to gain her attention. Behind him she could see Aksyonov moving toward the open door, and the second bodyguard exiting the other side.

Marissa was an ambush predator. If the world of covert kinetic problem-solving was an ice skating rink, the Navy SEALs or Delta would be an NHL brute squad. She was an Olympic figure skater. It took planning and finesse to execute her operations. While Marissa certainly was a weapon-selector-to-rock-n'roll kind of gal, that was never her entire plan.

No-Neck was within 5 feet when Marissa stumbled. The big man reached out to catch the falling woman. It was the act of a gentleman. A gesture she appreciated, not just because it provided the distraction she needed to reach into her bag.

The world seemed to slow as thousands of hours of training and countless real-world operations coalesced into that moment. It was this training and preparation that separated the dead from the living.

Gripping the pistol she drew it from the handbag and punched it into the bodyguard's throat even as his big hands caught her shoulders. Her finger tightened on the trigger and applied the required 5.5 pounds of pressure. The two rounds fired in rapid succession severed the man's brain stem.

It was like flipping a light switch. One moment No-Neck was saving a falling heiress and the next nothing. Just like that, chivalry was dead. Marissa growled to herself as the rotor wash blew some of the blood spray and tissue fragments back at her. She stepped to her right, searching for her next target as No-Neck's body collapsed.

The pilot, still holding the door, stared in wide-eyed disbelief as she rotated. The bimbo walking toward the wrong helicopter had transformed into the Angel of Death. They made eye contact for the briefest of moments before she shot him twice in the face, the pair of bullets entering just above his nose. He was dead before he hit the ground. He was just a pilot for hire, but it didn't matter. He was an obstacle in the way of her mission. Nothing more.

The rotor wash ripped the door from the falling pilot's dead hand, slamming it closed in the billionaire's face. A single threat remained. Unfortunately, Marissa's shot was blocked by the helicopter. Before she could get into position, Mr. Murphy and his pesky law decided to crash the party.

Seeing the pilot drop, the second guard coming around the nose pulled his pistol and began to fire at her. It was an impressive show of speed, but Marissa believed speed without accuracy was just a waste of bullets. The first shots were not even close as he loosed them in a panic.

Falling to her knees, she heard more bullets snap through the air. She'd dropped out of the line of fire, but that wouldn't last for more than a second or two. The second protector might be a slight upgrade from No-Neck. Or maybe not. But the fact that he had his gun out and was shooting unsuppressed shots was a problem. Like most major cities in the United

States, NYC used a ShotSpotter reporting system.

A series of microphones placed throughout the city listened for the sounds of gunshots. Upon detection, the network would alert the police to the location of the shots fired. The NYPD discovered soon after installing the system that close to 75% of the gunshots in NYC went unreported. Now that advanced detection system would be sending patrol units in her direction. Her location in the financial district ensured an especially swift response.

Marissa could see his feet as he completed his path around the front of the helicopter. His mistake was twofold. Not knowing where his shots had gone and lowering his weapon prematurely. The maxim had been drilled into her from day one of Project Olympus: confirm the kill. That split second bought her enough time to send him four memoranda detailing his tactical deficiencies, two of which he took to heart.

Rising from her knees, she opened the door and pointed her gun at an enraged Russian.

"Do you know who I am?" Aksyonov bellowed. People's ability to lie to themselves never ceased to amaze Marissa. Here was a man who wasn't in control of the situation but refused to accept that reality.

Sticking the muzzle below his chin, she caressed his cheek with her left hand, speaking to him almost sweetly. "Oh, Sergej. I know exactly who you are. The problem is, you don't know who I am."

Reaching into her bag, she pulled out the zip ties and handed them to him.

"Put these on," she shouted to make herself heard over the rotor noise. Aksyonov glared at her but complied with the order. After she'd slammed the door, Marissa moved to the cockpit and climbed inside. She and the other assets at Project Olympus had received extensive flight training in both jets and helicopters. She hadn't logged much time in the S-76, but she knew enough. The other plus was the radios would still be set to the proper frequencies.

Marissa donned the headphones and took time to adjust the seat, ensuring she could engage the tail rotor pedals. Returning the engines to full power, she noticed her passenger inching toward the door. A pistol tap on the clear partition and a motion for him to sit back down made him rethink his plans. She should've just secured his hands behind his back. Picking up the approach chart, Marissa verified the correct frequency before requesting takeoff clearance. Out of the corner of her eye, she saw three black suits racing toward her with guns drawn.

Aksyonov saw them, too. "When they get here, I'm not going to let them kill you. No, you'll pay for this. Maybe if you play nice, I'll just put a bullet in your head after I'm done with you."

Marissa took a deep breath and quelled the urge to shoot this piece of garbage in the face. She also begrudgingly appreciated the inconvenience the CIA team had to deal with in Andorra. Aksyonov needed to stay alive.

Reinforcements hadn't been part of the plan, but she judged there was enough time to take off before they got into effective weapons range. That didn't mean the suits wouldn't start shooting before then.

As she listened for her clearance, she wiggled her fingers, then grabbed the cyclic and collective. Pulling up on the collective, she smoothly applied power to bring the big corporate helicopter off the ground. She hadn't flown a helicopter in years, and it showed. The aircraft danced slightly as Marissa took off over the Hudson River, leaving a bloody mess on the pad.

Marissa was too preoccupied with the mechanics of keeping the giant bird in the air to clock the moment the three bodyguards lowered their guns and turned their attention to hauling confused passengers from a black tour helicopter. Nor did she notice when they pulled alongside her over the Holland tunnel.

Her plan to have a nice flight to Teterboro Airport in New Jersey was wrecked by rounds cracking through her door window and out the windshield. It appeared as though their rescue plan was to crash the helicopter, hope the boss didn't die in the wreck and then fish him out of the river. It wasn't the plan she would have made, but they seemed committed to it. Aksyonov seriously needed to tighten up his hiring process. It wasn't like he didn't have the money to afford the best protection.

She immediately dumped power. As she applied right pedal and pushed the cyclic forward and to the right, the corporate aircraft turned and dove. The S-76 was leagues above the tour helicopter in terms of power, and

Marissa used it to her advantage. Pulling in all the power the big girl could give, she sped toward the Manhattan skyline.

Marissa knew she was on a ticking clock even before she crossed the shoreline. Air Traffic Control would alert Homeland Security and the NYPD to the erratic aircraft, so she started talking to Air Traffic Control in an attempt to delay the alert.

"Mayday, Mayday, November One Two Three Five One has lost tail rotor command."

The mayday call told ATC that she had a serious emergency and they would be attempting to clear the airspace and get emergency response units toward her. A helicopter's tail rotor counteracted the torque effect that would cause the aircraft to spin at slower speeds. The emergency procedure for a loss of tail rotor was to increase airspeed, a fact with which Air Traffic Control would be familiar. The deception wouldn't last long. ATC would soon figure out she didn't have a real emergency, but this was just a stopgap.

She had to get the helicopter on the ground and retrieve what she needed without delay. There were unambiguous orders not to kill the Russian under any circumstance.

As soon as she touched down, hundreds of police would be converging on her location.

If her handler had been mad about the situation in Turks and Caicos, he would be livid with these results. The best thing she could do now was to achieve the mission's end goal.

She blazed across the shoreline at around 200 mph. People below her ran screaming in terror, likely believing another attack was underway. ATC buzzed in her ears, demanding updates. She ripped off the headset. There was no time for them and she needed to focus on flying.

Marissa continued descending until the S-76 was around ten feet above the rooftops of Canal Street. Then she flew east. She needed to land to gain some time and distance. What had begun as a covert action would now be international news this evening. Win or lose, this would be an epic entry in the CIA's mission chronicles. Hopefully, the person who had had the good idea to force her back into service would get fired.

Banking hard left, she buzzed over Little Italy, heading back north. As a New York City native, she knew there were green spaces large enough to land. But like everything in life, location was key. Central Park was the obvious choice. But she dismissed it. Too far away. She hadn't seen the black tour helicopter follow, but her situational awareness was limited to the cockpit. It could be right on her tail for all she knew.

She traveled north along Broadway, and just as she crossed W. Houston Street, she saw the answer. Decelerating the helicopter in a descending left turn, Marissa lined up an approach with Washington Square Park. It would be tight, but she was confident she could fit the S-76 on the ringed pathway. People stared dumbstruck at the descending aircraft. This wasn't something they saw every day, but this was New York and probably something they'd missed in the news. Unfortunately, they all had plenty of time to whip their phones out and video the entire event.

The landing was bumpy, not her finest hour. Pulling the engines to idle, she leapt out of the pilot's door and climbed into the back. She began running her free hand across Aksyonov's body in a pat-down search. She pulled each object out as it was found. Phone, wallet, and various pocket litter. Finally, Marissa found what she was looking for in his left pant pocket.

"What's the pin?" she asked, activating the device.

"Why don't you go…" his following words were cut short by Marissa shoving the barrel of her gun in his mouth. The force of the blow slammed his head against the headrest. He gagged, and his eyes watered as she leaned in close. She had to hurry. It might already be too late.

"Why don't you think long and hard about what you're gonna say next. Another comment like that, and I'm going to start cutting things off," she said as she pulled the karambit out of her bag.

"Do you understand me?" He nodded vigorously. Pulling the gun out of his mouth, she repeated her question holding up a small device about the size of a USB drive. The object in question was a hardware wallet used to store cryptocurrency keys offline.

"What's the pin?"

"8-6-7-5-3-0-9"

She entered the number without wasting time to see if he was serious. True to his word, the device unlocked.

"Jenny, I've got your number," she muttered as she began to work. Working from memory, she sent the Bitcoin and Ethereum to the accounts she'd been instructed to use. She noted with interest a balance for a currency that hadn't been mentioned. The Agency didn't say anything about securing the device, just making the transfers. This was supposed to look like a robbery after all. Might as well give it a bit more authenticity.

After she had finished her work, she dropped the hardware wallet on the floor. It had been three minutes since she'd landed, and the crowds still kept their distance from the aircraft. The unexpected landing, and approaching police, made them wary.

As soon as her feet hit the ground she sprinted west, leaving the giant helicopter in the middle of Washington Square park, its blades still turning. She could hear sirens wailing and people shouting as the remaining onlookers parted to get out of her way. The NYPD was closing in, and her first order of business was to get outside the search cordon. The only description the police would have was a small Hispanic woman, if they even got that right. There were lots of brown-skinned people in NYC, and she planned to use that to her advantage.

After several blocks, she slowed and merged with a crowd headed toward the Christopher St. Station. Continuing past the station, she ducked into a thrift store. Five minutes later, she emerged in jeans and a hijab. The Islamic population in New York had been growing for years. She was now just another Muslim woman strolling at her leisure through The Big Apple.

15

Naomi

The Bat Cave - Baltimore, Maryland

Naomi sat at her desk, staring into space over the top of the file she was supposed to be reading. Over and over she replayed the meeting at Peregrine. She was missing something. Derek's outburst was understandable, maybe even valid. Still, Sarah abruptly asking her to leave like that didn't make any sense. Once the initial sting had passed, she'd realized…it was almost like Sarah didn't want her there when the discussion continued.

She picked her phone up and considered sending another message before putting the device back down. Over the past few days, she'd tried reaching out more times than a love-sick teenager. Her calls went straight to voicemail, and the text messages had yet to be answered. Why was she being ghosted?

Across the room, Clark paced like a caged lion. He did this when he was trying to piece a puzzle together. Also, true to form, he was eating. This time it was pork rinds. Naomi felt queasy just thinking about them.

She had intended to enlist his help in finding a reason to return to Nigeria, but she came back from her weekend in Miami to find their current case had accelerated. Now the team was laser-focused on tracking the money trail. Questioning Danjuma would have to wait.

NAOMI

Naomi turned back to the intelligence reports in front of her. Realizing she'd reread the same sentence six times, she stood up and stretched. She needed to get her mind off its hamster wheel. The Bat Cave had a small gym, really more of a closet, with a pull-up bar, a bench, and some free weights. But it worked when she didn't have time to go to her gym.

Grabbing the pull-up bar, Naomi started a max set. She'd been stuck at 34 for the past couple of weeks and wanted to break through that plateau. The first twenty were quite quick. Behind her, a pork rind crunched.

She hated that sound. The deep-fried pig skins were a disgusting abomination that should never have been invented. The junk food was worse than the pickles on the pizza she'd seen in Miami. Closing her eyes and willing away the distractions, she continued the climb to 35.

"Why do you do those?" Clark asked through noisy chewing.

Naomi ignored him as she pulled herself up again for 33. Lowering herself back down, she alternated, first releasing her right hand to shake out her arm and then her left. Taking a deep breath, Naomi pulled herself upward, back and arm muscles burning as her chin rose above the bar.

Crunch, crunch. "That doesn't look like much fun."

"I'm trying to relax. It helps me think," Naomi growled.

Crunch, crunch, crunch. "If you wanted to relax, we could go on a bike ride. A nice 20 miler always does the trick for me."

Despite his poor eating habits, Clark was in fantastic shape. They had worked out together many times over the years, but his favorite exercise was on his road bike. It was also the solitary workout in which the former professional cyclist could best her.

"If you don't shut up, I'm going to get down off this pull-up bar and shove it…"

"Okay, okay, I'm leaving," Clark huffed.

As the sounds of crunching pig skin receded, Naomi pulled. Her arms shook as they worked in concert with her back muscles to lift her higher. Inches of upward movement seemed like miles, and her arms felt like concrete.

Her chin rose above the bar, and it clicked. As though someone had turned the light on in a dark room. She could now see the puzzle she'd been trying to put together by touch. Dropping off the bar, she strode back into the workspace. She'd broken past 34, but would have to celebrate later. Her rate of movement and the look on her face must have alarmed Clark. He dropped the bag of pork rinds into the trash.

"Alright, I'm done with them," he said, raising his hands in surrender.

"Shane, have you made any progress on the crypto front? I still can't believe someone up the chain signed off on Clark's idea to rob Aksyonov." Naomi said.

"Yeah, we certainly kicked over a hornet's nest on that one," Clark agreed.

"But we did gain access to the crypto wallet," Shane interjected.

Most of the covert activities orchestrated by the CIA were, by nature, illegal. But there existed shades of illegality. Kinetic action against targets on US soil was of the Congressional hearings and most of the 7th floor at Langley getting fired variety.

"I wonder who they got to do it?" Clark mused.

"It was Special Activities Division," Shane said with a wink. Shane was the organization's resident 'barracks lawyer.' The role of barracks lawyer was a time-honored tradition involving a junior member overhearing a partial conversation of a higher-ranking person, taking that information completely out of context, and claiming to be an expert with inside knowledge. Most things Shane said outside the scope of his job needed to be taken with a generous helping of salt.

"Don't think so. I've worked with those cowboys; they're not that surgical," Clark scoffed.

"Who do you think it was then?" Shane asked.

"A secret assassination program. Definitely something sub rosa. All the reports seem to indicate it was the action of a singleton the authorities have been unable to locate. Who else would have those kinds of skills?" Clark asked.

Naomi agreed with Clark, but she doubted it was a secret wet-work unit. She'd been there, done that, and knew they didn't hand out t-shirts. Naomi also knew her name would be on the shortlist when they decided to give targeted killing another go. On the other hand, she was likely acquainted with the person. The list of people with this level of skills wasn't that long.

"The problem with that theory is the CIA doesn't assassinate people. It says so right on the website," Naomi said dryly.

"Riiiight." Clark rolled his eyes.

"The United States doesn't negotiate with terrorists," Shane proclaimed, slamming his fist on the table.

"What?" Clark looked at the analyst as if he'd lost his mind.

In Naomi's opinion, they'd both lost their minds. She wished Jan, the other analyst, was back from vacation. The Zen redhead was a sunbeam of sanity in the wilderness of weirdos.

"Oh, sorry. I thought we were just repeating the nonsense politicians say," Shane replied.

Naomi pursed her lips. If she didn't cut this off, it would devolve into silliness again. "Back to the topic at hand. Shane, have you made any progress in tracing the funds since you got access to the wallets?"

"Not really. The money was deposited into a Swiss bank account."

"Which means we're not going any further. Good grief, sometimes I hate the Swiss and their stupid banking privacy laws. Hey, let's set up banking with zero transparency. I'm sure no one will abuse that system. Just out of curiosity, which bank is it?"

"Banque Suisse."

"Of course it is," Naomi growled.

Their hunt for an arms dealer selling US military weapons to terrorist and criminal organizations had been traced to Banque Suisse. That line of inquiry had been shut down when the seventh floor informed Naomi and Clark that a number of accounts supporting black ops were held at the bank. She was sick of these companies who could do whatever they wanted and never be held accountable because the US government relied on them for critical services.

"Ok, so if the crypto line is effectively dead for now, where are we with walking back the money coming from various companies. Any red flags?"

Clark stepped to his workstation and tapped a few keys. "A couple, but the biggest is an oil company called Gazovaya. We don't have access to their internal records. But their operation doesn't have the equipment to extract the amount of crude they would need to make the kind of money we're seeing exit the corporate accounts."

"Either they're charging way above market price, or someone is laundering money," Shane concluded.

"Where is Gazovaya's primary operation again?" Naomi asked.

"Nigeria," Clark answered.

Everything keeps coming back to Nigeria.

"It's clear they're laundering money. Why else would it be routed in the manner it has been? This goes well beyond tax evasion," Naomi said.

"We're all in agreement here. Aksyonov is routing money through Gazovaya. What's the point?" Clark asked.

"I don't think he's routing money through it. I think it's the origin of the funds. At least for him. I bet if we find the source of the money before Gazovaya, we'll get more clarity on the entire situation. Right now, it doesn't make sense why a Russian billionaire would funnel money into North Korea. What does he stand to gain from North Korea having an enhanced missile program?" Naomi asked.

She tried to keep the excitement off her face. This was a perfect opportunity to return to Nigeria.

"I think a little chat with our old friend Danjuma would benefit this investigation. If memory serves, he's pretty tight with the oil companies. I bet we could persuade him to get us some inside information on Gazovaya." Naomi hoped she sounded casual, as if reconnecting with their old informant was an idea she'd just had in the moment.

"He's not going to be happy to see us," Clark warned.

"Maybe not, but he will be happy when I let him leave the meeting to go back home to his family," she said. Chains rattled deep within the pit of Naomi's self-control. The dark angel was awake and she was smiling.

16

Isaac

Abuja, Nigeria

I wonder who gets hired to design airports. With a few exceptions, they all look the same. One design to rule them all. Incandescent lights, lightly colored walls, and an obligatory strip of gray running along the floor. From time to time, someone will decide to get a bit creative and change the place they put Starbucks.

Exiting the jet bridge into the Nnamdi Azikiwe International Airport terminal, I noted the airport in Abuja didn't fall outside of the standard deviation. I might have been in any of a hundred different municipal airports in Europe or North America.

The humanity flowing by was attired in everything from traditional African prints to blue jeans and t-shirts. Within the first 15 feet, I saw a jet-setting couple with designer luggage and an old woman who looked just like an ancient, gnarled tree on the Serengeti carrying her possessions in plastic shopping bags. Despite knowing better, I half expected to come across someone herding goats and chickens through the terminal as well.

While I had conducted operations on the African continent, this was my first time in Nigeria. I was underwhelmed. As is often the case, the intelligence workup I'd read had been academically helpful but failed to convey the true state of the location.

Nigeria is a resource-rich country, particularly in the area of oil. But an ineffective central government, poor infrastructure, and rampant corruption had robbed the country. What could be a prosperous nation lived in decidedly sub-standard conditions. The flourishing Islamic terror culture added a little extra something to the ambiance but did nothing to move Nigeria higher on my bucket list of places to visit.

We had landed in Abuja, the capital city. I'd read it was one of the fastest-growing cities in the world. While the government had made progress in combating the rampant corruption that left close to 65% of the country's population in extreme poverty, its effects were plain to see.

The trip through customs was no worse than a visit to the DMV. We were posing as American YouTubers, there to hike Aso Rock, the 1,300-foot monolith which was the city's most recognizable feature. Our collection of drones, GoPros, and laptops was ostensibly to film this endeavor.

Sarah played her role of bubbly, personable media director to perfection. Her French lilt disappeared, leaving behind an indefinite but obvious American accent. She excitedly directed the customs officers to our channel so they could check out the other videos we'd made and encouraged them to join our six million and growing subscriber list.

The channel hadn't existed 48 hours earlier, and the videos featured on it utilized the deep fake wizardry attributed to Jimmy's proof of life video. According to Mike, millions of bots out there were just waiting to follow you and pretend, much like Pinocchio, they were real boys, too.

Honestly, I don't know what he did. I tried to listen while he told me about it, but I found myself daydreaming about the beaches of Haleʻiwa. The North Shore of Oahu had to be my favorite place in the world. The ocean was amazing, the weather was nice, the food was great, and people left me alone. If I ever decided to leave Peregrine and hang up my hat, that's where I'd be going.

Our onscreen personality was none other than Mr. Derek Russo, who, true to form, collected the attention of most women and many men as though they were Pokémon, and he was determined to catch 'em all. This left me to be the unnoticed equipment wrangler/tech guy. I was more than happy to be invisible, but the tech guy…not so much. Turns out that even without Mike's mind-numbing, nerdy lecture about the equipment, I still knew more than the Nigerian customs officials.

Instead of attempting to be covert and secret squirrelish, we'd decided to hide in plain sight. The idea was to be stereotypical American tourists so no one would believe we were on a clandestine mission to kidnap and question a Nigerian information broker. After all, everyone knows American spies use Canadian passports to get into other countries.

I was glad to be on a mission. As baffling as it had been to learn the CIA didn't believe Jimmy was alive, at least it ended our period of inaction and waiting. I couldn't understand how the Agency had concluded the video was fake. Then again, my level of understanding of the technology in question would earn me a juice box and an invitation to sit in the corner while the adults talked.

"It's too bad your gal pal couldn't make it," Derek said, grabbing his backpack and leaving me to deal with the pelican cases of equipment and accompanying customs forms. He had thrown himself into the prima-donna-don't-carry-your-own-stuff lifestyle.

"She said she had another job interview," I shrugged. A knowing smile passed across Sarah's face, but she said nothing.

"I don't know who she interviewed with, but based on the news coming out of New York City, I think she got the job," Derek grinned.

"She didn't say she was going to New York," I countered, unsure why I was defending Marissa in this verbal joust. She hadn't told me she was going to NYC. But it didn't require a genius to put things together. The timing of her flight plus the stories about shootouts, a low-flying helicopter, and a kidnapped Russian billionaire had dominated the news cycle for several days equaled a pretty clear picture.

"Did she say she wasn't going to New York?" Derek asked.

I let the comment go, opting not to be pedantic. Derek was like a brother to me, and it showed when we bickered.

"I think that's our ride," Sarah said, pointing to a black Land Cruiser. I had seen the vehicle and reached the same conclusion several moments earlier. A boy who looked no older than 19 leaned against the truck. His rolled sleeves suggested that his biceps were larger in his imagination than in reality.

Derek, who had real biceps to show off, said, "Sun's out, guns out," and offered the young Nigerian a high-five that transformed into a back-thumping bro hug.

Selma's contact had turned out to be the owner of a private security firm catering to NGOs doing humanitarian work in the region. It sounded as if the two of them had been as thick as thieves during her time in the Army. When he'd started his company, he'd wanted her to work for him, but the overseas hardship duties weren't appealing. He'd helped them secure a safe house and had sent them a local driver. Supposedly his best.

"Samuel?" Sarah asked, approaching the young man with a warm smile.

"Yeah, that's me. Let's get your bags in the back. You've got to be hungry," he said, fishing a key fob from his pocket.

"Something to eat would be great. Where would you recommend?" Sarah asked, still in character. Despite seeing it dozens of times, I always found Sarah's ability to transform herself impressive.

I missed the answer as I moved to the trunk and began loading our bags. I doubted it would be anywhere good or interesting. If the airport was any indication, they rolled the sidewalks up after dark around here.

"Shotgun," I called as Derek opened the front passenger door. He rolled his eyes and got in. I preferred to be driving, but if I couldn't do that, shotgun was the next best thing. Irritating Derek was a side benefit.

"Gotta get out, bro. I called it." I pulled the door back open.

"You can't be serious."

"I am."

Derek looked to Sarah, who shrugged and said, "Rules are rules. If we didn't have them, the world would collapse into anarchy."

I decided to throw in the warning I'd received from an old Gunnery Sergeant for good measure.

"*First it's hands in the pockets, the next thing we know, Cuban paratroopers are landing in Florida.*" That particular bit of sage advice had been offered when

I'd asked him why Marines Corp standards prohibited us from putting our hands in our pockets even when it was freezing outside.

"Cuban paratroopers?" Derek asked.

"They're waiting for any chance, even if it's something like Marines with their hands in their pockets," I deadpanned. "Or people who don't honor the rules of shotgun."

"Fine," he grumbled.

The dark, arid landscape offered nothing interesting to look at as we drove the lonely road connecting the airport with the city of Abuja. I settled in for a boring drive, when the monotony was wrecked by a pair of trucks blocking the road, their light bars flashing.

"Is this something we need to worry about?" I sat up straighter in the seat.

"No, no. Standard police checkpoint. You don't have any weapons or drugs, do you?" Samuel asked.

"No," I said, thankful there was nothing for the police to find. There would be tactical kit waiting for us in the safe house. We'd have to be careful. No one wanted to get into an altercation with the good guys.

"We'll be fine. The police are just inspecting for contraband and looking for drunk drivers," Samuel assured us.

"Would an investment into their retirement account help speed things along?" Derek asked. The police were known to be corrupt in this part of the world. Bribes were the cost of doing business.

"Maybe, unless we happen to get two honest cops. Then we set ourselves up for more problems. If they want money, they'll tell us," Samuel explained.

We were 100 meters away from the trucks when I got my first good look at the officers. Two stood in front of the vehicles. Another four were visible behind the trucks. Olive drab uniforms with black body armor that read 'Police' matched the pictures I'd seen during the intelligence briefing. Each officer had an AK-47 assault rifle slung in front of him. Something about the situation bothered me, but I couldn't put my finger on it.

One of the officers held up his hand, indicating we should stop. A spotlight from each truck flared to life, illuminating the interior of our SUV. Samuel complied, brought the Land Cruiser to a stop ten meters from the checkpoint, and flipped the headlights off. Both officers raised their weapons at the same moment Samuel swore to himself.

"Those aren't real police," the driver hissed.

That statement prompted more cursing from the backseat. The details that had been bothering me snapped into focus like a parachute opening. There was no one in the driver's seats to move the trucks, and the uniforms didn't appear to fit right. The searchlights were blinding, and I was now unable to see the four men behind the vehicles.

As far as situations go, this wasn't great. We were confined in a vehicle without weapons against a larger force. The two men approaching us were ready to engage. Their overwatch was coming from guys with standoff distance and positioned behind the cover of vehicles. They also benefited from the concealment of blinding mini-suns.

I didn't bother asking Samuel if he was sure or how he knew. The men's odd behavior combined with the mismatched details was enough for me. I would've given anything for a firearm. A cursory check of my pockets revealed my only weapon was a pen I'd somehow pocketed after filling out the customs form. The pen might be mightier than the sword, but how did it stack up against assault rifles?

"Do you have a gun?" I asked, praying the answer would be yes.

"No." The response was a bucket of ice water, dousing my hope and shocking me with his stupidity. Here was a security contractor in Nigeria without a weapon. It made about as much sense as wearing a raw steak swimsuit in the piranha tank.

The two faux officers split to approach either side of our vehicle. At least they weren't shooting. Maybe we could talk or bribe our way out of this. The man on my side indicated I should roll down my window. I could hear Samuel in a heated exchange with the other fake cop.

"He says we all have to get out of the vehicle," our driver informed us as the thug on his side wrenched the driver's door open.

On my side, the not-a-cop leaned in the window, confident in his status as the apex predator. I found myself with a new best friend invading my space. Spotting Sarah in the backseat, his gaze turned lecherous. He spoke to his partner in some language I didn't recognize. The guy on the driver's side took a step back.

A crocodile grin spread across his face. He yanked the back door open with a shout that brought the four other men moving toward our vehicle. This situation was turning less than ideal. Sarah wasn't a defenseless lamb, but she was also in a poor position and outnumbered by far. I had no intention of sitting quietly while some flea-bitten losers gang-raped Sarah. Alfred had once told Batman there wasn't any point in doing a bunch of pushups if he never used the muscles he'd built.

I glanced back at her. A silent understanding passed between us. The world was full of horrific things people did to each other, but in my book, rape and child abuse were crimes deserving of death or worse. As my gaze crossed the windshield, I saw the beast of my dreams staring back at me. A prehistoric wolf with glowing red eyes. Its mouth curled in a snarl.

Pulling the pen from my pocket, I swung it upward toward not-a-cop-2. He saw the motion at the last moment. A jerk of his head caused me to miss the artery I was aiming for. Instead, the cheap pen lodged in his windpipe. Anticipating his reflex to step away from the SUV, I hauled myself halfway out the window after him.

Grabbing the hanging AK-47, I dropped back into my seat and pulled the weapon across my body. My new best friend's torso was dragged through the window. Extending my seatbelt, I began to loop the excess around his neck with my right hand while maintaining control of the rifle with my left. After I had wrapped it three times, I locked the fabric in the crook of my elbow to free my right hand but keep tension on the seatbelt.

My new bestie thrashed and clawed at the safety belt now strangling him. Grabbing the back of his head, I smashed his face over and over into my knee until his hands fell limp. A dark wet spot spread across the knee of my pants.

Great. Now I have blood on my jeans.

When I saw Derek open his door, I knew he was moving to grab the sidearm off my prisoner. Grabbing the pistol grip with my right, I flicked the safety selector to auto before pushing Samuel back into his seat to clear my line of fire. Then I torqued my body, extended my right arm, and pulled the trigger. The booming staccato of the rifle in close confines was deafening, and the acrid smell of gun smoke assailed my nostrils.

This is possibly the most gangsta way I've ever shot someone.

The burst wasn't the finest example of marksmanship, but it did its job. Sarah was on the man as soon as his body hit the road. Pulling his sidearm, she shot him twice in the face, ensuring he stayed out of the fight. Sarah then unloaded the rest of the clip at the four advancing men now illuminated in the spotlights. Her goal was suppression rather than accuracy. A way to buy herself time to retrieve the rifle from the fallen man at her feet. One hostile dropped, and the other three wisely retreated to the cover behind the trucks, not wanting to be in an open kill zone.

The opposition had yet to fire a shot. Their shock was understandable. One moment they were heading over for a rousing evening of rape and murder; the next, their would-be victims were fighting back and had their number down by half.

Once behind the vehicles, the remaining three sought to rectify their ballistic silence. Their response came from a time-honored technique known as spray and pray, which is known and practiced throughout the world. It is simple and inelegant. I didn't know how often those prayers were answered, but in my experience, I found fortune favored the proactive. To be honest, I preferred the aim and hit your target approach.

Bullets began to ricochet off the SUV's frame. Behind me, I heard Derek firing. The windshield spiderwebbed and Samuel's body jerked with the impact of the bullets.

It's time to get out of the vehicle.

The first step in assisting casualties during a firefight is to return fire and suppress the enemy. I had to clear the kill zone. I couldn't help Samuel if I was dead. Dropping my AK-47, I grabbed the chin and back of my new bestie. In a decidedly unfriendly gesture, I twisted, snapping his neck. The resulting crack was all I needed to hear to unbuckle and shove my door open. Sarah had pulled the rifle off her man. She was now contributing to the rock-n-roll concert in the middle of the road.

ISAAC

Exiting the Land Cruiser, I joined the gunfight. Muzzle flashes pointed to the source of the death flying around us.

"Moving," I called, advancing toward the police trucks in a shooter's crouch.

"Covering," I heard Sarah yell back. There is a maxim observed by Special Forces worldwide. *'Don't move faster than you can shoot.'* It doesn't do any good to close with your target if you can't effectively engage it. Despite years of training, the animalistic impulse to run was still there.

I felt more than heard Derek following close behind me. When the rubber met the road, the pretty boy was a guy you wanted on your team. Without a doubt. Popping up from behind the truck, one of the men swung his rifle in my direction.

Most companies have mandatory training, and Peregrine is no exception. Our last seminar was on conflict resolution. Sarah claimed it checked the box for federal contractor requirements, but I suspected she just liked tormenting us.

In the spirit of my recent training, I presented my own five bullet plan to de-escalate the situation. My counterpart found the proposal impactful, and several points blew his mind. Conflict resolved.

Derek's pistol barked, dropping another man, while Sarah finished her prolonged conversation with the third gentleman from Nigeria. Derek and I moved around the trucks, weapons up, and ready to engage. The three men appeared dead, but rounds into each head made sure they were no longer a threat.

"I think I found the real police," I said, gesturing at several bodies stacked in the truck's bed.

"This is so weird. Why were these guys impersonating them?" Derek asked.

"I don't know, but I don't believe in coincidences. We have to assume we were the targets until proven otherwise," Sarah said.

"If we were, it was the worst interdiction I've ever seen, and I've worked with the SEALs. It was more like they were playing cops, and then they saw Sarah," I said.

"This is my fault? I was asking for it?" she asked. I started to make a tactical retreat from the conversation when I noticed the twinkle in her eyes.

"Where's Samuel?" Derek asked.

So much for buddy aid.

I'd eliminated the threat but forgotten to return and render assistance.

"He's been shot and needs you to look at him," I said. While we all had combat medical training, Derek was a certified EMT and filled the position of team medic. He gave me a look that said *You've got to be kidding* before trotting off toward the bullet-riddled SUV.

"Let's do a quick site exploitation and get out of here," Sarah said as she started going through the pockets of the dead man closest to her. While she checked the bodies, I did a hasty search of the two trucks. They reeked of stale cigarette smoke. In the second truck I found something that made me feel like I had jumped out of an airplane and forgotten to take a parachute.

Walking back to Sarah, I showed her what I'd discovered. Printouts with our pictures and flight itineraries. Someone had known we were coming. We were being hunted.

"We need to go now," she said.

"Yes, but we shouldn't take these weapons with us. We don't want to be caught with guns that can be traced back here," I said. I didn't know if it would matter in the end. The investigating police would know that someone had left the scene. But we couldn't be too careful.

The most important thing was to clear the area before whoever sent these guys turned up and discovered we were still alive.

Sarah agreed. She and I wiped down every inch of the weapons we were holding before dropping them on the ground. I retrieved Derek's weapon and gave it the same treatment.

"He's going to need a doctor, but he's stable for the moment," Derek reported when we reached the Land Cruiser. I noted the plastic taped over Samuel's bared chest and a tourniquet on his left arm. A gauze bandage wrapped his right shoulder.

"Let's move him to the back seat. We'll drop him at the nearest hospital.

ISAAC

I'll drive," I said, showing Derek what I'd found. His eyes widened, and he nodded. Sarah had already climbed into the front passenger seat. Derek would ride in the back to keep an eye on Samuel until we could get him better help.

I felt terrible about the idea of ditching Samuel in front of a hospital. Yet, we weren't in any position to be answering questions. We needed to get to work and find answers to our own questions. The luxury of taking our time and establishing a pattern of life was gone.

17

Jimmy

Undisclosed Location

Zhao walked into the observation center where a bank of monitors showed live feeds of their current prisoners. The Eden Initiative was unraveling. He still couldn't believe the audacity of Sergej's abduction and subsequent robbery. Who had done it? Surely not the Americans. There was no way they would allow such a reckless stunt in the middle of New York City. They would have just arrested him at the airport. Still, it would be hard to make someone of Sergej's status disappear. This felt more like something the Israelis would do, but why in NYC?

The loss of the funds he'd been carrying had been a setback, but it was not insurmountable. Alexander had seemed more annoyed about the action against Sergej than the loss of millions. Sergej, of course, was vowing revenge on whomever had dared to attack him.

"Has he moved?" Colonel Zhao asked the tech monitoring the surveillance feeds. The big American was sitting on his bed with his back to the wall, knees pulled to his chest.

"No, sir," the tech responded. While officially, everyone was supposed to address each other with the title of Comrade, that didn't happen in reality. Mao had urged the Chinese to use the salutation to show everyone was committed to the communal struggle. However, Zhao's research indicated it was more effective and productive not to force subordinates to address their superiors with the title. People felt more comfortable recognizing someone as a superior than pretending they were all equals.

It had been several days since Zhao believed they had broken James Taylor. Since then, there had been no signs of deception or attempts to withhold information. Despite the cooperation, Taylor maintained his story about the mission in Nigeria. He and his Marines had been training with the Nigerian Special Forces. They had just been the closest team available when the CIA needed additional assets to take down a series of weapons caches. Zhao's own information confirmed this story.

His title of Colonel was a bit of a misnomer. While he had been a colonel in the People's Liberation Army (PLA), he was no longer in the military, having transitioned to the Ministry of State Security. Still, he enjoyed the title, which was a useful misdirection when conducting interrogations. James Taylor and Matthew Hassan were not the first enemy soldiers he'd questioned, but they were the highest value by several orders of magnitude. Zhao had found his enemies had an easier time talking when they thought the conversation was with another soldier. This ploy hadn't worked with the Americans.

Zhao had seen the news of the failed Nigerian raid along with the rest of the world. The Americans had been nosing around in Nigeria. Much to his shame, it was Alexander who'd connected the dots between the inconsistencies at Gazovaya and the American activities. He'd also alerted Zhao that two Americans had survived the raid and been captured by Boko Haram.

Zhao despised the terrorist savages and gladly would have sent a kill squad to erase the camp. So, grabbing two potentially high-value American soldiers was more than enough of an excuse to act. He'd convinced his bosses that this was too good of an opportunity to pass up, with the added benefit that the American government already thought they were dead. In a true measure of joint cooperation, Alexander had given Zhao the location of the prisoners, and Zhao had supplied the manpower to get them out. Chinese Special Forces were working in the region, so it hadn't been that difficult to retask those units.

The PLA had acted with remarkable speed, but it still wasn't quick enough. The proof of life video had complicated matters. Fortunately for Zhao, the CIA had requested assistance from the NSA's Computer Network Operations. While Zhao was stationed in Washington DC years ago, he had managed to turn a low-level NSA employee. That man was now one of the best hackers in the US's premiere penetration and exploitation unit.

Andrew Brock, a married man, had fallen prey to one of the classic blunders: the honey pot. The entire act was captured on Hi-Def video. The Chinese government never asked him for any classified information, instead using him as a tool to rid themselves of troublemakers. On close to a dozen occasions over the past decade, the Chinese had alerted him to or arranged for a security flaw that would allow the US to take action against individuals of interest. The timely discoveries helped to solidify the hacker's credibility and move him higher into the organization.

While Brock was no longer married, there was no going back. So, when the call came instructing him to make sure the video from Boko Haram was declared a fabrication, he had no choice but to comply. With the United States government believing the video was falsified, no one was looking for James Taylor and Matthew Hassan.

* * *

Jimmy stood across the street looking at The Meatball Shop. It was one of his favorite eateries in New York City. He remembered discovering it on a walk with Isaac, while his friend shared about his plan to leave the military. Jimmy had been torn between encouraging him to step into a private sector startup and advising him to stay.

Looking back, he realized that he might have been jealous Sarah had asked Isaac to help her start the company and not him. It would have been easy to attribute Sarah's favoritism to a relationship between her and Isaac. But the truth was, he didn't know if the two were involved. Sarah and Isaac had posed as a couple for several weeks during an operation in Dubai. They

JIMMY

were inseparable, seeming to have their own inside jokes, but that could have just been them maintaining their cover. Isaac was always private about his relationships, and Jimmy wasn't one to pry.

In the end, they never made a move against their target, and Sarah disappeared back to whatever black project she worked for at the time. Although there must have been other teams hunting their target, as he died from tetrodotoxin poisoning from an improperly prepared piece of fugu several weeks later. The chef maintained his innocence all the way to his execution.

Working with Isaac was fun, but they both knew it couldn't last. As they each advanced in rank, it would be impossible to continue working together on a daily basis.

That conversation was a turning point for Jimmy as well. He left ISA soon after Isaac and returned to the Marine Corps. It had never been done before. The move angered many senior officers, and it was clear to him that his days of career advancement were over.

Jimmy started to cross the street toward the cafe when the door to his cell opened, ripping him from his happy place. The happy place was a tactic he'd learned years ago and was how he dealt with stressful situations that were out of his control. Before his capture, he'd used this technique right before a mission when he needed to relax his mind.

Outwardly he didn't react, forcing Colonel Zhao to walk up and shake him several times.

"James! James, I am very sorry to bother you, but I need to ask you a few more questions."

Jimmy rotated to face the chair being brought into the room. Zhao sat down, crossed his right leg over his left, and folded his hands on his knees. This body positioning told Jimmy that his Chinese captor had more than a few questions to ask. They would be here for a while, but it wasn't like Jimmy had anywhere pressing to be.

"I know you were in Nigeria training their Special Forces. The news and the Nigerians have confirmed as much. But training Nigerians isn't all you were doing in that country, was it?"

"No. We also assisted with several weapons raids across the country," Jimmy said, shaking his head. He was tired of this line of questioning. It felt like he'd been asked the same questions a hundred different ways, but he didn't allow his frustrations to show.

"Were there any data uploads before Boko Haram showed up?"

"I don't remember. It would have been standard practice, but I don't know if it took place. I was busy trying to prepare our defenses," Jimmy answered.

"James, I'm trying to get you out of this facility, but I need your cooperation. Yes, it is true, you will never return to America. But you also don't need to spend the rest of your days imprisoned here," Zhao said, sounding comforting and friendly. Jimmy nodded in acknowledgment of this statement.

Since Jimmy had begun answering questions and cooperating, the Colonel had reverted to his previous persona. He was kind, almost grandfatherly. True to his word, life had gotten better. Zhao was letting him read. Books were the primary way Jimmy passed the time, except for the periods he spent in his happy place. It was more important to be able to survive and fight another day than it was to die protecting information. Particularly things that could be obtained through public channels or were no longer current.

"I understand you don't know if it went through. Do you remember seeing Mr. Hassan working on uploads or data collection? Did he tell you about anything they found?"

Jimmy shook his head. "I took part in the weapons raids but wasn't responsible for intelligence collection."

"James. Boko Haram stole a critical piece of technology. It would be something very similar to what the United States might use. The encryption on this device would also allow those animals to expand their communication without the Nigerian government being able to stop them," Zhao said. His voice sounded strained. Like his self-control was on the verge of cracking. Jimmy didn't want to return to the hostile interrogations of the past, so he decided to try and help.

"I do understand the dilemma. We were looking for intelligence against the weapons operations. Things like maps, hard drives, and USB sticks would have been transmission priorities over a phone that would take time to exploit."

* * *

Numerous non-verbal cues told Zhao that Taylor was telling the truth. Zhao also noted that the prisoner had begun referring to the United States as a 'them' and not an 'us.' Clearly, Taylor's loyalty to his country was breaking. It was also a giant leap forward for him to volunteer information without being asked.

Alexander was a fool to allow people to use beta versions of satellite phones that utilized the HERMES network. It would be a huge problem if the United States discovered a second-rate terror group was using cutting-edge technology connected to a satellite not available for public use. Anyone with half a brain would start taking a hard look at HERMES. Discovery of the weapons systems aboard would be inevitable.

Zhao was now confident there was no way to confirm or deny whether the sat phone had been located. In the meantime, Alexander was continuing on with business as usual. Zhao thought it was a dangerous and foolish play to use the Russian to funnel money into North Korea. Especially after the recent robbery. It seemed improbable that Sergej was just randomly mugged by a woman with the skills to take out two highly trained bodyguards, steal and successfully land a helicopter in the middle of a city park. So far the assailant had managed to evade capture, leading Zhao to suspect that the Americans had conducted the hit. But that was not his area of concern. Alexander seemed confident in Sergej's abilities, so Zhao would continue to do his part.

"Thank you for the information. I believe they were preparing your food as I came in. I'll make sure they hurry." Zhao rose, pleased to see a grateful look on Taylor's face. Walking back into the command center, he issued the necessary orders to have their source in Nigeria picked up for questioning. Gazovaya had a team of Wagner Group mercenaries who could grab the informant in a matter of hours. The informant might be able to tell them if the phone had even been there at the time of the raid.

18

Naomi

Dulles International Airport, Virginia

"There's our ride," Clark said excitedly, pointing to the Lockheed L100 Hercules sitting on the Dulles ramp. The aircraft was the civilian version of the famed C130 used by the United States, Canada, and Great Britain. Originally designed as a troop and cargo transport, the airframe was the longest continuously produced military aircraft. The four-engine turboprop workhorse was capable of using short, unimproved surfaces for takeoff and landing, making it ideal for work all over the globe.

"It certainly is, and we're going to feel every bump and jostle for the sixteen hours of flight time," Naomi grumbled. Clark loved this kind of stuff. Naomi, on the other hand, wished the CIA would come up with a hedge fund cover like Clark's favorite novels. Then they could travel in style in a rock star jet. Instead, they were stuck on cargo planes and ocean freighters. On occasion, they got to fly commercial, but always in economy class. So much for the glamorous life of being a secret agent.

MerchWork, Naomi and Clark's cover organization, had a standing contract with a dozen charitable organizations that sent food and medical supplies to Africa. The next scheduled shipment had been two weeks away, until an anonymous donor purchased 15 tons of rice for immediate delivery to the needy children of Nigeria. With the current price for rice sitting at $500 per ton, the excuse for entry into Nigeria had cost the Agency $7,500 USD. Naomi thought it was pretty good money management on the sliding scale that was US Government spending.

"We could've taken a private jet nonstop, which would've taken 10 hours," Naomi said.

"So, now you're James Bond? International assassin, licensed to kill?" Clark asked.

"Of course not. James Bond is British."

"And a man."

"And a man," Naomi agreed, thinking of how nice Sean Connery had looked in his tuxedo.

Several men moved around the lowered ramp, checking the cargo to ensure everything was secured correctly. The loadmaster walked over to Naomi and handed her the shipping manifest.

"Everything is locked down, Ms. Kaufman. The pilots are doing their preflight checks, and you should be good to go."

"Thanks, I really appreciate this. I know it was last minute and everything," Naomi said.

The loadmaster shrugged, pulling off his hard hat to wipe his brow. "It is kind of odd for a shipment of rice, but if I wasn't doing this, it would be something else."

"Well. Nonetheless, thank you," Naomi said, patting the man on the shoulder and walking up the ramp.

"Pilots said we're all set. They're going to start the run-up," Clark called over his shoulder as he busied himself with securing his hammock. Naomi flipped down one of the webbed seats that lined the interior, wishing she'd had the same idea.

* * *

Abuja, Nigeria

NAOMI

Naomi and Clark pulled into the large auto body shop. After landing, they'd picked up their car, a small, nondescript sedan, and begun their surveillance detection route. The SDR was basic tradecraft that would flush out all but the top-tier observers. The idea was to run a route highlighting recurring people or vehicles. The drive around the city was a welcome reprieve from the endless droning of the turboprops. Although the flight hadn't been all bad. The refueling stop in The Azores had been a welcome chance to stretch their legs.

Despite the late hour and growing darkness, the sounds of air-powered impact tools greeted them as they walked toward the garage entrance.

"It's odd that an information broker would run his operation out of a car repair business," Clark said.

"Not that odd. We work for a logistics company, and Hercules Mulligan, one of the legendary spies in American history, was a tailor," Naomi said.

"I'm impressed you know who Hercules Mulligan is. Most people have never heard of him or know he saved George Washington's life on more than one occasion," Clark said.

"I wouldn't be too impressed. I'd never heard of him before I saw *Hamilton* last year on Broadway," Naomi said as they walked through the front door. It was like stepping into the bedroom of a teenager. The difference being a smell of hydraulic fluid mixed with motor oil rather than a persistent haze of cologne. The posters of scantily clad women and general disorder were par for the course.

"It doesn't matter how you learn about history, just as long as you do," Clark said affably.

"Hey, I got into an accident with my rental. I need to get it fixed before I take it back to the airport," Naomi said to the young woman behind the counter.

Without looking up from her smartphone, she said, "We don't work on rentals. Gotta go to the shop across town for that."

"We tried there, but they were closed," Clark said.

"We're closed, too."

"Your sign says open," he protested.

"Nope. Closed."

Although the phone was silent, Naomi could see the game Candy Crush reflecting off the woman's glasses. She understood the need to do mindless things to pass the time. Some people enjoyed playing games on their phones. Naomi's pastime was reading fantasy novels. She had just started a new series, *The Legends of the First Empire,* and was looking forward to returning to her book. The only thing stopping her was the minor issue of getting information relevant to national security from a duplicitous Nigerian information broker.

"My friend told me to come here. Said Danjuma had a friends and family special, and he could hook me up," Naomi countered.

"You don't look like Danjuma's family," Candy Crush shot back.

"We're friends, and we'd appreciate the help," Naomi said, emphasizing appreciate.

"I don't think he's even here. Let me check," the woman said, stuffing the phone in the back pocket of her jeans and walking toward the back room.

"I don't think he's even here. Let me check," Clark mimicked in a high falsetto. Naomi tightened her lips to deprive Clark of the satisfaction of seeing her smile. She'd discovered that any amusement shown on her part only encouraged this type of childish behavior.

They both knew this was all part of the dog and pony show. The NSA was tracking Danjuma's phone, and as of 5 minutes ago, it had been right here. Unless they were updated that the device was mobile, there was no reason to think he was anywhere else.

Several minutes later, the woman returned and sat back down behind the counter, resuming her game.

"Is he here?" Naomi asked.

"He's here, but he's busy. Said come back in the morning, and he might be able to help."

"Does this feel like a trap to you?" Clark muttered.

"Everything feels like a trap to me," Naomi said.

"Do you think we should come back later or maybe just poke our heads in the back and see if he can squeeze us in?" Clark asked.

"I mean, we came all this way. I don't have anything better to do, do you?"

"Better? Yes. Not dying is better," Clark said.

"Stop being so melodramatic. You've got to go big or go home," she said, smiling and waiting for the reply she knew was coming. Sure enough, Clark did not disappoint. "You're underestimating my willingness to go home. It's literally my only goal."

With their course of action decided, the pair approached the doors leading to the back of the shop. The woman didn't look up from her phone as they walked behind the counter and through the swinging door to the back. The door behind the counter led to a hallway. A long window looking out onto the garage floor ran along the left side. The four bays were occupied by vehicles in various states of disassembly.

"Looks like inventory procurement would be a better description than repair shop," Clark noted.

Naomi pointed to the stairs up to an office overlooking the shop floor. She still hadn't told Clark she planned to ask Danjuma about Jimmy's video. He likely assumed that subject had been settled. Something bothered her. It didn't make sense that Peregrine, with all their skills and resources, had come to a different conclusion than the NSA. She wanted to believe she had all the relevant facts, but was experienced enough to accept she had to act with the information available.

There were so many unanswered questions. Even accepting the video was a hoax. Where did Danjuma get it? He almost certainly didn't know why it had been made, but he likely knew who had created it. It seemed the opportunistic dirtbags didn't realize the overwhelming nature of the evidence of Jimmy's death. But that still didn't explain why it had been sent to Greggor. Why not make it public? A captured Special Forces operator would be a huge bargaining chip. It would also put a massive target on the group who had him.

"Mind if we come in?" Naomi walked into the office as though she'd been invited. An outstretched hand indicated they should sit in the chairs in front of the desk.

After Naomi and Clark sat down, Danjuma looked them up and down before saying, "You Americans seem to have more car troubles than most."

"Our car is fine. We need to discuss an oil company," Clark said without preamble, which surprised Naomi.

Danjuma's head bobbed up and down as though he had been expecting this. "Oil is very important in Nigeria and especially here in Abuja. It's a very expensive discussion. Which company are you interested in?" he asked, smiling broadly.

I wonder what discussions we could have with him that wouldn't be expensive?

Naomi knew the CIA would pay his price. Within reason. But first, she needed to figure out whether he knew anything worth paying for. On the other hand, Danjuma bore the burden of convincing them he had something without giving anything of substance away for free.

"Gazovaya," Clark said, and Danjuma's eyes widened with genuine surprise.

"The first thing I can tell you is that it's very dangerous to go poking around Gazovaya. That you can have for free," the Nigerian said.

"What kind of dangerous? I might be in the market for it," Naomi said.

Danjuma looked confused, so Naomi clarified her statement. "What's so dangerous about Gazovaya?"

"It's owned by Russians."

And you win the 'obvious statement of the night' award.

"We know that. Can you provide insight into the company's internal workings," Clark asked.

"Could you be more specific? I know many people who work at Gazovaya. But they are in many different departments. I need to know who to ask."

"Internal financial reports. We suspect they're funding terrorists," Naomi said, careful in her wording of the statement. She wanted to imply things without stating them outright. It was better when people thought they could read between the lines.

"You think they are funding Islamic terror outside of Nigeria?" Danjuma asked, taking the bait. This was not at all what the pair of CIA agents suspected. Islamic terror was a favorite target of the CIA—everyone knew that. Naomi offered a coy shrug.

"Can you get those records?" Clark asked.

"It will be difficult and very expensive. I will need to…" The room went black before Danjuma could finish justifying some exorbitant price. Inky black wings flared open, and Artemis rose from her dark pit like a wraith. Naomi's pistol was in her hand. The chair she'd been sitting in clattered to the floor. Clark rose a millisecond slower, his weapon also out and at the ready.

The powered tools, which moments before had provided a steady cadence, were now quiet. The sudden silence was deafening in its totality.

"The backup power will be on in a few moments. There is no need for panic." The calm in Danjuma's voice told Naomi this wasn't unusual, but she didn't believe in coincidences. Her training and life experience had taught her to be suspicious of everything.

Naomi pulled her phone out to turn on the flashlight function. Noticing a lack of cell service as she unlocked the device. "Do you normally lose cellular coverage when the power goes out?"

"No, and it's most odd. The backup generator should have come on by now," he said, a note of concern entering his voice.

"Seems the landline is down as well." Clark held up the handset on Danjuma's desk.

Through the large bay window, Naomi could see the street lights emanating through the garage door windows. The dark angel was screaming for her to move.

Naomi grabbed the Nigerian by the shirt and hauled him around the desk.

"Whatever this is, my men will deal with it," Danjuma protested.

"We've got to go. I'll lead. You make sure he doesn't get lost," Naomi said, swinging the door open. Clark grabbed Danjuma by the shoulder and pushed him out the door after her.

"Where are we going," the Nigerian said, attempting to pull away from Clark. His outburst was rewarded by a pistol to the back of the head.

"Shut up and keep moving," Clark growled. The men below were now calling to each other. Naomi could see the silhouettes of AK-47s. She wasn't sure which was worse, whoever had turned off the lights or the half dozen men waving assault rifles. It also didn't help that she was now kidnapping their boss.

"Tell them to lower their weapons," Clark said.

Before Danjuma could say anything, the door leading to the lobby swung open and dark figures flowed in. They were moving fast, long guns up and scanning for targets. Naomi could tell by the silhouettes they were wearing night vision. She could hear faint popping as the muzzles of the first two shooters flashed.

Muted thuds told her that at least two Nigerian thugs were down. The lack of return fire indicated the defenders didn't realize they were under attack. They had likely never heard the sounds of suppressed weapons.

These were the people who'd killed the power and jammed the cell service. Professionals who outnumbered her and Clark and outclassed the local talent.

"Contact front. Get down," Naomi hissed. They had to get off these stairs. She opened fire at the lead man. The boom of the handgun shattered the relative silence. She felt the concussion of the shots in her chest. Automatically compensating for the weapon's recoil. The first shooter dropped. The second turned with incredible speed and began firing controlled pairs at almost the exact moment Clark loosed his first shots.

Three AK-47s opened up. The thunderous noise bounced around the garage bay. The muzzles flashed like a beacon to each shooter's position. On the plus side, Danjuma's men now realized they were under attack. However, they'd already lost half their number, and those left were shooting at Naomi and Clark.

She had five steps to go.

Rounds pinged off the metal stairs and railing as the CIA agents rushed to get clear of them.

Three steps to go.

The dark angel hadn't felt this alive in a long time. Time was a fluid concept that had now slowed for Artemis. She noted that the three Nigerian goons were no longer shooting at her. That left the two dark shapes moving toward her.

NAOMI

One step remaining.

The barrels of the invaders flashed, looking like a sparking lighter. Behind her, she heard Clark grunt and his weapon go silent. She found herself falling backward as the slide of her pistol locked open. Naomi had always suspected her life would end like this, but she hadn't thought it would be tonight in a dirty Nigerian chop shop. Her body hit the floor she'd been trying so hard to reach minutes ago. The pistol flew from her limp hand, skittering across the concrete floor in front of sightless eyes.

19

Isaac

Abuja, Nigeria

As we pulled away from the Federal Medical Center, Sarah was on the phone with Selma. In the rearview mirror, I watched several people in medical scrubs rushing toward Samuel. Selma would alert her friend to his driver's situation. Samuel was just minding his own business, doing Selma a favor. Next thing he knew, he was in the middle of a shootout before being dumped at the hospital.

"He deserves better than this," Derek said from the backseat. Sometimes I felt like he could read my mind.

"We owe him, but we have a mission to accomplish right now," Sarah said. We drove for a while in silence, the tension thick and heavy like freshly poured concrete.

"This should be it," Sarah noted, pointing to the next house up the street on the right. Like all the other residences, the safe house was surrounded by a cinder block wall, making the neighborhood look like a series of miniature compounds. As we pulled up to the gate, I punched in the code Selma had given us, sighing with relief when the iron gate swung open.

Several pelican cases were waiting for us in the living room. After clearing the house and ensuring we were the only ones there, we inspected the equipment.

ISAAC

The biggest downside of having a third party deliver your tactical equipment is the lack of control over the type and condition of the weapons. But having an Army vet running security ops in Africa as our supplier felt like a safe bet. If all my dreams came true, there would be suppressed HK417s with 300 Blackout ammunition. An M4 Carbine was much more likely, but I would be ok with an old but functional AK-47. The Russian-built assault rifles were basic, yet reliable.

"Is this a joke?" Derek asked when the first case was opened. What lay before us wasn't even in my top 10. In fact, had I had a list, this particular weapon wouldn't have been on it.

"On the plus side, we're not going in unarmed," I said, picking up one of the crossbows. I had attended a week-long training event during my secret squirrel days to familiarize us with unconventional armament. I had used the weapons on several occasions. Hunting trips weren't exactly tactical environments. Bambi and Turkey Tom weren't trying to kill you. The closest I'd ever been to using one in a tactical situation was on the other side of the TV screen when Rambo was administering justice.

As a young Marine I had a running joke with a few buddies about how much fun it would be to take the USS Constitution out to fight Somali pirates. I had daydreamed more than a few times about being on that old 1700s warship with era-appropriate weapons such as cannons and muskets. There had been no doubt in my mind that Marines with swords and muskets would be more lethal than pirates with AK-47s. I must have sent my suggestion memo to the wrong department because I was still waiting to hear back from someone to follow up on that idea. Maybe they had finally decided to get back to me.

Right now I was wishing that we hadn't left those guns in the middle of the road. How was I to know we'd get crossbows and tomahawks instead of firearms? I didn't feel like I was to blame for failing to forecast this particular outcome.

"These are nice," Sarah said, who seemed unperturbed by the current loadout. I had to admit they were superb bows. The TenPoint Havoc RS440 was 3 inches shorter than an M4 carbine and quieter than the best-suppressed rifle in the world. It was as close to a silent ranged weapon as possible. The downside was you had to reload after every shot.

"We can't operate with these," Derek said, putting the weapon back in the case and snapping the lid closed. I didn't disagree. It might be fun for a safari hunt, but it was impractical for a tactical operation. If Danjuma had actionable intel, we could start planning a mission to get Jimmy back. The best bet was Boko Haram had him. After all, a raid against one of their weapons caches had resulted in his capture. Even three people who had as much experience as Sarah, Derek, and I were still an inadequate raiding force. Heavier firepower wouldn't change it from a near-certain suicide mission, either. But that was a chance I was willing to take if we could get some intel and better guns.

Sarah nodded in agreement and pulled her phone out. "I'm calling Selma to get the address. We'll trade these out and then go see Danjuma." She stepped out of the room to make her call.

Several minutes later, she returned, shaking her head. "We can't exchange these until tomorrow."

I shrugged. "It's not ideal, but we're just going by the shop to chat with Danjuma. We'll be able to upgrade before we need to do anything. But we do have to go tonight. Someone knew we were coming. Speed is of the essence." I knew it was a bit reckless and cavalier, but what were the odds we'd get into two unplanned altercations in a single night? Besides, crossbows were an upgrade over the mighty ballpoint pen.

"That's why we should ensure we have the right equipment," Derek said.

"Fast and good is better than perfect and late," I said, and Sarah nodded in agreement.

"Seriously? We're really storming the castle with knives, axes, and crossbows?" Derek asked.

I looked at Sarah and winked. "It's ok. This is a safe space. You climb into bed. Mama and Uncle Isaac will take care of the big, bad Nigerian informant."

Derek huffed. "Ok, but why the crossbows? Couldn't he get us some long guns?"

"It was a mix-up. These were supposed to be for a hunting trip in the north, but the cases got switched. I guess they had to turn the other vehicle around and bring them back," Sarah said.

"That would have been fun trying to explain suppressed rifles," I said.

"He can't even get us a few pistols? That would be better than this," Derek said.

"I don't know. The crossbow has a better range than a pistol. Plus, what's Danjuma going to think when three intruders show up armed with these?" Sarah asked, holding her bow up.

"We're not even going to need them," I said.

"That's what they said about the important kit in Black Hawk Down," Derek countered.

I rolled my eyes and continued to ignore the drama queen. Derek could lay it on a bit thick sometimes. "I think I'd be more worried about the guys with bows than guns if it was me. That's a different level of crazy."

"Exactly," Sarah said with a wicked smile. I'd seen that look before, and it didn't bode well for the Nigerian's long-term survival prospects.

* * *

"Drone is launched," I said for Mike's benefit. We didn't have the bandwidth to provide him with remote access to the drone. The communication setup we were using at present combined line-of-sight encrypted radios with a call over the cellular network so Mike could join in. A redundancy that allowed the team to stay in communication.

I would be controlling the drone. Mike had a far more critical job. He needed to monitor the local law enforcement and military. It would be up to him to stall or delay them in any way possible if they were alerted to our presence. To this end, Mike had infiltrated many of the networks and computer infrastructure in and around Abuja.

Mike had tracked Danjuma to an auto repair shop. Through a combination of computer wizardry and the Dark Side of The Force, he had determined the information broker ran his operations from the shop. This evening Mike politely asked the Nigerian cell network for Danjuma's location. Or maybe he wasn't polite. Courtesies aside, he was still at work. Sarah, Derek, and I were hunkered down in a trash-strewn alley waiting on the drone to get over the target.

The mechanic shop was just coming into view. Lights shone through the garage door windows into a nearly empty parking lot. The street lights flickered as though debating whether they would continue working all night.

"That's odd," Mike said. His tone was curious, but it made the hairs on the back of my neck stand up.

"What's odd," I whispered as I instructed the drone to hold station over the target building. Sarah gestured for us to start moving, and I gave her a thumbs-up, falling in behind her with Derek picking up rear security. With part of my attention focused on the eye in the sky, I needed the others to pay attention to the situation immediately around us.

"Someone else is in the power grid system," Mike responded distractedly.

"Is it a system administrator or an authorized user?" I asked, straining my cyber security knowledge to come up with those terms. Sarah held up a closed fist, and I stepped into the deep shadow of a doorway. A Sprinter van flew past our position.

"No. Too noisy. They're brute forcing their way through the firewalls," Mike said.

"Are they a threat to us?" I asked.

"No. Maybe. Probably not."

"Can you stop them?" I said as the van pulled into the parking lot.

"Of course, but not without revealing our own presence in the system," Mike said.

"Do not compromise yourself," Sarah said. As she spoke, the garage went dark. I flipped the camera on the drone to night vision in time to see the van door slide open and shooters come piling out. They double-timed it toward the building, the telltale shape of suppressors on the end of their barrels. This wasn't good.

"Mike, what just happened?" I said.

No response.

"Mike, are you there?" I asked again, looking at my phone. No signal.

"Comm check," I said.

"Lima Charlie," Sarah said, followed by Derek.

"It's a hit. They're going for Danjuma," I said. Sarah brought her weapon up and started moving toward the target. Derek and I fell in behind her. No questions were asked, and no further explanation was required. The tactical situation had changed, and so had our plan. Someone was moving to capture or kill the information broker. We had to assume the worst-case scenario. Someone was trying to kill him, and I wasn't ready to lose our one good lead on Jimmy's whereabouts.

Our approach brought us behind the van. A guy stood next to the open passenger door smoking.

Ole Smokey Joe is going to find out cigarettes are bad for his health pretty soon.

I saw another man sitting behind the steering wheel in the driver's side view mirror.

"Derek, you have the guy on the passenger side. Isaac, cover me. I've got the driver," Sarah whispered.

Derek stopped and took a knee to cover his target. Sarah moved like a liquid shadow, taking an approach angle that allowed her to advance unseen by Smokey Joe. I moved close behind Sarah, covering her advance. Reaching the back of the van, she lowered the crossbow, holding it with her right hand. With her left, she grabbed the tomahawk vertically sheathed along the small of her back.

"Green," Derek said, letting us know he was ready.

Sarah was at the edge of the driver's side door when he sensed something was off. As the man started leaning to look out the window, Sarah's swing caught him in the right cheek. The slash must have severed his tongue and stopped his jaw from moving, because the only sound he made was a wet gargle. Pulling with the handle, she used the tomahawk to drag him part of the way out the window like a hooked fish. Swinging her crossbow up she fired an arrow from contact range right into the base of his neck.

"Reloading," Sarah said as she pulled an arrow from the front-mounted quiver.

I heard a metallic pop from what I assumed was an arrow puncturing the side of the van. Derek must have missed. Stepping around Sarah, I navigated the front of the van. I'd taken no more than four steps when Derek called, "Target down. Reloading."

Gunshots rang out. A pistol being fired rapidly. A second joined a moment later. Someone was fighting back.

Now there are two groups in there. Both with guns. Fantastic, we just brought crossbows to a gunfight.

The reloading process for the crossbows was a significant drawback. We had practiced at the safe house and could each consistently complete it in about 20 seconds. That was forever in a firefight, considering it took maybe a second and a half to reload an assault rifle. From the size of the van, I estimated there could be up to eight shooters in there, and that wasn't counting the two I'd just heard. We needed a lot of bullets to either miss us or not be fired. We'd each come with 5 arrows. A choice that was now feeling like a severe lapse in judgment.

The decision was made worse by the fact that the driver wasn't armed. He'd doubtless been a local hire paid to drive the vehicle. It would have been nice to get our hands on a couple of those suppressed rifles I'd seen the assault force carrying.

What is the deal with drivers not carrying guns around here? It's like it's illegal or something.

"Did your guy have a weapon?" I asked Derek as he came trotting up.

"Nope, not unless you count the lighter and cancer sticks."

I shook my head. "Those take too long and are unreliable. Too many lifelong smokers making it to their eighties and nineties."

So, whoever we're dealing with doesn't trust the locals with bang sticks.

"How are we doing this then?" Derek asked.

"Normally I'd suggest multiple points of entry, but I think we need tight fire discipline tonight," I said.

"Agreed, don't waste shots," Sarah said as what sounded like two or three AK-47s joined the contest to shoot the most bullets the quickest.

Great, more people with guns. This is turning into a three-ring circus, and

ISAAC

the clowns haven't even arrived. Hopefully, someone in there is trying to keep Danjuma alive.

"Did either of you see radios on the bodies?" I asked, focusing on the problem at hand.

"Nope," Sarah said, followed by a "negatory" from Derek.

"Copy. I've got point," I said, moving toward the front door. Based on the men we'd just taken down and the lack of communications equipment, the assault force would likely assume everything behind them was clear. It might be our sole tactical advantage.

Moving toward the front door, I glanced behind me out of habit to ensure the stack was following. Unlike his shot, Derek's claim of target down had been partially accurate. While his man was deceased, he was still standing pinned to the van by an arrow through the neck.

I clenched my teeth as a small bell rang when I pushed the front door open.

So much for entering unannounced. Hopefully, the sound of gunfire would cover it.

Just as the thought went through my mind, the pistols and AK-47s went quiet.

A small whimper from behind the counter alerted me to a young Nigerian woman curled in the fetal position.

"Civilian," I said to let Sarah and Derek know the person I'd found wasn't a threat.

The door behind the counter led to a hallway. A long window looking out onto the garage floor ran along the left side. Through the window, I could see the street lamps shining through the windows on the garage doors. Several figures moved through the pools of light. The outline of night vision goggles on their heads clearly visible.

My night just kept getting better and better.

Stacking up next to the door, I pointed to my eyes and held up four fingers to tell the team I could see four hostiles. I placed my hand on the doorknob, steeling myself to swing it open silently and enter the room.

"HEY! Can you guys hear me?" Mike's voice came booming through my earpiece at a volume that felt loud enough to wake the dead. My hand squeezed the pistol grip of the crossbow, but years of good trigger discipline kept me from reflexively firing. *'Keep your finger straight and off the trigger until you're ready to fire'* had been a favorite mantra of my drill instructors back at Paris Island.

Pulling my hand away from the doorknob, I double-clicked the radio to tell Mike we could hear him, but talking wasn't an option. Thankfully he understood.

"Roger. I copy. I have your locations inside the building. Do you want me to turn the power back on?" Mike asked. I looked back at Sarah, who gave me a brusk nod. Turning the lights on would give us a momentary advantage over the guys with night vision. It would blind them for a few seconds. That small advantage often separated the living and dead. I wished I had a firearm right about now.

"Switch it on in five," I said.

"Coming on in five," Mike repeated.

Closing my eyes and placing my hand on the doorknob, I prepared to enter the garage bay. The lights came on like a soundless flash bang. When I opened my eyes, I jumped at the sight of a guy through the window on the other side of the door. I'd missed him standing in the deep shadows of the corner of the room.

Turning the knob, I slammed the door into him as he tried ripping the NVGs off his face. I pushed hard on the door, and pinned him between it and the wall as Sarah and Derek moved into the room. Arrows flew from their weapons as I sighted in on my own target, a shooter standing partly behind a car in the second stall. Using the reflex sight on my bow, I placed the reticle on his chest and pulled the trigger.

The arrow flew at 440 feet per second, crossing the room in the blink of an eye and burying its razor tip in his heart. I dropped the crossbow, and pulled on the door to release the pressure holding the man in place. A jab from my left hand snapped his head back. Throwing the door closed, I caught his right hand with my left as he attempted to draw his sidearm. Then I stomped on his foot to force him to take a step backward and provide the opening I needed to pull my knife.

A knife is not my preferred method of termination. While I don't like to kill people in general, I don't lose sleep over ending bad guys. My loss of sleep comes from my fallen teammates whom I failed. The strike to the neck was quick but messy.

Looks like we're doing laundry tonight.

I ignored the mess and the coppery smell assaulting my nostrils to liberate the rifle and begin scanning for targets. Derek and Sarah were crouched behind a row of large tool chests trying to reload their weapons. The enormous rolling cabinets were painted fire engine red and stood almost five feet tall. Between the steel exterior and the tools inside, they were a good choice for cover and concealment.

There had to be a dozen bodies strewn across the shop, and three were piled at the bottom of the stairs to the second floor. I hoped Danjuma wasn't among them. Sudden recognition flared, drawing my gaze back to the pile at the stairs. Naomi Kaufman's lifeless eyes stared back at me. Clark Martinez was beside her. Neither of them was moving.

What on earth are they doing here?

Before I had time to think about it, the final shooter announced himself by popping up from behind the hood of a car in the third stall. I assessed my tactical situation as his gun rose to sight in on me.

Rookie move to stand in the open without cover.

His gun was rising, and I was out of position, also not great.

So I ran. And promptly slipped in the pool of blood growing around the man I'd just killed. The fall saved my life but wounded my pride. I hoped there was no surveillance footage. Bullets sparked off the concrete floor and metal walls as I scurried to the relative safety of the tool chests.

"Where'd you get the gun?" Derek asked.

"The guy over there gave me his," I said.

"That was thoughtful. It would have been nice if he'd had two," Derek said as rounds thudded into the toolbox. Next to go was the large glass window behind us, which shattered as more bullets sought to make our acquaintance.

"You two argue about the stupidest things at the dumbest times. Derek, if you want a gun so bad, go ask the guy out there for his," Sarah said.

I leaned around the edge and fired back. I'd gotten off two shots when the next pull of the trigger resulted in a soft 'click.' A weapons malfunction. Mr. Murphy was in party mode tonight. I soon discovered the problem. The casing of the last bullet was stuck in the chamber. The gun was useless. Throwing it away, I began to reload the crossbow. I looked around the side of the tool chest, hoping to re-establish the shooter's location. I saw him moving toward our position. There was no way I could reload my crossbow in time.

"He's advancing on us at 2 o'clock. You need to take him out," I said, wishing I had a loaded weapon. Without a word, Sarah and Derek rose as one. The shooter was too close. There wasn't a prayer he'd miss. In fact, a wide burst could hit them both. Once again, I would be the one to survive when others didn't. I reloaded as quickly as possible, expecting to hear muffled pops and see one of my friends fall, their dead eyes accusing me.

20

Naomi

Abuja, Nigeria

Naomi was tumbling into the blackness of the abyss. Panic exploded from her chest, and she screamed soundlessly into the dark. She hit the rocky ground with an impact that should have killed her or at the very least broken every bone in her body, but there was no pain. A familiar wasteland stretched before her in what appeared to be a twilight haze, yet she was unable to distinguish any light source.

She closed her eyes, willing it all to go away. This was a dream, and she'd wake soon. For a second, Naomi wondered if she was dead. The inability to remember how she'd gotten here began to gnaw at her.

"Naomi. Naomi, you have to get up." The voice was soft, like a gentle breeze blowing through silk curtains. She opened her eyes and found herself staring into a face she'd know anywhere. It was her own. But not now...this face was young...a teenager...that was how she looked when...

No, No, No, No! We are not reliving that moment in time. This is just a dream. I'm going to wake up any second.

"Naomi, you have to get up." This time the voice was louder, more insistent. Opening her eyes again, Naomi saw smoke behind her younger self.

"Who are you, and why are you here?" Naomi asked.

The face smiled, and for the first time, she noticed the eyes were burning.

"I'm Artemis, silly. This is where I live until you let me out," she said, holding up hands that were shackled with thick chains. Naomi was in the abyss with the dark angel. What she'd thought was smoke were actually Artemis's wings.

"We used to spend so much time together, and now I'm stuck here. Why did you abandon me?"

"How do I get out of here?" Naomi asked, ignoring the question.

"Walk through the door," Artemis said, pointing to a door made of light that Naomi had never seen before. Pulling herself to her feet, she walked toward it.

"Take me with you," Artemis pleaded. Naomi ignored her and continued walking. A terrific crack of thunder rent the air and forks of lightning impacted the rocky ground, leaving small craters in their wake. Twilight had turned to darkness. Aside from the sporadic lightning, the only sources of light were the door in front of her and the glow behind her emanating from Artemis's eyes.

"HEY! I'm not done talking to you. You owe me!" the dark angel shrieked in fury. Naomi turned to look at her. The chains holding Artemis were white hot and the ground beneath her feet glowed red as though there was a dormant volcano just waiting to explode.

"Without me, you would've never survived. I made you what you are, and now you're just going to walk away from me?" Artemis yelled. The thought of releasing the dark angel usually felt so good. Yet, this time, Naomi shook her head at the being of rage and fury.

She felt tears roll down her cheeks, only then realizing it had started to rain. Naomi heard the sizzle of the falling drops hitting the chains. The dark angel had spoken the truth. Naomi wouldn't have survived without her, but Artemis's time in control was over. The light shower transformed into a downpour and streams of water ran through the ruts in the ground.

Steam rose from the molten rock and Naomi watched fixated as the chains and the ground cooled. Wreathed in darkness, Artemis strained against her bindings. Malice and fury radiated from her, reaching for Naomi like outstretched claws, desperate to maintain the status quo.

NAOMI

"No," Naomi whispered for the last time before turning around and continuing toward the door. She could feel the heat from those eyes on her back, but she couldn't turn around. She knew if she did, she'd be lost forever. It was a logical thought. One rage and fury could never understand. She put her hand on the doorknob.

"Who do you think helped you cope after he..." the dark angel continued. Naomi opened the door and stepped through it. Light exploded into existence. This was how she had imagined the dawn of creation while she was attending Hebrew school.

* * *

She was lying on the stairs, having been knocked down by Clark, Danjuma, or both. Were they dead? She remembered everything now. The mission, the firefight, and her head impacting the metal railing. That must have knocked her out. Clark's gun had gone silent before she fell, and he wasn't moving. She felt sluggish, with a massive headache. She knew she hadn't been shot. At least not today. Trying to stand now would cause her to lose her lunch on the garage floor. All at once, the door in front of her slammed open, smashing into the shooter on the other side of it.

Naomi's brain worked in overdrive to assimilate all the data it was receiving. None of it made sense. Isaac Northe was coming through the door, followed by Sarah and Derek. Were those crossbows? Arrows flew, but her brain was taking so long to process things. She could feel the dark angel screaming to be freed.

Isaac was a hurricane of violence as he killed the man behind the door. Their eyes met for the briefest of moments, and then he dove across the floor as someone shot at him from the other side of the shop. He disappeared behind the massive tool chests. She could hear their voices but couldn't make out what they were saying. Isaac leaned around the toolbox, shooting. The large glass window exploded.

Why did he stop shooting? Where were the police?

A curse followed by the rifle being thrown told her the gun was either out of ammo or had malfunctioned. There was pressure on her shoulder. Her mind must be clearing. She was probably still in shock and likely had a concussion.

Naomi could see the shooter. He stood up from behind the car and began to cross the shop floor. He was going to kill the Peregrine team, and all she could do was watch. She felt the *tap tap* at her shoulder again. Turning her head to look up, she saw Clark's bloody hand trying to give her his pistol. The shooter was ten feet away from the tool chests. Out of the corner of her eye, she saw two figures rise from behind cover.

Summoning every ounce of her willpower, she reached toward the offered weapon. Two arrows flew, and the long gun spat. One of the arrows caught the shooter in the shoulder, and the second flew by, missing the neck by inches. Naomi's fingers wrapped around the pistol grip. He was so close there was no need to aim. Just point and shoot. She pulled the trigger once, twice, again, and again.

Naomi jumped. Isaac was in front of her. One hand on her elbow and the other on the empty pistol she was still trying to fire. "Hey. Good to see you. Why don't you let me take this? You got him." Isaac's voice was reassuring. She felt like a shipwreck victim when the rescue swimmer arrives. The conditions of the storm hadn't changed. She wasn't any less tired trying to keep her head above water, but now there was hope.

"Building is clear," Sarah said from somewhere to her side.

"Can you sit up?" Isaac asked.

"Yes. I think so. Can you check on Clark?" Naomi asked as she sat up with assistance.

"I'm fine, although Danjuma seems to still be out cold," Clark said from behind her. She turned to look at him and immediately regretted it as a wave of dizziness hit her. Derek had somehow climbed the stairs and now sat next to Clark, bandaging his right arm.

"Through and throughs on the forearm and bicep," Derek said, answering her unasked question.

"We need to get going," Isaac said. "The police have been alerted and are about five minutes out. Mike is trying to delay them, but there's only so much he can do."

"There's going to be a lot of scrutiny here. The police are corrupt but not completely incompetent," Sarah said.

"It's not every day you come across something that looks like a scene from a Quentin Tarantino film. Nigerian thugs and what I'm guessing are Russian mercenaries killed with arrows," Isaac said.

"I'd pay to see that movie," Derek said, helping Clark to his feet.

"Who would you want to play you?" Isaac asked as he helped Naomi stand.

Naomi had experienced some strange things in combat, but hearing two guys talk about watching a movie based on the firefight they'd just been in was a first.

"You mean if I couldn't play myself," Derek said.

"Obviously," Isaac said with a grunt as he lifted Danjuma into a fireman's carry.

"Would you boys mind waiting until we're off the X to discuss your Hollywood careers?" Sarah asked. Naomi saw a flash of a smile as she asked the question.

"Do you need any help walking?" Sarah asked Naomi.

"No, I should be fine. What are you planning on doing with him?" Naomi asked, gesturing at Danjuma.

"We were going to question him here, but that's not really an option. I think our best bet is to take him to our safe house unless you have a better idea."

"Yes. Let's get out of the country," Naomi said. Everything was happening so fast. There was no contingency for how things had just gone down.

"Do you have a way to do that? We flew commercial," Sarah said.

"Nothing glamorous. We have an L100 Hercules at the airport. The flight crew is with the aircraft. They could be ready to go by the time we got there."

"We'll take it. We need 2 minutes to collect our bags from the safe house," Sarah said. Naomi nodded, and Sarah walked off to talk to Isaac and Derek. Naomi heard sirens in the distance as they stepped out into the parking lot. She was thankful the police response had been slow to this point.

"Is this your car?" Isaac asked, pointing to the sedan she and Clark had arrived in. Naomi nodded and climbed into the passenger side as Derek took his place in the driver's seat. Clark climbed into the backseat. Opening the trunk, Isaac unceremoniously dumped the unconscious Danjuma inside before squeezing into the backseat with Clark and Sarah.

Sarah called her logistics specialist, who advised them to drop the kit at the safe house and clear the area. Her contact would be able to recover everything.

Naomi picked up the phone to make her own call. She needed the pilots to get the bird ready for immediate takeoff. The pilot picked up on the second ring. "Hello?"

"Hey, we're headed to you. We need to leave. Now!" Naomi said.

"Understood. We'll be ready," he said, ending the call.

Naomi was surprised to get a call back less than a minute later. "Did you already file a flight plan?" The pilot asked her.

"No. Why?"

"There is already a plan filed and approved. We've been given priority clearance." The hair on the back of her neck stood up. Someone had known about their need for a quick exit and filed for the crew to expedite the process.

Who would be able to do that?

Her mind picked out a probable answer a moment later. "Thanks for the heads-up. We'll be there in a sec. I want to be moving as soon as we're on board," Naomi said to the pilot before disconnecting.

"My flight crew just informed me that their flight plans were filed and approved. They are cleared to leave as soon as we get on the plane," Naomi said, turning around to look at Sarah. She felt terrible for them, crammed into the backseat like that, but Clark and Isaac had opted to pass the time by playing on their phones. Naomi knew Clark liked to play Boom Beach and Clash of Clans. She wondered what type of mindless entertainment Isaac enjoyed. It was surreal and oddly normal. A welcome change from the shootout that had taken place less than 10 minutes ago.

"That's great news," Sarah said.

"Yes, except they told me they didn't file the plan."

"You just said…"

"A plan was filed and approved. Seems someone decided to expedite things. Do I have Mike to thank for that?" Naomi asked.

"I'm sure I don't know what you're talking about. Hacking into air traffic control systems would be illegal and most unethical," Sarah said with a straight face, but the glint in her eye confirmed Naomi's suspicions.

"You said the NSA verified Jimmy's proof of life video as a fake. Just out of curiosity, did the CIA techs come to the same conclusion?" Isaac asked, looking up from his phone.

"Well, no. The CIA team believed the video to be real. That's how the NSA became involved. We wanted CNO to look at it to see if they could come up with any data we could use for a target package," Naomi said. She knew she shouldn't be telling Isaac this, but it wasn't anything more than she'd already told him.

"So, the CNO team discovered it was a fabrication? That's a pretty impressive forgery," Isaac commented, returning to his phone.

"Again, no. It was their star golden boy hacker, Andrew Brock. Everyone else missed it," Naomi said. Isaac nodded but didn't comment. His attention was now focused back on his phone.

21

Marissa

Highway 90, New York

People with options and resources don't make a habit of traveling via Greyhound bus. But that was where Marissa found herself. Sitting in a semi-comfortable seat in the back row, watching the landscape fly by in the late night hour. The young woman five or six rows ahead of her undoubtedly wished she had more options. She introduced herself to Marissa while they waited at the terminal for the bus to arrive. Her name was Roxanne, but she went by Roxy. She attended school at Mohawk Valley Community College in Utica, New York. Marissa had smiled and given her name as Angelica. The authorities were looking for a single woman and Roxy might prove to be a good cover. Marissa was never one to turn down a tactical advantage.

Since getting on the bus, Roxy had found herself the object of unwanted attention from the two redneck boys across the aisle. Maybe they were still in high school. Marissa couldn't tell anymore.

The situation irritated her for several reasons. The first was Roxy had yet to stand up for herself and tell the little trolls to leave her alone. Marissa suspected Roxy would stay quiet and hope the boys got bored or an opportunity would arise to escape the situation. The second and truly frustrating part was Marissa couldn't intervene. Doing so would draw all sorts of unwelcome attention. A short, brown woman giving a couple of jocks a beatdown would be more than memorable.

It had taken far longer to escape New York than she planned. Originally she'd have landed in New Jersey, and then been able to disappear anywhere the interstate system would carry her. However, being trapped within the confines of Manhattan had complicated matters. The NYPD and what she assumed was Homeland Security had locked down the island. She'd spent two nights in battered women's shelters, taking advantage of a hot meal and a place to lay low.

Marissa had no way of knowing what kind of information the local and federal agencies had about her. There was no reason to risk capture at the transit checkpoints. Well-versed in the science of manhunts, she knew there was a literal clock ticking for the pursuers. If they didn't locate her in 48 to 72 hours, they would assume she'd somehow slipped the net and left the area. After that, the search radius would grow by the hour until it was unfeasible to search the zone.

Technology was a problem because of continuously improving facial recognition software. Algorithms never got tired or bored. She doubted there was a good picture of her face. On the other hand, her height, approximate weight, hair, and skin color would have been recorded and loaded into the search criteria. There was also a strong possibility that some sort of gait analysis had been performed. The way people walked, shifting weight from one foot to the other, length of stride, and foot positioning created a unique signature. Tier-One operatives would change how they walked to throw off human and digital observation.

A train heading north had taken her across the Spuyten Duyvil Bridge and into Yonkers. From there, it had been reasonably simple to make her way into Connecticut. Buying a last-minute bus ticket with cash didn't raise an alarm like it would with an airplane ticket. She'd thought about stealing a small plane, but that would create more problems than solutions. So here she sat on a bus headed to Canada. Miami was where she really wanted to go, but honestly, she didn't see a way that was ever going to work.

The CIA had been her handlers for a few weeks, and already the risk and recklessness of their 'job requests' was increasing. They saw her as a weapon, valuable for the violence she could bring to the fight, but of no intrinsic worth. When she ended up dead on one of these missions, they wouldn't even bother to recover her body.

She thought about the team at Peregrine. Colleagues but also friends. They had each other's backs. She'd wanted to join their pack for the protection they might be able to provide her, but she saw now that was foolish. If anyone could help her with the CIA it was Naomi, but she didn't seem open to the idea.

Realistically, what did she expect to happen even if she could join Peregrine's happy little family? Was she going to date and marry Isaac Northe one day? Have a couple of kids and become a suburban housewife? Maybe she'd have a minivan and join the PTA. That would be a blast. Sitting around at soccer games listening to bored housewives complain about their husbands while checking out the hunky coach who wore his shorts just a bit too tight. The idea of that lifestyle bored her enough without having to live it.

Maybe Isaac could quit Peregrine, and they'd travel the world together. Isaac could go pro foodie, and she could take pictures of all the interesting locales. The list of places she wanted to travel to was endless. It might be nice to be able to go to Tokyo or Bangkok without needing to commit mass murder. Marissa smiled at the thought of walking down the streets of Florence, Italy listening to Isaac describe the culinary perfection they'd just enjoyed at some new hole-in-the-wall restaurant.

It might have been the drone of the bus motor, or her fatigue, but it took the logical part of her mind a few minutes to kick in and recognize that she was indulging in fantasies like a schoolgirl with a crush. She snapped herself to attention, figuratively and literally. She had to pull it together. They'd gone out for a couple of meals, that was all. Marissa doubted Isaac had any idea she was interested, if you could even call her that. Most men were clueless, but Isaac wasn't most men. He checked so many of her boxes, including his attention to detail. Granted, Isaac had taken a drugged coffee from her, but that could be excused. He was someone who could take care of himself. Isaac understood the world wasn't a fairytale where good always triumphed. Maybe most important, he seemed to actually listen when she talked.

None of these feelings outweighed the fact that going back to Miami could implicate Isaac and the rest of Peregrine in the recent operations she'd undertaken. That would negate any goodwill she'd generated with them by turning over the phone and video of Jimmy Taylor. She wasn't stupid enough to throw away the potential of their help in the future for a silly infatuation. Facts would always win over feelings. She was a highly trained, deniable, and disposable asset. Who knew what the CIA would force her to do next? She had to remain practical if she wanted to live past Tuesday. So, she headed to Canada.

Marissa gritted her teeth as she saw one of the boys slide into the seat next to Roxy with the other hanging over the back of his buddy's chair. She wished the woman would just punch one of them in the face. A broken nose could help back them off...or make things worse. It was hard to tell at this point. She chafed against the need to stay quiet and unnoticed. Marissa wasn't a white knight who needed to ride to the rescue of every damsel in distress, but there was something different about this. There were echoes of her last mission with Project Olympus.

She closed her eyes and told herself that no action was required. Staying under the radar was far more critical than telling some kids to mind their own business. Marissa needed to figure out her next move once she got to Canada. Should she stay there or go to some place like Iceland? She could also catch a flight to Brazil or Chile. She could possibly find work and protection with any one of the major cartels. Colombia was out. That place was so infested with CIA and other federal agencies that there were entire apartment buildings used as American safe houses.

The idea of living in Toronto appealed to her. Metropolitan areas were easy places in which to disappear. Diverse populations and ready access to people who could help establish a new identity, for a price, of course. Money wasn't an issue. She had more than she could spend in this lifetime. Sergej Aksyonov's generous donation had seen to that. The biggest dilemma was what to do. Maybe she would pursue the life of a freelance photographer.

But there she went again, drifting off into fantasy. It didn't matter where she went or what she did, the Agency would find her. They undoubtedly had a whole team working that problem set right now, probably just across the hall from the section tasked with covering her trail.

There would be critical equipment malfunctions and corrupted files, which would make it next to impossible to positively ID her. There wouldn't be enough evidence to prove the CIA had interfered in the case. Experienced investigators would be able to read the tea leaves and recognize the Agency's involvement, but they'd be powerless to come after her with anything concrete.

Life as an assassin, first for the CIA and then for Banque Suisse, had taught her the importance of cybersecurity. More often than not, it was possible to locate a target by following their digital footprint. Marissa frequently changed phones and SIM cards and stayed off social media. She didn't feel the need to help someone track her. One of her few vices was her Pinterest account. There were several photographers whose work she enjoyed, even though she wasn't connected with them.

The two young men, who Marissa had learned were named Lonny and Riley, had moved past what could be considered juvenile fun to expressing amorous intentions. Lonny was a rodent with protruding front teeth. Riley looked like a down-home farm boy, complete with overalls. Lonny sat in the seat next to Roxy and seemed to be the leader.

Marissa could see in the reflection of the bus window that Lonny was attempting to grope her.

"Stop it! Stop it!" Roxy shrieked as she pushed Lonny's questing hands away. Riley laughed as though her protestations against the assault were the funniest thing he'd ever heard. Leaning over the back of the seat, he licked the side of her face. Roxy tried to slap the big farm boy, but he caught her hand. Lonny moved in, achieving his intended goal.

Marissa had seen this behavior before and knew where it led. In college several frat boys had been 'flirting'— as their lawyer had later called it—with a young woman in one of Marissa's classes, when things 'went a little too far.' She'd reported the incident, but one of the boys was the son of a high-powered Congressman. During the trial, the young lady, who worked two jobs to pay her way through college, was accused of being everything from a prostitute to a trailer trash gold digger who had set the boys up in order to profit from a settlement.

Ultimately the boys had been acquitted of all charges. The young woman dropped out of college, unable to deal with the shame and ridicule. Several weeks after leaving, she was found dead of a painkiller overdose in her bedroom at her parents' house.

Marissa knew these boys would ultimately win in this contest of wills. The bus was two-thirds full but empty in terms of decent human beings willing to intervene.

Marissa felt her soul shrivel a little bit more as she stifled the urge to get involved in the unwanted love connection. She hated the other passengers on the bus for not doing anything to help the young lady. But more than anything, the dirty feeling of self-loathing was drowning her.

Another scream from Roxy prompted the bus driver to get on the PA system and tell everyone to get back to their seats. The boys' movement back across the aisle reminded Marissa of buzzards slowly flapping away from a carcass in the middle of the road. An oncoming vehicle might have interrupted them, but they'd be back.

Picking up her phone to distract herself with Pinterest, she was surprised to see that she had an unread message from Isaac in her Signal app. Butterflies took flight in her stomach, like when the cute boy in school had passed her a note all those years ago.

```
Isaac: Can you talk?
```

The message had come in just a couple of minutes ago. She should ignore it. Cutting ties and disappearing meant she couldn't afford the contact. She chewed her lip for a second, then against her better judgment, tapped out a quick reply.

```
Marissa: What's up?
```

She smiled as a message bubble told her he was typing.

```
Isaac: How was NYC? Looked like someone threw quite the party.
It's been all over the news.
```

Marissa was uncertain how to respond to the obvious insinuation.

```
Marissa: It was fine. How's Nigeria? Sorry I couldn't go.
Isaac: Not as boring as I'd hoped, but we have Danjuma. Also ran
into your girl, Naomi. She's giving us a lift back to the States.
```

Marissa stared at the last message for what felt like a lifetime.

What did he mean by 'ran into your girl'? Why was she in Nigeria? Had they gone together?

She suspected Naomi had a thing for Isaac. The way she watched him when she thought nobody else was looking. Did Isaac realize? Did he reciprocate?

Through sheer force of will, she shut down that line of thinking. Her mom had always said Puerto Ricans were passionate people. Marissa considered herself to be pretty logical and levelheaded, except when it came to the ugly green monster. She didn't wear jealousy well and knew it.

```
Isaac: So I was wondering if you could do me a favor?
```

Marissa felt her breath catch. It was such a stupid thing to get emotional about, but when was the last time someone had asked her for a favor? Or had asked her anything, for that matter? Project Olympus, Banque Suisse, and now the CIA…they didn't make requests. They issued orders. Years of having no autonomy, of being owned by puppet masters who cared more about mission accomplishment than if she lived or died. And now Isaac threw it out there, like it was nothing.

MARISSA

'I was wondering if you could do me a favor.' What did that mean? What kind of favor could he possibly need from me?

```
Marissa: Maybe... strongly depends on what it is. I'm terrible at
baking cupcakes.
Isaac: LOL, no, I can handle the cupcakes. I'm trying to find out
why the CIA believes Jimmy's video is fake.
```

Now that sounded interesting. Her brain rapidly scanned through scenarios. If she agreed, they would owe her a favor in return. She might end up corroborating what Naomi had said—that the video was a hoax. That wouldn't make Isaac or Sarah or anyone at Peregrine happy. But they weren't the type to shoot the messenger.

Or, she might discover that the CIA knew the video was real and was intentionally covering it up. They could be denying its validity for their own nefarious purposes, and leaving a US service member to rot in the custody of a terrorist organization. If she found proof of that then maybe, just maybe she would have the leverage she needed to get them off her back for good.

```
Marissa: You have my attention. What do you need?
```

Several minutes passed before Isaac responded.

```
Isaac: Seems CNO's star hacker flagged the video as a fake.
Marissa: Do you have a name and location?
Isaac: Andrew Brock. Severn, Maryland.
```

And just like that, her plans changed. She wouldn't stand out in Maryland any more than she would in Toronto. And if someone put two-and-two together to connect her to the helicopter hijacking, that was the CIA's problem. If they wanted her to keep doing their dirty work, they'd get her out. And if not, she'd go to prison. Not an ideal option. Still, it wasn't like she was free now. But she could be. If she did this favor for Isaac and found the answer he wanted, the Peregrine team would be in her debt and she might be able to tell the CIA where to go. It was worth the risk.

It crossed her mind that some people, like Sarah, were willing to take these kinds of risks for other people, not just themselves. She didn't relate. She thought it best she not mention that to Isaac.

* * *

The driver announced they'd be stopping in Fulton for a half-hour in the next ten minutes. Marissa opened Google Maps and began weighing her future travel options. Her tactical center assessing risk vs. reward and possible second and third order effects of each decision.

When the bus stopped at the Pilot Travel Center, Marissa shuffled off the bus behind the rest of the passengers. The truck stop was devoid of activity at this early hour of the morning. Two cars and a cruiser refueled across from an eighteen-wheeler. Half a dozen semi-trucks idled in the parking lot, their drivers getting much-needed sleep.

The Travel Center was indistinguishable from the countless others Marissa had been in throughout her life. The fluorescent lights were hurting her eyes after hours on a dimly lit bus. Her first stop was the coffee stand. Gas station coffee was rarely good. At this hour it was guaranteed to have sat for so long it'd peel paint. That didn't matter. She just needed something hot.

Her fellow passengers moved mindlessly among the aisles, looking for something to eat. An announcement informed all who were concerned that shower #3 was now ready. Marissa mulled over what it would be like to live life on the road, where a truck stop was your source of a shower. She imagined it was a liberating nomadic existence for many people who lived this life, one that allowed them to experience a freedom most others never knew.

Browsing a wide assortment of tools covering the back wall, she grimaced at her first sip of the scalding hot, large black coffee. The two loudmouths from the bus were bouncing around as though the early morning hour had no effect on them. As they entered the restroom, Marissa turned and followed, grabbing a hanging tire iron as she passed.

Both looked like they had spent a lot of time in the gym, and Marissa was sure they were stronger than her. If she were entering a straightforward fight like a boxing or wrestling match, there'd be no hope of victory. The agenda this morning didn't include boxing. They were at the urinals laughing and joking as she entered.

A criminal trial had already taken place in the court of Marissa's mind and a verdict had been reached. Guilty. The sentence was death and she was here to carry out the execution. There would be no threats or second chances. Time to put these animals down. If they didn't hurt Roxy, they'd just end up hurting someone else in the future.

Neither noticed her until she was within four feet of Riley. As the bigger threat, he needed to be taken out first. Both cursed and tried to look at her, but their instinct to not expose themselves limited their range of motion. With the tire iron in her right hand, she swung like Serena Williams returning a hot volley.

The back of Riley's skull gave way as the blow sent it into the dirty tile wall. Death was instantaneous. Lonny wasn't nearly as lucky. As the farm boy collapsed in front of her, she popped the top off her coffee, throwing the scalding contents into the remaining would-be rapist's face. With a scream more animal than human and all dignity forgotten, he brought his hands up to protect his burnt face. Marissa's swing missed as Lonny slipped on the pee-slicked floor.

"Hey, what's going on out there?" a voice bellowed from one of the stalls. Marissa hadn't bothered checking if they were alone. It didn't matter. This wasn't an assassination that had to be deniable. It was the termination of two rabid animals before they could bite anyone else.

From his knees, Lonny tried grabbing the urinal to pull himself up as Marissa sidestepped left to get a better angle. Her second attempt found its mark after she dropped the coffee cup and switched the tire iron to her left hand. The lip of the latrine caught him in the throat, crushing his windpipe as his face smashed into the urinal cake. She brought another blow down on the top of his head to crush his skull.

"Is everyone alright out there?" Marissa heard as she walked out of the bathroom, dropping the tire iron in the trash can. Before she exited, she tapped the service button.

For all the violence and shouting in the bathroom, no one in the central area appeared to have noticed. Exiting the Travel Center, Marissa pulled out her phone to check her orientation one last time. Then she walked over to the cruiser bike, and removed the fuel hose.

The keys left in the ignition had been helpful. Most people in rural areas like this assumed no one would steal their vehicle. She headed toward a small airstrip nearby. By the time she arrived at the airport, the bike would have been reported stolen. It would be much easier to locate than the plane she was about to steal.

The ride to the Fulton County Airport six and a half miles from the truck stop took 15 minutes. As the wind blew through her hair, she thought about the misery and trauma she'd saved Roxy. The little piece of her soul that had shriveled on the bus began to revive. There was something redemptive about sparing someone else pain.

22

Alexander

Zurich, Switzerland

A lexander restrained himself from throwing his cup of tea against the wall. The delicate blue and white tea service had been a gift from the Danish Royal family and was over 200 years old. His portfolio of European royal artifacts rivaled most museums. Housed in an underground vault below his Geneva estate, the private collection was a favorite among his wealthy investors and donors.

Zhao's mole in the NSA had provided the identities of the people who'd initially given the CIA the proof of life video. Peregrine, Inc. concerned Alexander. He didn't know how they'd gotten ahold of the video, but having a group of ex-military and ex-intelligence operators looking into this wasn't what he needed. They had already created enough problems for him. He needed to control and mitigate the possible damage. Through his contacts in Interpol, Alexander had had their passports flagged and hired several private investigators to keep an eye on their activities.

When he'd learned they were traveling to Nigeria, it was the perfect opportunity to get rid of them once and for all. Not only had they survived the ambush, but they had managed to eliminate the mercenaries Zhao had sent to collect the Nigerian informant, and had disappeared with him to boot.

The intercom buzzed, followed by the voice of Kirsten, his executive assistant. "Sir, you have a call on line one. Mr. Zhao." They spoke French unless it was absolutely necessary to converse in another language.

Hopefully, Zhao had some good news for him. The Eden Initiative was close to its final stages. It wouldn't be long now.

Alexander picked up the phone and recited the familiar Mandarin phrase. "Hello, friend."

When Zhao cleared his throat before speaking, Alexander knew the news wouldn't be good. "We have a problem. My NSA asset, Mr. Brock, is gone."

Alexander took a deep breath, letting it out slowly before speaking again, this time in English. "What do you mean he's gone?"

"He hasn't responded to any of my messages in two days," Zhao answered. The Chinese intelligence officer was becoming increasingly unreliable. Despite being old friends, Alexander contemplated terminating their business arrangement. It would be helpful if Zhao could complete his part of the plan, but he was no longer indispensable. The biggest hitch in the project was Alexander now found himself without the services of an assassin. That wasn't strictly true; there were people he could call, but none of them had his former asset's skill level.

"What steps have you taken to locate him?"

"After the first 24 hours, I sent people to his house. His car is there, but no one is home. I have sources in the hospitals and the police departments looking, but nothing so far." Alexander massaged the bridge of his nose with his thumb and pointer finger. Since manhunting wasn't his specialty, he had no ideas or suggestions to offer. He had people for that. Zhao was supposed to be one of them.

"You need to find Mr. Brock. What he knows is dangerous. In fact, when you do find him, put a bullet in his head," Alexander said.

"Kill such a highly placed asset? The Americans will be suspicious when one of their top computer people gets murdered. They are a formidable opponent when they decide to truly hunt," Zhao said.

Alexander laughed out loud for the first time in a long time. "My old friend. You forget that we're about to render their technological advantage

ALEXANDER

useless. Shortly there will be much more for them to worry about than a dead hacker."

The Eden Initiative would be a great realignment to force ecological accountability. The planet wasn't a charge card mankind could just keep swiping. The bill would come due and humanity would pay with its own extinction.

"I have another meeting. Keep me updated," Alexander said. He was about to hang up the phone when Zhao cleared his throat again. He had something else to say, something he felt Alexander should know.

Alexander sighed, "Is there anything else I should be aware of?"

"Yes. It's just that I don't think we will find Brock."

"Why not?"

"My people entered the house. As I said, he wasn't there, but we found his phone and computer. His wallet in a bowl with his keys on the counter. It appears as if he simply walked out of the house."

Alexander's irritation began to rise again. He should have been informed of this development straightaway. "Who took him?" Abduction was the only explanation that made sense.

"I don't know, but we have the phone and computer. They're in diplomatic pouches headed here right now."

"Find out. Get this sorted." Alexander hung up the phone before Zhao could say anything else. It was settled. His former boarding school classmate had outlived his usefulness. He'd call The Sicilian. Alexander didn't like him. He was messy and sadistic, traits Alexander found both unsavory and unprofessional. But he was reliable. He'd thought about tipping the police off to The Sicilian several times. He would do it after Zhao was taken care of; it would be his penance for his old friend dying badly.

The intercom buzzed again. "Sir. Your next appointment is here. Should I send him in?"

"Yes. Thank you, Ms. Hoek." The Dutch woman was decades his junior and had worked for him nearly as long. There'd been a brief tryst early in her employment, but Alexander had realized quickly that Kirsten would be far more valuable as a gatekeeper than a lover.

The office door opened, and a thin man walked in. Disheveled gray hair and a rumpled brown blazer gave him the appearance of an absent-minded but brilliant academic. He appeared to be much older than his thirty-five years. An overstuffed folder with papers protruding at odd angles would have completed the look. The mathematician preferred to use a MacBook. Otherwise, the stereotype held true.

"Good afternoon, Dr. Linter. Please have a seat. Would you care for a spot of tea?" The academic smiled and nodded as he settled into the seat. Pressing the intercom button, Alexander spoke quickly. "Ms. Hoek, tea for Dr. Linter and me." Every asset needed special handling. Dr. Linter needed to feel like an essential and valued member, so there was extra hand-holding when they met.

Without being asked, the mathematician launched into an update. "The simulations are coming along nicely. I believe we could wipe out the GPS constellation with four missiles, but the data from North Korea is a cause for concern. I don't think…"

Alexander waved his hand dismissively. "Let me worry about the launches. I just need you to tell me where to shoot. What's our launch window?"

"We need a precise positioning of the GPS constellation in order for this to work. That configuration only occurs once every 42 days." The mathematician gave a short chuckle. "The ultimate answer."

Alexander didn't know what he was talking about and didn't care enough to inquire about the joke. Instead, he smiled and offered his next question. "Are you certain targeting the GPS system will have the desired effect?"

Dr. Linter looked as though the answer should be blindingly obvious, but Alexander didn't care enough about this man's opinion of him to be insulted. "GPS satellites are little more than incredibly accurate atomic clocks which transmit a time signal back to Earth. Disruption would have the immediate effect of shutting down all navigation and grounding air traffic. Basically, everything we do depends on accurate time. From the time stamps on banking transactions to the rules governing the internet. The system will begin to break down when the data packets passed between computers are no longer in sync. Loss of accurate time puts everything controlled by a computer at risk." All of that made sense to Alexander, but critical systems would have redundancies.

The conversation paused while Ms. Hoek brought in the tea service and poured a cup for each man.

"Milk and sugar, Dr. Linter?" she asked as she prepared Alexander's tea.

"Yes, please." The words were polite, but the tone said anyone who drank tea without milk and sugar was an uncultured savage.

Alexander waited to continue until his executive assistant left the office. "Aren't there ground-based backups?"

"Yes, but those are a stopgap. After a few hours, time would start to slip. It only takes a fraction of a second. The cloud would fail, and with it, all the services hosted there. Mobile phones would no longer work, and the power grid would collapse within the first 24 hours because the transmission networks would no longer be able to balance the load. In short, computers, communication, power, and transportation. All rendered useless."

"The internet as we know would be dead. Everyone scrambling to access any GPS and communications system that are still operational." The plan would provide the leverage needed to make environmental changes. Changes that would provide a sustainable world for future generations. It was far past time to stop letting the greedy little children drive the bus.

"The elimination of these targets will induce a cascade of destruction?" Alexander asked.

"Yes, The Kessler Effect is a theoretical sequence of annihilation that would exterminate all the satellites in orbit."

"This would include HERMES?"

"It would take a while, but yes. The GPS constellation is in Medium Earth Orbit, whereas HERMES is in High Earth Orbit. They'd be hit in the expanding debris cloud."

"But HERMES would be able to fire before being eliminated by this wave of destruction?"

"Yes, of course. The entire sequence can be modeled with all fragmentations and trajectories accounted for. That's how we're able to establish that the Kessler Effect is possible. We will schedule the launch so that the tungsten projectiles will be passing through low Earth orbit when the key satellites are destroyed."

It was the master stroke. The prime solution would obliterate the technology which created globalization and the industrial engine that powered the planetary decimation. The struggle for survival would force local communities to band together instead of meddling in other people's affairs.

Dr. Linter paused and ran his fingers across his eyebrows before continuing with a slightly pained expression. "The biggest problem is the North Koreans. They aren't capable of this level of precision."

Alexander interlaced his fingers and nodded, smiling pleasantly. Much to his annoyance, Dr. Linter was correct. Despite the massive amount of money and technology that had been provided to North Korea, they were still not capable of reliably hitting a target. Much less one in space.

"Of course. I'll handle that aspect. I'd suggest you make sure your own house is in order before worrying about someone else."

Dr. Linter sputtered at the rebuke, but before he could speak the intercom buzzed. "There's an urgent call on line one, sir."

"Dr. Linter. I'm so sorry. I must take this call. I appreciate you coming by. I'll be in touch." The dismissal was understood. The scientist rose, looking mildly perturbed, and left.

Alexander lifted the receiver and switched to Russian. "Hello, Sergej."

23

Isaac

Peregrine Office - Miami, Florida

"You kidnapped an American citizen?" Derek said for the third time. Peregrine and Marissa were gathered in the conference room, and everyone was seated except Derek. Sarah presided over the head of the table, arms folded across her chest. Selma sat with her fingers steepled, and Mike clacked away on his laptop. I couldn't remember the last meeting Mike attended where he wasn't doing something other than paying attention.

"Yep." I leaned back in my chair, savoring another sip of my coffee. The fruity notes in the light Ethiopian roast. I'd picked up a bag from Per'La, a local roaster in Miami. I was pleased with my decision to use the French Press.

"You just can't do that," Derek sputtered.

Did he expect me to deny it?

"Seems like he can," Mike said without glancing up from his keyboard. From the corner of my eye, I saw Sarah's face. I wasn't the only one trying hard to control my expression.

"He's an American citizen and works for the NSA," Derek continued.

"Is he always so prudish? I'm pretty sure most of us have kidnapped someone from their home," Marissa said, as if abduction was something normal adults did on Saturday mornings.

Derek turned on her like Doc Holiday spinning to face an opponent in a duel. "Why are you even here? Who invited you?" Marissa made pistol fingers and extended her arms to point at Sarah and me before dropping her thumbs in a shooting gesture. Her flippancy only seemed to enrage him further. "Have you questioned him? Is he dead? If not, where is he, and what will you do with him when you're done?"

"Yes, no, safe, TBD," I said.

He didn't seem to follow my answer. "What?"

I ticked the items off on my fingers as I spoke. "Yes, I have questioned him. No, he's not dead and is in a safe location. His fate is yet to be determined."

Sarah leaned forward, resting her forearms on the table. "What did he tell you?"

"Nothing of value. Brock's acknowledged working for the NSA, but I haven't had a chance for an in-depth interrogation. To be honest, I'm disappointed in him. Spies these days have no sense of class or decorum. Zero points for just blurting out that he works for the NSA. This is why I could never turn my life into a thriller novel. Everyone knows the top secret government men are trained to resist torture for years and never give up a single bit of information."

"That and the non-disclosure agreements you've signed," Sarah said dryly.

Ok, so the non-disclosure agreements will definitely limit my literary future.

Derek's next retort was angry and pointed. "What's your heat state? The last thing we need is the police getting video of you grabbing this guy off someone's Ring doorbell camera."

I shrugged. "You'd be amazed what people will do if you just ask nicely."

"It helps when they get the memo," Mike muttered. I froze, waiting to see if Mike would say anything else.

Derek apparently had his subsequent sarcastic statement locked and loaded and didn't hear Mike. "You just asked nicely? I'm not an idiot. How long does he have before he bleeds out? How many bones did you break? Does he still have all his fingers and toes? You can't do this to American citizens. You're turning into the monster you used to be. Have you started drinking again? I should turn you in right now."

I ignored the monster comment and the accusation that I'd fallen off the wagon. He wasn't wrong; there were periods of my life when I hadn't been a great person. I'd learned a while ago that you could do great things in service of your country and still be a garbage human being. Sometimes there isn't a lot of difference between the hero and the villain they fight.

Out of the corner of my eye, I saw Marissa start to rise. Sarah shook her head, and Marissa dropped back in her seat.

That's interesting. Marissa looked ready to jump into a fight with Derek but deferred to Sarah.

It was bait that I wasn't interested in taking. Derek said all kinds of things in the heat of the moment. He always joked it was his Italian passion running hot.

All appearances of amusement were gone as Sarah rose from her chair. "Are we done? We have a mission to accomplish. I stood in this room not so long ago and gave a speech about Jimmy being abandoned by his government. We still have no sanction, and our actions are 100% illegal. Let me be very clear. I don't care what laws we must break to get Jimmy back. He's family. Derek, get on board or get out, but stop acting like a pedantic child. Isaac, you should have included us in this. Marissa, this is a team operation. I don't care what you do in your free time, but if you ever try to split my team, I'll end you." Sarah's usually subdued French lilt came through like the beam of a lighthouse at night.

Sarah locked eyes with me, and I nodded in understanding. I watched as she looked at each person in turn. When she got to Derek, I saw him study her before pursing his lips and nodding. I could understand and even appreciate his rigid moral belief system, but I trusted Sarah. I hadn't known her CIA callsign had been Athena until recently, but it fit perfectly. She excelled as a leader and tactician.

"So, where is Mr. Brock?" Sarah asked.

Our logistics specialist cleared her throat. I'd almost forgotten about Selma. "He's at a property in the Glades." I'd asked for Selma's help after we'd grabbed Brock. Leaving Sarah out of the plan hadn't been the best idea, but other than that, it had gone much better than I'd expected.

Sarah glared. "You were part of this little free-for-all, too? I expected better from you. How about you, Mike? Were you involved in the kidnapping of Andrew Brock?"

Mike didn't answer. The rapid eye movement told me he was focused on reading something. He began to type before hitting what I assume was the return key. Taking his hands off the keyboard, he picked up the Rubik's cube and began to solve and shuffle the squares in rapid sequence.

"Yes, he knew about it. He's the one who located Brock for us," I answered on Mike's behalf. He was locked onto something, and it was dumb to pull him away to answer a question I could field for him.

"So, Derek and I were the only ones left out?" The silence in the room answered loud and clear. My reasoning for keeping Derek in the dark had been well-founded, but Sarah…

"I'm sorry about that," I mumbled, feeling ashamed that I hadn't trusted her.

She took the proverbial knife-in-the-back in stride. Looking right at me, she asked, "What has Brock told you? Why did he tell the CIA the video was a fake?"

"He insists the video is actually fake," I said.

"He's lying," Mike said still staring at the computer. At that moment, all we heard was the scratchy metallic sound of his cube's spring as he twisted and spun the puzzle.

"We all believe that. It's why we're here," Sarah said gently.

Sarah's ability to pivot and address personal issues while maintaining mission focus was incredible. One moment she was chewing me out for an unsanctioned action. The next she was walking around the table to provide emotional support to a team member. Sarah sat beside Mike and placed a hand on his forearm. He shuddered and took a deep breath before sagging back in his chair. The pressure he felt right now had to be incredible. The weight of his brother's life hanging in the balance. The burden of all the experts saying that he was wrong. His team acting on the credit of his word alone.

ISAAC

"What are you working on?" Sarah asked so softly I almost didn't hear it.

"When Isaac and Marissa grabbed Andrew, they forced him to unlock his phone and laptop, so I could remotely access it. I haven't found anything interesting, but I uploaded a little script. Carmen Sandiego," Mike said.

"Like *Where in the World is Carmen Sandiego?*" Derek asked.

"Yes. Exactly."

"I love that show," Selma said, smiling and nodding her head in approval.

"Did you ever play the game?" I asked.

"One of my favorites. An absolute classic," Selma answered.

"Let me guess, this program steals stuff and leaves hints for you to follow and figure out where it is?" I asked.

Mike had set his cube down and looked around the table as people spoke. I remembered too late that an obvious yes or no question for everyone else was an invitation for him to jump into a nerdy techno-rant. I had no one to blame but myself.

"Computer devices are a bit like Schrödinger's cat."

"Leading this team is like herding cats. I completely understand why Schrödinger put his in a box," Sarah muttered.

Mike either didn't hear Sarah's comment or chose to ignore it. "The outcome is variable until you open it up and look. Observation of the object fundamentally changes its state. With a computer, it requires memory to look at something. Carmen Sandiego infiltrates that systems memory by..."

"Does it tell you where the other computer is?" I interrupted.

"Yes, and it also..."

I had to short-circuit this before it became self-sustaining. Mike had literally spent hours telling me about a program he'd written. I had heard and recognized his words to be English. I even knew the definition of most of them, but I'd still had no idea what he was talking about. "I'm sure what it does is impressive, and how it does it is a work of art. Unfortunately, aside from Selma, you are the only one here who can fully appreciate its amazingness."

Selma shook her head. "This is zero-click tech. The Israeli firm NSO Group are pioneers in the field. They basically invented the exploit."

Understanding blossomed. Seeing the world through Mike's eyes must be a little like being a fully equipped Spec Ops team sent back to the Revolutionary War. Night Vision, infrared lasers. You'd be able to see spectrums invisible to everyone else. Communicate in ways incomprehensible, and perform at a level never before seen. Arthur C. Clarke was 100% correct when he wrote, "*Any sufficiently advanced technology is indistinguishable from magic.*"

And once again, Mike was all by himself. It had to be lonely, being able to see things that seem obvious to you, but no one else understands. We were witnessing the magic of Mike. The perfect alignment of talent and purpose.

There was something I needed to know. "If your program just tells you where it is, why did you name it Carmen Sandiego?"

"I was watching the show when I named the file." Mike's answer made me laugh. He just used what was in front of him without premeditation or trying to be clever.

"Have you gotten any results from Carmen yet?" Sarah asked.

"No location, but someone has taken the devices from Andrew Brock's house."

This didn't make sense to me. "Why do you think someone has taken them if you don't have location data?"

"I've lost connection with both of them."

Marissa and I seemed to be on the same train of thought. She asked, "Would you lose connection if their batteries died?"

"Yes, but the batteries didn't die." Mike seemed confident. While it didn't happen all the time, it wasn't uncommon for him to just answer the question asked. Despite how irritating it was to get information when he was like this, the team all knew he wasn't trying to be difficult.

"How do you know?" I asked.

"They both went offline at the same time." His answer made sense now. Going offline at the same time meant one thing.

"Someone put them in a Faraday bag?" I asked. The bag, lined with a metallic mesh, was designed to block electromagnetic signals. It was a common tactic to put an electronic device in a Faraday bag to prevent it from being tracked or hacked.

"Yes."

I gave a short pump of my fist.

"Why are you excited about that? Losing connection with the devices seems like a bad thing." Derek said.

"Andrew is working for someone who doesn't want the US Government looking for Jimmy. Why else would there be such a push to stop the hunt for him?" I asked.

Derek threw up his hands. "I dunno. It seems like a long shot."

I wanted to start pointing out all the other things we'd done that had been long shots. Seeming to sense my desire to argue, Sarah shot me a look that said, 'Shut it down.' Her eyes scanned the other faces around the table before coming back to rest on me.

Why does she keep looking at me? Oh yeah, I'm the one who kidnapped a top-secret government hacker. Probably shouldn't do that next time if I don't want to get looks from the boss.

"Mr. Northe and Ms. Diaz, since the two of you thought it necessary to bring Mr. Brock down to our corner of the Sunshine State, I have a few questions I'd like to ask him. Mike, keep working here. If you learn anything, give me a call. Isaac, Marissa, and I will go pay Mr. Brock a visit."

24

Naomi

The Bat Cave - Baltimore, Maryland

Naomi was torn between going off the reservation to join Peregrine in the hunt for Jimmy, and staying on the trail of whomever was supplying money to the North Korean missile program. Officially, investigating Sergej Aksyonov was priority one. But it felt more like an errand to clear up the curiosity of some department head than a matter of critical importance. The US was continually monitoring the DPRK. Any threat to America or her allies would be detected well in advance.

The situation with Jimmy, on the other hand, felt like a place where she could actually have an impact. Danjuma had confirmed the CIA's initial analysis. Nothing in this shadow world of smoke and mirrors could be taken at face value. Not even the seemly obvious conclusion that Boko Haram had created Jimmy's proof of life video. She didn't know how, but the US chasing its tail about a phantom soldier who might still be alive could be used to someone's advantage.

The Nigerian terrorist group was bush league in its technological capabilities. They couldn't have made a deep fake even if they wanted. It lent credibility to Danjuma's claims that he'd just been a broker looking to sell the information. Naomi didn't believe for a minute that he was in the dark about the buyer's identity, but that was a problem for the people interrogating him. She wondered if the Nigerian would ever breathe free air again. Prisoners in Guantanamo were being released, but that wasn't the same as being held in a CIA black site.

Naomi had requested satellite analysis for all known Boko Haram strongholds. The terrorist group was declining and had few significant locations remaining. Africa in general and Boko Haram specifically weren't high priorities on anyone's to-do list. There was no telling how long it would take for some desk jockey to get to it. Hopefully, they didn't receive the request right before lunch or on a Friday, then it'd never get done. There was also no way to elevate the urgency of the request without revealing that she was still looking into a closed case.

All she and Clark could do right now was to plod along the money trail. Why did someone want to enhance the North Korean missile program? Naomi felt this was where the focus should be, instead of worrying about where the money came from. It was like being concerned with where the arsonist bought the gasoline while the house burned.

"Hey, Clark. You got a minute?"

"Sure, what's up?"

"Why would someone want to improve North Korean missile accuracy and effectiveness?"

Clark leaned back in his desk chair before swiveling around several times. "Because someone wants to level the playing field?"

"That seems unlikely. The DPRK is unstable, and bringing them up to par with everyone else would destabilize the entire region."

Clark nodded, considering Naomi's point. "That's true. There's no telling who they will shoot or for what reason. That's exactly why China, their strongest ally, has been reluctant to help them."

"Shoot someone. That's a valid reason. What if whoever is funding them has a target no rational country would engage?" Naomi mused.

"Nothing else makes sense."

"The problem is the range. We can't eliminate anything based on the range of their weapons anymore. They are capable of hitting anything on Earth.

Last week they launched a satellite, and yesterday they shot it down."

"Why would you launch a satellite just to shoot it down?" Clark asked.

"Why do they use anti-aircraft guns to execute political prisoners? Apparently just because they can."

Clark pointed with his chin, and Naomi turned to see Shane waving his hand. "What's up, Shane?"

"The satellite analysis you requested of those sites in Nigeria has come back. Must have been a slow day, or someone is trying to earn analyst of the month."

Naomi walked over to Shane's computer. "Open it up. Let's take a look."

They flipped through a dozen pictures of three different sites. All of them featured buildings that bore signs of continuous fighting. Bullet-pocked walls and piles of rubble scattered around. Many of the structures were little more than two or three walls that had yet to collapse. Camouflage netting was sporadically stretched over areas Naomi assumed the terrorists wanted to shield from aerial observation. Included were analyst markings noting the location of weapons and fortifications. They looked like the rebel strongholds they were.

"There's nothing here. We know now for certain that Boko Haram had Jimmy. Still, there's nothing to confirm he was ever in any of these locations," Naomi said while wondering when she'd started calling the Marine Special Operator by his first name.

Clark gave a soft snort. "What were you expecting? A building tagged with 'Gunny Taylor was here'?"

"That would have been helpful, but no. Maybe increased guard activity or vehicles that looked out of place," she said. Naomi turned to walk back to her workstation. What was the next move?

"Hey, wait just a minute," Shane called. "When I put in that analysis request, I also reached out to a buddy over at JSOC and asked him if he had access to anything in our area of concern."

Naomi whipped around, staring at the analyst. She couldn't believe the stupidity that had just come out of his mouth. Their operation at the MerchWork facility was top secret and compartmentalized.

"You did what?" A certain amount of crosstalk took place, but that was all through secure channels. Even if he was talking with someone from the Joint Special Operations Command, it was a massive violation of their OPSEC.

"Uhhh mmmm…" Shane stammered, taken aback but the sudden fury. She wasn't sure what he'd expected. Maybe a high five and a 'tell me what you got'?

Naomi started slowly walking back toward him. "What did you do?"

"I was chatting with him."

Naomi placed both hands on his desk and leaned to glare at him. Her voice low and threatening. "Where? Where were you so stupid as to be having a classified conversation with someone without clearance and or need to know?"

"It was secure. We were chatting on the internal JSOC messenger," Shane said, holding his hands up defensively.

Clark cocked his head. "How were you using that messenger?" I know you used to work there, but…"

"Well you see, when the CIA recruited me, everything happened so fast that the JSOC System Administrators never revoked my access." Naomi felt a wave of relief wash over her. She wasn't happy Shane talked out of turn, but it wasn't as bad as she'd imagined.

It's still a security problem, but at least not on our end.

"Then you asked him for any intel JSOC might have about the area?"

Shane looked relieved that he wasn't about to be punched in the face. Though the jury was still out on his continued employment.

"He sent me a video that he said was kinda odd. A drone waiting to support a SOCOM unit recorded a raid. They saw the raid after the fact. Apparently, so much nonsense happens in Africa, and Nigeria in particular, that no one thought anything of it. He remembered it when I asked and sent it over just a little bit ago."

It was the absurdity of the world that they lived and worked in. Someone could witness a raid and not report it because it was either normal or didn't impact their job.

The video looked like the typical Drone TV Naomi had seen a hundred times before. Based on the zoom, the aircraft was just loitering, likely observing an area before air or ground assets moved into the sector. Off to the right of the screen were several clusters of buildings that appeared to match the photos of the largest stronghold they'd just been examining.

Whatever the drone was doing, its focus wasn't on the Boko Haram fortress. At the far corner, Naomi could see four aircraft moving toward the cluster of buildings. The aircraft were following a riverbed, flying nap-of-the-earth. The riverbed passed within 500 meters of the encampment. She knew from experience the helicopters would follow the river and pop up close to the objective.

"Those look like US birds," Clark said. The lead and trail helicopters looked like AH-64 Apache gunships. The two in the middle appeared to be UH-60 Black Hawks. There was something off about the aircraft, but she couldn't put her finger on it. Maybe they were just an older variant of the legendary utility helicopter.

"It's not the 160th. They don't use Apaches," Naomi said. The 160th Special Operations Aviation Regiment was the premier and preferred method of travel for US Special Operations. The Night Stalkers were the best pilots in the world, but their choice of gunship was not the Apache. Instead, they opted for AH-6 Little Birds or, when heavier firepower was needed, a highly modified Black Hawk known as a 'DAP' or Direct Action Penetrator.

This must have been a conventional force or, a Spec Ops team getting a ride from a conventional force. It would be next to impossible to find out who ran this operation. It wasn't like there was some database or master operations center that coordinated all military and intelligence action. That was to say nothing of the FBI and DEA running their own little covert ops. Even the NYPD had representation around the globe.

"The Virginia National Guard is a very long way from home," Clark said. He referred to the fact the United States Military operated at such a high tempo it had to constantly pull in National Guard units to support the mission. The citizen soldiers were often asked to take on the same hazardous missions as their active-duty counterparts.

NAOMI

At the point where the riverbed was closest to the terrorist camp, the helicopters popped up over the trees. The Apaches split left and right, opening up with their cannons in seconds. A line of tracers reached from the attack aircraft. Fingers of death snuffed out several guard positions before the defenders knew they were there.

The Black Hawks raced in to join the fight. Door guns added to the stream of tracers annihilating the compound. Sporadic muzzle flashes told her the defenders were shooting back. The home team was no match for the attacking force's superior firepower and night vision capabilities. Naomi noted that the Apaches hadn't bothered trying to dominate or subdue the entire area. The concentration of fire indicated a specific target. Naomi was willing to bet the raiders had solid intel on their objective.

Moments later, her suspicions were confirmed. The Black Hawks were on the ground. Men poured out, weapons up and firing as they moved toward the closest structure. Naomi glanced at her watch when the birds touched down. Fifty-three seconds later, the men rushed back toward the helicopters escorting two people. The closest Apache fired two missiles into a bunker that foolishly decided to start shooting at it.

The edge of the video started sliding toward the raid as the drone banked away from the ground action. The view of the action below would disappear in the next few seconds.

"Pause that. Back up a couple seconds. Right there. Can you zoom in on that guy?" Naomi said right before the two Black Hawks left the frame.

Shane paused the video at the prescribed spot and zoomed in. Naomi squinted, looking closely at the screen. She could see a person but could not make out clear features. "Can you get in closer?" Shane zoomed in further. Naomi sucked in a breath. Looking up, staring into the camera, was the face of Jimmy Taylor.

He's alive, and someone got to him before me.

"What is this?" Clark asked as he pointed to the shoulder of one of the men escorting Jimmy. The man was wearing the flag of the Chinese government.

"The Chinese took Gunnery Sergeant Taylor?" Shane asked in shock.

The dark angel screamed so loud Naomi squeezed her eyes shut and clenched her jaw. Shadow wings flared open, and Artemis's eyes burned. The chains holding her now gone. The dark angel rolled her neck and stretched her arms. A single beat of wings launched her into the air.

"This proves without a doubt the video of Jimmy was real. Andrew Brock lied," Naomi said. She would kill that duplicitous hacker if it was the last thing she did.

"Not just Taylor. There's someone else," said Clark.

By the time the terrorist camp came back into view, the helicopters were gone. It had taken the Chinese team less than ten seconds to hustle Taylor and the other person onto the aircraft. Naomi, Clark, and Shane spent the next thirty minutes going frame by frame. Whoever the second man was, he never looked up toward the camera. Could it be Matt Hassan? His body had never been recovered either. Now that they knew for certain Jimmy had survived, it seemed possible that Hassan might have as well.

Naomi stood up and looked at Clark with a wolfish grin. "It's time to hunt."

25

Marissa

Everglades National Park, Florida

The property Selma had mentioned had an off-the-grid prepper vibe. The house looked to have started out as a single-wide trailer. A mix of sheds, shipping containers, water reclamation tanks, and solar panels was arranged in a chaotic manner reminiscent of a chair and blanket fort a child might build in the living room. The drive had taken ninety minutes, nearly all of them on US HWY 41 heading west.

Sarah had decided to have Derek and Selma stay and work with Mike while she, Marissa, and Isaac went to visit Brock. Marissa figured Derek's self-righteous outburst had gotten him uninvited, whereas Selma and Mike had better things to do than persuasively asking questions. Besides, too many cooks in the kitchen never produced great results.

Marissa hadn't come with Isaac when he and Selma had brought Brock out here. She'd had to take care of a few things and sleep. She hadn't gotten a solid night's rest since before she went to New York.

Stepping out of the car, Marissa was assaulted by a smell that was a cross between sulfur and rotten eggs. The odor so pungent it nearly made her puke.

Trees and sawgrass covered the wetlands surrounding the property. It looked like a perfect environment for all sorts of animals she wouldn't want as neighbors.

"Why would anyone live out here? It stinks, plus it's probably crawling with snakes."

"More than likely, and they get pretty big out here," Sarah said. Isaac shivered and touched his pistol. Sarah noticed his reaction, laughed, and gave him a bump with her hip. "Isaac here is scared of snakes." Hip bumps were familiar gestures and it struck Marissa as odd. She knew Peregrine was a close-knit team, but could there be something more to Sarah and Isaac? She immediately dismissed the thought. Isaac didn't seem the secret affair type, and Sarah wasn't a cheater.

"Snakes are evil through and through. Especially ones that can grow over twenty feet long and weigh more than 200 pounds," Isaac said. He scanned the yard perimeter as though he suspected a monster python was even now trying to sneak up on him.

"That's a BIG reason not to live here," Marissa said.

Isaac looked at her and tapped his nose twice. "Yep, let's not keep Brock waiting. He's probably lonely and could use some company." As the women followed Isaac, Marissa changed her assessment of the house. This place screamed serial killer.

Brock's kidnapping had been pretty standard in Marissa's experience. Bag over the head, zip ties on the wrists and feet, and tossed in the trunk. So, she hadn't given much thought to his imprisonment situation. Her particular skill set didn't usually include her target remaining alive, much less the logistical problem of keeping them hidden for an extended period.

Whatever she might have expected, seeing him in a crocodile transport cage wasn't on the list. It was a great idea and appeared to work better than chaining him to a radiator. The rectangular enclosure forced Brock to lay curled, not allowing him to stretch out. The head and foot of the cage were locked doors that let someone get behind an animal, no matter which way it faced.

This room was on a completely different level. The sloped concrete floor with the drain in the middle could have been dismissed. However, the embedded I-bolts with steel rings gave off a slaughterhouse, torture room vibe. She'd seen a setup similar to this in Columbia in one of the cartel prisons. Fortunately this place was much more sterile and Marissa appreciated the lack of body parts that looked like they'd been removed by cocaine-fueled psychos wielding chainsaws.

Marissa knew from SERE training that lying in a confined position for extended periods became excruciating. Plus, there were the psychological effects of not having freedom of movement. Marissa was confident that once removed, Brock would be cooperative to avoid going back into that cage.

Isaac walked up to the cage. "Good afternoon, Andrew. How are you doing?"

The angry response indicated a man who hadn't yet come to terms with his current situation. "I think I've proved that I'm not going to talk and I'm not a security risk. You've gone too far, and I'm going to make sure your contract gets canceled."

Sarah looked at Isaac. "What's he talking about? What contract?"

Isaac shrugged. But the smirk on his face said he was proud of himself. "When he answered the front door, I told him I was with an NSA counterintelligence project codenamed Loki. The contract would simulate abductions to ensure its top-level employees weren't a security risk. I told him we were in the beta phase right now, just working out logistics, and since he was a pretty big guy, I didn't want to get hurt trying to force him into the vehicle."

All of this was news to Marissa. Isaac had sent her around to the back and asked her to enter through a top window so they could clear the house at the same time. It had been odd how quiet Brock had been on the drive, but she'd assumed that Isaac had just knocked him out. As far as the part about not getting hurt, that was funny. Andrew Brock was a pretty big guy and a definite departure from the pasty, chunky programmer stereotype. Still, he was nowhere near the size of former Navy SEAL Charles Greggor, whom Isaac had taken apart in a close confine fight.

"He believed you?" Sarah said incredulously.

Isaac waved his hand at the cage. "I told Brock if he didn't believe me, he was welcome to check his email. A memo was sent out ten days ago, giving people a heads-up that this was in the works. I had Mike write a fake memo and insert it into his work email."

Marissa was impressed with Isaac's planning and ingenuity. It showed his abilities to socially engineer people and the extent of government absurdity. The fact that one of its highly placed employees would believe the farce would be mind-boggling to most people. There was a pause while Brock's brain glitched trying to process the deception. The silence shattered with a string of expletives that would have been at home in an online Call of Duty game.

"Seems like he knows it's not a training exercise," Isaac said dryly. Marissa still couldn't believe he'd talked a guy into willingly climbing into the trunk of a car zip-tied in under three minutes. Then again, it hadn't taken much to convince her to ditch her trip to Toronto to kidnap some hacker in Maryland. He knew which cards to play and which buttons to push. That was dangerous, and it made Marissa like him even more.

Brock's rage ignited. He started thrashing and kicking the cage door. Rocking back and forth in a futile attempt to free himself.

Sarah sighed like a patient mother dealing with a toddler tantrum in the candy aisle. "Get him out of there." Isaac gave a thumbs-up and walked to the cage door behind Brock's head.

Unlocking the door, Isaac reached in with incredible speed, using both hands to fishhook either side of Brock's mouth and yank him out of the cage. Still restrained, Brock could not break his fall to the concrete floor. Brock was much feistier than Marissa expected a middle-aged hacker to be. Maybe he took karate on the weekends. Whatever his experience, it hadn't trained him to fight a former Spec Ops guy while restrained, but it didn't stop him from trying.

Rolling to his side, Brock pulled his knees to his chest and rolled down onto them before raising his torso. The movement from his back to his knees was fast, and Isaac congratulated him with a knee strike to the face that broke his nose and returned him to his back again. The crack of his skull on the concrete floor also knocked him out.

Marissa looked over at Sarah, who watched the entire scene with arms crossed and a dispassionate look on her face. She shook her head before realizing that her own hands were still in the pockets of her jeans. Isaac wiped the saliva off his fingers onto Brock's shirt.

"I thought we came here to question him," Marissa said as Isaac started walking out the door.

"We did. I just need to get a few things before we wake Sleeping Beauty," Isaac called over his shoulder.

Several minutes later he returned, wheeling a waist-high tool chest. Sarah raised her eyebrow upon seeing the assortment of items on the top of the rolling cabinet, but said nothing.

Sarah looked to Marissa. "Today I'm going to be good cop, Isaac will be bad, and you're the floater."

Marissa grinned and cracked her knuckles. "Okay, so how are we going to play this?"

26

Isaac

Everglades National Park, Florida

The video of Jimmy had replayed over and over in my mind for the entire drive. He sat in that wooden chair, hands tied behind his back. He'd been tortured but was unbroken. Unbroken and alive. That was the critical detail, the essential element that made this a rescue mission, not a campaign of revenge.

On the flight back from Nigeria we had questioned Danjuma Adebayo, the information broker whose life we'd saved. We'd learned Boko Haram had captured Jimmy after the rogue drone, under the direction of Charles Greggor, had massacred the raiding force. Boko Haram then reached out to Danjuma to try and ransom Jimmy back to the US.

Danjuma said they wanted to keep it quiet because they were more likely to get paid if the exchange was done secretly. The logic made sense. If the Nigerian snitch was to be believed, Jimmy's location had been purchased with cryptocurrency by an anonymous client on the dark web.

I believed Danjuma's claim, that he never knew where Jimmy had been held. He'd completed the financial transaction and connected the two parties. For all he knew, the American government could have made the purchase. Jimmy was just another commodity to sell. I wanted to throw him out of the plane, but Jimmy's situation wasn't his fault. You didn't blame the dung beetles for rolling poop into balls; that was just their nature. The bigger question for me was why he hadn't contacted Naomi with the information? He was supposedly in bed with the CIA.

The focus of this interrogation needed to be on Brock's role. Brock was directly connected to the people who had Jimmy, and it had to be a nation-state. There were two principal reasons to buy Jimmy: to use him as a bargaining chip, or because he had something of value. So far, there had been no attempt to use him as leverage. Quite the opposite, this demonstrated a persistent and active attempt to cover up the fact he was still alive. That pointed to option two: clearly, Jimmy's captors believed he possessed valuable information.

"Wake him up," I said. Marissa had been standing behind Brock, but backed up when she saw Sarah grab the garden hose coiled in a corner of the room. Sarah sent a jet of water straight into Brock's face. He gasped, eyes opening wide as he jerked his head to get away from the stream.

He immediately entered bargaining mode. "Why are you doing this? What do you want? Do you want money? I can get you money. Whatever you want, you don't have to do this." Tossing the hose in the corner, Sarah moved to stand in front of him.

Sarah's voice was kind as she squatted down to bring herself to his eye level. "Sorry about that. We needed to wake you up and I figured water was preferable to slapping you. My colleague is going to ask you a few questions and then we'll see what we can do to get you back home, ok? Why don't you take a breath and we'll get started."

Brock nodded shakily and tried to control his breathing. He didn't appear to notice Marissa closing the gap behind him.

"Do you think you could take these handcuffs off? They're digging into my wrists," Brock said.

Sarah shrugged and pulled a key out of her pocket. "I suppose I can do that. This is a relationship of trust. Please don't make me regret doing this for you." Walking around to the back of the chair, she removed the cuffs.

It was a calculated risk. The big man had years of karate training. But Marissa stood behind him holding a gun. Moreover, Sarah had extensive

Krav Maga experience and I'd watched a few Kung Fu movies. I felt pretty good about the situation.

I picked up a meat tenderizer and began to bludgeon the ribeye steak on the cutting board in front of me. The swing of the spiked metal kitchen tool produced a thud that reverberated through the thick maple cutting board. Brock winced at the sound of each blow.

Convinced I had his undivided attention, I set the tool down and glared at him. I needed to make it clear I was not the good option in this scenario.

I felt like a Bond villain with my henchwomen standing nearby.

"Do you remember being asked to analyze a video of a captured American?"

Brock stared at me, a look of recognition passing across his face. He shook his head. "No. I've never done anything like that. I work on the penetration of mobile devices." Brock had recovered quickly, but to those trained to read micro-expressions, it was a neon sign screaming *I'm lying!*

I sighed, and Sarah stalked forward. Brock held his hands up defensively, giving her a choice of which wrist to grab. She chose his right. Torquing it clockwise and extending it away from his body, Sarah delivered a vicious throat punch. She grabbed the back of his head and pulled it into a knee strike to his face. I was sure the speed and violence were far beyond any choreographed karate kata he'd ever done.

Allow me to introduce Sarah Powers. She doesn't appreciate it when people lie to her, especially on the first question.

If Sarah was still playing good cop, I needed to reassess my role as bad cop, otherwise Brock might not survive long enough to answer any questions.

"That probably wasn't the most fun you've had this week. We're going to try this again, and while I admit my colleague might have overreacted a bit, you did lie to me on my first question. That's not a great way to build a relationship of trust."

Brock was bent over, coughing, with blood pouring from his nose. I saw Marissa smirk behind him. It would seem I'd said something amusing. "Since I already know you performed analysis on a video, we're going to move to the next question." He nodded in agreement.

"And you just got beat up by a girl," Marissa interjected as though Brock needed reminding.

This hadn't been part of the plan, but I'd improvise, adapt, and overcome.

"Why did you report the video was a fake?" I asked.

Brock offered a casual shrug. "Because it is a fake. There were markers showing it had been altered. Most people wouldn't have found them. It's an impressive forgery, but still a deep fake." He sounded sincere and I'd seen no evidence of deception.

Is it possible he's telling the truth and Mike just missed something?

I was at a crossroads. On one side, Mike believed the video was real. A Nigerian informant also believed in its validity enough to broker a deal to sell Jimmy to the highest bidder. On the other side was a well-respected NSA hacker with an impressive track record saying the footage wasn't real. Whatever he'd shown the other NSA and CIA analysts had been enough to convince them. He appeared to be telling the truth now, but he had lied to me on the first question.

The decision wasn't a hard one. Mike had never lied to me. I would believe him until proven otherwise.

A wide leather belt sat on the tool chest next to the cutting board. I picked it up and walked toward Brock. Holding the buckle, I let the rest of the belt uncoil to the floor. His eyes flashed and he gripped the arms of the chair as he stood. It seemed Brock still had a bit of fight in him after all.

With my right hand, I whipped the belt at his face. He took the diversion, grabbing at the flying leather strap while I punched him in the side of the neck with my left. His head snapped back toward the impact. Using the tension still on the belt to stabilize my movement, I rotated on my left foot and drove my right knee into his chest. The blow sent him back into the chair and almost tipped it over. Yanking back down on the belt, I freed it from his grasp.

To my surprise, he started to rise again. The cold steel of a pistol barrel against the back of his head froze him in place. Grabbing his right arm, I cinched the belt around his wrist and pulled him toward the tool chest. All the while Marissa kept the weapon pressed to his head.

I put his hand on the chopping board next to the piece of steak. Brock tensed his arm to pull it away when Marissa leaned in close to his ear and purred. "If you move your hand, I'm going to start putting holes in you." Brock wilted.

I picked up the tenderizer and held the belt taut. "Let's try that again. Why did you say the video was fake?"

Brock's tone and speed of response demonstrated his will to fight was broken. "Orders. I've been working for the Chinese for years. My handler told me to be on the lookout for a video of a captive American. The CIA approached us and asked for help digging out any clues that could lead to his recovery. I was told to discredit it. So I planted markers in the video that could indicate a deep fake."

"Why would your handler tell you to discredit the video?" Sarah asked.

"I don't know." Sarah raised an eyebrow and he stammered, "I don't know, but I suspect the Chinese have him, and they don't want anyone to know." His body language indicated he was telling the truth, or at least he believed what he said.

Now we were getting somewhere, and I had some questions. Slamming the tenderizer into the steak inches from his hand I asked, "Why? What would make you think they have him?"

Brock shied away from me. "The voice signature in the video was Nigerian. The American was reported dead after the failed raid on a Boko Haram weapons cache. Intercepted communication between a Nigerian informant and a suspected Boko Haram device. That device was traced to a stronghold in the Sambisa Forest. A stronghold that has since been raided by Chinese Special Forces."

None of what he said by itself was conclusive. Each point was circumstantial at best. However, compiled circumstantial data could be used to build a clear, actionable case.

So, he knew the Chinese government was holding an American service member. No, it's more than that. He'd actively aided a foreign power in ensuring my best friend never returned home.

"Why did you do it?" I asked, anger bleeding into my tone. I was coming close to losing all objectivity.

"They forced me. I had to," Brock whimpered.

"Not the video. Why sell out your country to the Chinese? Did they pay you? Is that the money you were offering me? Got a nice little fund tucked away in a secret bank account? Are you planning to retire to some tropical island and live the good life?"

"No, no, no. They didn't pay me. One of their agents seduced me, and they recorded it. Threatened to show my wife." Brock laughed bitterly. "We're not even married anymore. We divorced after I caught her cheating on me. But they helped me advance in the NSA. Created vulnerabilities in the devices of high-ranking party members for me to discover."

"And they used those leaks to shift and manipulate the balance of power," Sarah said.

Brock nodded.

"Who does your handler work for?" I asked. It would help to know where to start looking if we knew which organization of the Chinese government had Jimmy.

"What do you mean? I told you the Chinese government."

"Oh, come now. You're a smart guy and pretty good at digging up information. There's no way you didn't find out who held your leash."

Brock nodded, acknowledging the truth of my statement. "His name is Zhao. He works for the Ministry of State Security."

"Where is he?"

"Who?"

"The American."

"I don't know. Honestly, I don't. I would tell you if I did." The pleading tone in Brock's voice made me want to punch him in the face. My best friend was being held captive because a computer nerd couldn't honor his marriage vows.

"I believe you. Would Zhao know where he is?"

"Yes. Definitely."

He's pretty eager to get someone else in the crosshairs. Misery isn't the only thing that loves company.

"Where is Zhao?"

"I'm not sure. But I traced his calls a few times. They always led back to an IP address in Hong Kong."

Hong Kong and this Zhao guy were good threads to start pulling. I couldn't think of any further use for Brock. My literary hero, James Reese, would have left Brock tied to a tree for something hungry to find. While the Florida Everglades was one of the few places on Earth alligators and crocodiles coexisted and it would be interesting to see which one found him first, I wasn't going to do that. He deserved to die, but I'd prefer him to have years to be tormented over his treason rather than a few hours of terror before he died. Then again, if we didn't get Jimmy back, I might just put him in the ground after all.

"I think we're done here," I said, slapping Brock on the shoulder and releasing the belt.

"What happens now?" Brock asked suspiciously.

"You're going back to Maryland. I'm sure the NSA has been worried sick about you. So, we'll write you a nice note explaining everything." The hacker's face paled and he looked like he'd rather go back into the crocodile cage.

"Don't worry about anything. I have a couple of friends. Great guys. Marines I used to serve with who are going to drive you back and make sure you get there in one piece. I'd hate for you to get kidnapped again," I said, pulling out my phone to make the call.

27

Jimmy

Central Barracks - Hong Kong, China

A soft knock on Jimmy's cell door woke him. Rolling out of bed, he pulled on a shirt and slid his feet into a pair of cheap plastic flip-flops, which were his only footwear. A stack of books sat on a small table bolted to the floor next to his bed. There was never a shortage of books.

Jimmy was a voracious reader like one of his heroes, General James Mattis. Jimmy had even gone so far as to ban his men from watching movies and playing video games in favor of reading while deployed. The warrior monk's quote, "If you haven't read hundreds of books, you are functionally illiterate, and you will be incompetent, because your personal experiences alone won't be broad enough to sustain you," was one of Jimmy's mantras.

Colonel Zhao had given instructions that he could have any book he wanted, with the exception, of course, of those China considered subversive. Besides reading, Jimmy had started learning Mandarin. Things had gone as the Chinese officer had promised. Cooperation had ended the torture, and now he could read and work out. The food was also much better. He still hadn't been asked to divulge anything that couldn't be readily obtained on the internet.

The best Jimmy could figure was the Chinese had some sort of operation in Nigeria. He'd been a target of opportunity, and he attempted to come to terms with the fact he might be an unwilling guest in China for quite some time. This facility didn't strike him as a long-term accommodation, and he suspected he would be moved sometime soon. He still hoped to escape, and continued working to stack the deck in his favor. That was part of the reason for wanting to learn Mandarin. He couldn't count on people's ability to speak English, and he needed to be able to communicate if he had any hope of returning to the United States.

The knock sounded again before the door swung open. Colonel Zhao walked into the small cell holding two mugs of steaming tea. Hot drinks were a luxury Jimmy had begun receiving soon after he became cooperative.

"Good morning, my friend. How did you sleep?" Zhao asked slowly in Mandarin. The Chinese officer had been supportive of Jimmy's efforts to learn the language.

"I am well. I fell asleep reading last night," Jimmy responded slowly. China's official dialect had a lot of sounds he'd never used before as an English speaker. Many of the words sounded similar, and he wanted to be sure of his pronunciation.

"Still reading *The Silmarillion?*" Zhao asked.

Jimmy had read The Hobbit on one of his deployments and found he enjoyed Tolkien. The English author had a way with words few others had ever achieved. Now that Jimmy had a surplus of time, he'd decided to embark on the literary quest of the history of Middle Earth. He had already burned through The Lord of the Rings trilogy and the Children of Huron. He slowed down a bit for The Silmarillion. It was denser, and he wanted to take the time to process Middle Earth's origin story.

"Yes." Jimmy paused, hunting for words he could use to answer the question. "I'm very happy for it."

"You're very happy for it?" Zhao asked, switching to English to make his point. Jimmy felt embarrassed, even though he knew the feeling was absurd on an intellectual level.

"I meant to say I enjoyed it."

Zhao nodded and slowly said the correct phrase while handing him a mug.

JIMMY

Jimmy accepted the beverage with a grateful smile, and repeated the phrase several times, committing the words to memory. Zhao nodded in approval.

"Let's walk," the Colonel said, nodding at the open door.

Jimmy had been out of his cell a few times to go to a small gym that he suspected had never been intended for use by prisoners. As was their custom, Jimmy remained quiet, waiting for Zhao to start the conversation. There was always an agenda, and small talk and questions had a way of relaying information, either directly or by inference.

Information was the only currency Jimmy still possessed, and he wasn't just going to give it away for nothing. His mom used to tell him that God had given him two ears and one mouth because he needed to listen twice as much as he talked. It was a philosophy that had served him well.

The pair turned down a hallway Jimmy had never seen. They walked into an empty conference room, where he came to an abrupt halt. For the first time in, Jimmy didn't know how long, he saw and felt sunlight. It streamed through the windows, bathing the room in a warm glow. He'd forgotten how much he missed the sun. The urge to run to the window and put his hands on the glass was overpowering. For some reason, he felt like crying. Yet, he fought down both of those impulses. There was no reason to provide Zhao with more insight and leverage.

"I often enjoy watching the sunrise over Victoria Harbour." Zhao's words hung in the air like a hawk circling high overhead. He never said anything without a point. "The building we're in is Central Barracks, but it used to be known as the Prince of Wales Building. The building's design is interesting. It's shaped like an upside-down gin bottle. The narrow bottom was a defensive measure to slow down invading forces. So many things change. This building, designed to be a fortress, was handed over without a single shot fired."

Jimmy blew on his tea to cool the steaming liquid as he stared out the window overlooking the harbor, waiting for Zhao to get to the point. He was now aware the skyline, of which he'd only caught a glimpse before, was Hong Kong. Why would they bring him here? There had to be so many places more secretive and secure. Maybe that was the point of hiding him on a military base in the middle of a large metropolis. Who would think to look for him in Hong Kong? Besides, everyone thought he was dead.

It didn't take long for his contemplative captor to continue. "I have a confession to make. Despite our best attempts to deceive the United States, they have determined that you and Mr. Hassan are still alive. Our governments have finalized a prisoner transfer. You will be flying back to the US by tomorrow afternoon. Professionally, I think there is more you could tell us. Personally, as a fellow soldier, I am happy you will be going home."

The information overload took an age to process. Was it true, or some kind of a ploy? If it was a trick, Jimmy couldn't see the end game. All he could do now was operate with the information he had available. If it were true, which was a big if, it would mean someone hadn't given up on him.

What was he supposed to say? Thank you for your hospitality. I appreciate that you stopped torturing me after I started providing information. That last thought brought on a fresh wave of shame. He'd given up on his government and discussed classified information. If only he'd held out longer. He should have known better. Kept the faith that the United States of America would never abandon him.

The tears he'd fought back at seeing the sun now ran unchecked down his face. Jimmy knew he didn't deserve to be saved after his loss of faith and betrayal. It would have been better to die before providing the enemy with something they could use against the government that had never stopped searching for him.

* * *

Zhao briefly considered placing a hand on the big American's shoulder but discarded the idea. He'd done his job, and now he had a phone call to make. "I have a few things to do. You can stay here as long as you like. I have ordered everyone to leave you alone. I'm sure you have a lot to process."

Turning on his heel, he walked out of the room, leaving the crying soldier alone. Zhao closed the door to his office and took a seat behind his desk.

JIMMY

Opening a drawer, he pulled out the encrypted cell phone he only used to call Alexander. Alexander answered on the third ring, greeting him in Mandarin, which annoyed Zhao. His pronunciation was terrible, and in all the years they'd known each other, he'd never bothered to improve.

The pompous Swiss banker believed the world revolved around him, and Zhao was tired of being wrapped up in his schemes. It was time to retire. He had more than enough money to live out his days in comfort with his wife. He was getting too old for all this intrigue. After this was done, he was out.

"How did it go?" Alexander asked.

"Just as planned. Both Americans believe they are going home. We will put them on a private jet with people claiming to be from the American consulate." Zhao wasn't sure why Alexander was asking about this. He'd already given the banker the information gathered from the two Americans. There was no legitimate reason for Alexander to have continued interest. It just wasn't in his nature. But Zhao squashed the alarm sounding in the back of his mind, flattered by the personal attention from his colleague.

The Ministry of State Security had ordered him to move the prisoners. They believed there was still valuable information being withheld. On days like today, he had to fight to stay focused. It would be so easy to mentally check out and stop playing his role. Soon the world would be in chaos in both figurative and literal terms. The global balance of power disrupted forever.

The GPS system was the lynchpin that enabled the worldwide internet. The internet would be gone along with the technology that depended on it. Technology gave countries like the United States and China huge advantages. Where would the mighty United States be without the ability to use smart bombs and drones? What would China do when they could no longer track their population? What would the Communists do when they had to answer to the community? The people would rise up and take back control, and he would be on an island far away from it all.

Zhao believed the orbital bombardment was excessive. He'd tried to talk Alexander out of the action, but on that point, there was no room for discussion. Did so many people need to die to save the environment? Alexander believed it would force the world's nations to listen to him and become more environmentally conscious. All Zhao knew for sure was that it would create a big mess—one he wanted to avoid at all costs.

"You're going to take them to the farm near Laughlin Air Force Base?" Alexander asked, even though Zhao was sure he already knew the answer.

For several years, the Chinese government had been acquiring farmland on the quiet near critical US Air Force bases. The farms produced crops while also serving as points of surveillance.

By purchasing the food grown at these farms, Americans were unknowingly funding Chinese espionage operations. Zhao still couldn't believe the US Government didn't put a stop to it. China would have never allowed it. But soon, it wouldn't matter. When the GPS system came down and technology failed, the US and Chinese governments each would be just as crippled as the other. He'd been preparing for this moment for years.

Zhao took his family on an annual vacation to a house in Fiji. His wife believed they rented the home, but he had purchased it in a secret deal years ago. It wasn't the biggest thing he could have afforded, but it still cost him several million in US dollars. After sending the two Americans off, he'd submit his retirement paperwork and take his family on vacation. He had several months saved up.

"There's no better way to convince them they are home and safe than by landing them in Texas and driving them past an American military base," Zhao agreed. "The interrogators will pose everything as a debrief and continue pumping them for information. They will say a lot more once they think they're safe and among friends. The best part is, we've hired some military contractors to meet them at the airfield and pose as their Department of State. A few of them even used to work for diplomatic security."

"Nothing like a cadre of bearded white men to lull them into a false sense of security," Alexander said.

Zhao had been a member of The Eden Initiative for almost two decades. What had started out as a few idealistic boarding school classmates had grown into a cabal with access to hundreds of billions in funding and the ability to influence global agendas. All in service of reversing the damage inflicted by the power-hungry proletariat puppets of the profiteering plutocracy. In the beginning, he'd been a radical true believer. Grandchildren had changed things. He still believed in the goal of preserving the planet, but now he was just so tired.

The old spy was ready for the missiles to launch and technology to fall. China and Alexander each had their hooks in him deep, and the only way to be free was to blind China and cut the lines to Alexander during the chaos.

"Does Dr. Linter have a firing solution?"

"Yes. However, the North Koreans aren't ready."

Zhao blew out a breath in disgust. "We would have been better off building our own launch facility in China."

"We both know the risk of discovery was too high. The North Koreans might take a bit more time, but with them, success is a near certainty," Alexander said.

"Of course."

Alexander cleared his throat. "I need to ask a favor of you. I have a business partner. A Sicilian who could use a little help. A logistics problem. I'd appreciate anything you can do."

Zhao smiled to himself. *Ah, this is why Alexander has been showing extra interest. He needs a favor.*

Zhao's ability to solve logistics problems like this was one of the primary reasons he would have a port to weather the coming storm. "Of course, my old friend. I am happy to do whatever I can to help."

28

Isaac

Peregrine Office - Miami, Florida

Sarah had ordered from Naiyana Thai for the dinner planning session. I was pleased and surprised to learn they were open. I have a working theory that the best Thai restaurants have arbitrary hours of operation. This place was no exception. Their spring rolls were extraordinary, but the best ones I'd ever eaten were from a small restaurant in Alabama, of all places. I'd been visiting a friend attending Army Flight training in Fort Rucker. He took me to a spot just outside the Daleville gate. That was a life-changing experience.

"I think we can agree Zhao is the next link in the chain," I said.

Selma nodded while scooping pad see ew onto her plate. "We could take one step further and say Hong Kong is a pretty good next step. Brock was a talented hacker, and if he traced him back there a number of times, it's likely his base of operations."

"What if it was a trick and Zhao, or whatever his name is, wanted Brock to think he was in Hong Kong to throw him off the trail?" Derek asked.

Mike shook his head, grabbed a spring roll, and took a bite before setting it back down and wiping his hands with a napkin. "No, it wasn't a trick. I met Brock before. At a Black Hat convention. He's the real deal. Except about the video, he's wrong about that."

I set down the Thai tea I'd been drinking. "He was told to lie about that. He 100% knew that video was real. I didn't realize you knew him. Was he a friend?"

"I said I met him, not that I knew him. We attended a seminar together."

Most people, upon realizing they had met the subject of an ongoing investigation, would have mentioned it. Mike wasn't most people. That data point hadn't been relevant to the equation. Relationships mattered, and I made a mental note to ask Mike outright if he had any connection to future targets. It might not change a course of action, but it was good to be aware of the variables that affected the team.

I set my chopsticks down next to my pad thai. "It sounds like Hong Kong is the next logical step. It may be beneficial to set up a base of operations there so we could react more quickly. I think Zhao should be our next target."

Sarah shook her head. "We still have the Federal Reserve contract to handle. I'm sorry, while I'm committed to the hunt for Jimmy, the reality is we don't have an actionable lead. This is still a business, and we still have to pay the bills."

I had forgotten I was scheduled to go to Denver to start the reconnaissance. It was embarrassing to get so wrapped up in the hunt that I lost sight of what was around me.

"I would certainly be in favor of dumping the contract if we had anything actionable," Sarah said before I could respond.

To my surprise, it was Derek who answered her. "We know Zhao is the next link, and he's been traced back to Hong Kong."

"That's true," Sarah agreed. "But Hong Kong is a big city, and we don't have anything other than a name. Likely a last name. How many people are named Zhao in Hong Kong?"

Mike's fingers flew over the keyboard, not understanding her question was rhetorical. "Over 12k. It's the 7th most common surname in China."

Sarah nodded. "So, a lot. The contract stays. We have tracking software on Brock's phone and computer, and we can act whenever they ping back. Let Mike hunt for Zhao. When he finds him, we can act then. We worked hard to secure that job, and we're not just going to throw it away because we wish something would happen."

Derek scratched the stubble on his chin. "Isaac, you're taking lead on the Fed job. It doesn't require any of the rest of us. At least not yet. Sarah and I could go to Hong Kong to be in a position to respond more quickly."

Selma had set her chopsticks down, shaking her head. "That's an unjustifiable expenditure. I'm sorry, that trip to Nigeria was expensive and we can't afford to move without…"

Mike whooped. "Got it!" All heads snapped in his direction. We waited to see what he said next. While less than common, outbursts such as these were also not unprecedented. With any luck it meant he had just located Brock's phone and computer. On the other hand, if we were in a commercial he might have just gotten a great deal on car insurance.

He most likely found the phone, but saving money is always nice; hopefully more than 15%.

Thirty seconds passed, and the only sound was the tapping of Mike's fingers on the keyboard. Mike didn't appear to notice we were waiting on him to continue. I cleared my throat. "What do you have?"

He stared at his computer, absorbed in whatever was on the screen. I stood up and walked over to his spot. Placing my hand gently on his shoulder, I squatted next to him. What I saw on his screen made no sense to me. At least it wasn't a car insurance website. "What do you have?"

"The location of Brock's computer," he said distractedly.

"You know where it is?"

"Yes."

My heart soared. Someone audibly gasped. It might have been me; I'm not sure. We'd been watching the news and missing person reports. There had been no public mention of Andrew Brock's disappearance. My former teammates had called about 30 minutes ago to let me know that they'd be dropping Brock off at the NSA campus's main security checkpoint. We didn't have any real evidence of his espionage.

The interrogation hadn't been recorded. Brock's confession wouldn't be admissible in court and video of the incident would only serve to incriminate us. The NSA would be curious about his unscheduled vacation and it would be hard for him to point a finger at Peregrine without implicating himself in treason. The mission was to find Jimmy. Any other justice was secondary.

We were pretty sure now that whoever picked up those devices would be connected to the Chinese. At this point, I half expected the devices to be pinging from inside an embassy. Infiltrating one of those would be a new experience for me.

"Ok, so where is it?" I prompted.

He finally stopped typing and looked up. "Hong Kong. Specifically, Central Barracks."

"Central Barracks? Like an army barracks?" Selma asked.

In answer, Mike pointed at the big screen on the far wall near where I'd been sitting. Looking up, I saw Google Earth zooming in toward what I assumed was Central Barracks. The building was a strange shape. It looked like an upside-down bottle of Jack Daniels.

"The computer is in there?" Sarah asked. Mike nodded. No one bothered asking him if he was sure. When it came to computer things, Mike didn't speculate, at least not voluntarily. He hated having to guess. The computer was there.

"I also found Zhao," Mike said, pulling up a picture of a Chinese man who appeared to be in his 70s.

"How do you know that's him, and how did you get that picture?" I asked. I hadn't expected Zhao to be so old.

"When they connected to the computer, Carmen went looking for an internet connection. That created a port to access, so I turned on the camera and microphone. I'm processing the conversation through neural machine translation."

"Do you know what they're saying?" Derek asked excitedly.

"For the most part. Machine translation isn't perfect, but it's a good on-the-spot option."

The fact he could remotely connect to a machine halfway around the world still blew my mind. The writing had been on the wall for years. The cyber arena was now where battles were won and lost.

"Ok, I get that, but how do you know that is a picture of Zhao?"

"Someone in the room said to go get Colonel Zhao. When he came into the room, he made the mistake of bringing his phone in. Like most people, he left the Bluetooth on, which I used to connect with his device. I don't understand why people do that. It's like walking around with an open invitation to steal your personal data. So then, when he left, he must have gone back to his office, and the phone helped me ID his work computer."

"Wait, what? You used Brock's computer to connect a phone and then jump to a computer on the network?" Selma asked. I always found Mike's computer wizardry amazing. Based on Selma's incredulous response, I didn't have sufficient technical knowledge to appreciate the feat he'd just accomplished.

"Yep."

"Are you sure it's the same Zhao who handled Brock?" I asked.

"No, but I can check. Give me a few minutes."

The rest of the room returned to eating as Mike opened windows and typed in commands. Watching him I felt the sensation of deja vu. It was just like the first time I'd ever watched an instructor pilot run through a startup checklist. The flurry of motion was mesmerizing.

"It's him. I ran him through facial recognition and confirmed he was stationed at the Chinese Embassy in Washington DC during the time Brock claimed to have been compromised. I have also confirmed the phone I connected with is the same one that's been sending encrypted messages to Brock's phone."

"Mike, I want to be you when I grow up," I said. He smiled, seeming pleased with the admiration.

"Does that mean you can track his phone?" Sarah asked.

"Yes."

Sarah stood up and looked at Selma. "I want to be in the air headed to Hong Kong in the next 90 minutes. Call Anthony at Global Biz Jets. He owes me a favor."

Selma's face paled. I could only imagine her mind racing through everything that needed to happen. She stood up and hurried out of the conference room toward her office. Her logistical magic was no less impressive than what Mike did on computers.

"Mike, pack the equipment you need. You're coming with us. Derek, pack the weapons and meet us at the general aviation terminal. We don't want to show up to a gunfight with crossbows again." That assault had gone well, but I agreed with Sarah. There was no reason to tempt fate a second time.

"Marissa?" The two former colleagues looked at each other, silently communicating. Marissa nodded her assent. "Give Derek a hand."

Derek scowled, clearly not thrilled to be working with the unemployed assassin. But he gave a thumbs-up and walked out of the room, headed to the offsite armory. Marissa stood and followed, not looking ecstatic about the assignment either. The door closed behind her, leaving Sarah and me alone.

Sarah smiled and flipped her ponytail off her shoulder. "Seems we have actionable intelligence."

"Seems so. I'll push the Fed contract back a few weeks."

"It's funny, the last time we worked together overseas, we had different employers."

"Hopefully, this doesn't take as long as Dubai," I said. That operation had been tedious and taken several weeks. Jimmy had been part of that mission. Most of it anyway. The assignment ended when the target died from a bad piece of fugu. I never understood the appeal of eating something with a real chance of killing you.

"That's true, but it was fun," she said with a whimsical smile.

"You might even have a chance to moonlight as a sushi chef," I said with a wink. I had no proof that Sarah had killed our mark, but leopards can't change their spots.

Sarah offered me a predatory grin. "Make sure you bring your game face, Honey Badger. I suspect we're going to need it."

29

Marissa

Gulfstream G-650 - Russian Airspace

Marissa had never stopped to consider how much it had cost Peregrine to rent the ultra-long-range business jet. But she did take a minute to appreciate that the last time she, Isaac, and Derek had been on the same flight, it had been the exact same model aircraft, and she'd nearly killed the two men.

Derek sat on one of the white leather couches reading a book called *Anathem*. Marissa wasn't sure what Sarah saw in him. Besides the fact that he was one of the best-looking men she'd ever seen in her life. Nice to look at, sure, but still a jerk. She'd tried hard to be friendly while picking up the weapons, but he'd just given her the cold shoulder. Every time she tried to make conversation, his replies were snarky. Marissa wanted to believe that Sarah was with him for some reason other than enjoying a sweet piece of eye candy, but so far she had no other insight.

Selma sat next to Derek, typing away on her laptop. Isaac and Sarah were huddled on the other couch, deep in conversation. Isaac looked up at her and smiled before resuming his discussion with Sarah. She felt her heart flutter and had to fight the inclination to wave.

Mike was camped out at the table near the back of the plane. He alternated between typing furiously and staring at the screen while playing with his

Rubik's cube.

It was an almost cozy scene. All of them in their places, a team preparing for a mission. Everyone doing their job, counting on the others to do theirs as well. Like a family, they relied on each other. And despite the disagreements she'd witnessed, they all seemed to genuinely like one another. She didn't know why she was here. She'd fulfilled the favor to Isaac when she'd found Andrew Brock. They were already in her debt. This was not her fight. So why had she stayed?

Isaac stood up. "Hey, come on over here. We'll review a few things before we dim the lights and rack out for a bit." Marissa stood up to join Sarah on the couch as Isaac went to grab Mike. It wouldn't do to start the meeting without the only person capable of finding Zhao.

"Isaac and I have been discussing this, and I believe we have a pretty good plan. This operation will start as soon as we can get off the plane. Sorry, Selma, that means you have a few more things to do, and you're on luggage duty."

Selma shrugged. "I'd rather be doing that than trying to kidnap a Chinese spymaster."

"Fair enough. As soon as Mike can locate Zhao's phone, we'll set up a surveillance box around him. We don't have enough people to keep eyes on him the whole time without burning ourselves. So, we're going to visually confirm that it is, in fact, Zhao carrying the phone," Sarah explained before motioning for Isaac to pick up the narrative.

Isaac leaned forward, scanning the group and making eye contact with each person. "This means we're going to be operating as singletons. This will be a bit more natural for the girls than the boys, but Derek and I have had enough experience to make this work. The biggest thing to remember is that we do have time, but we do not have government backing or sanction. There is no submarine in the harbor or helicopter waiting on a pad somewhere to whisk us away. This is 100% a kidnapping, and we are looking at life in a Chinese prison if we get caught. So, this needs to be very clean and very, very quiet."

Marissa never gave much thought to the legal consequences of her actions.

The possibility of jail time had never given her pause. She'd always assumed that one day things would go wrong. Either she'd die or get arrested. She wasn't destined to have a future in which she sat on her lanai sipping tea and watching the sunset over the rolling ocean surf. People like her didn't get happy endings.

Isaac turned to look at Mike, leaning back, playing with his Rubik's cube. The squares turned slowly, almost seeming lethargic. "You told me you had some tech to help us on this operation, didn't you?"

Mike's eyes lit up as he jumped from his chair and hurried to the back table. A short while later, the hacker was back and handing out strange-looking eyeglasses. Isaac was the first to put them on. "What do you think?" He asked no one in particular.

Marissa covered her mouth. "They're just so…"

"Flattering?" Isaac asked with a waggle of his eyebrows.

"Ugly," Derek said.

"Awful," Sarah agreed.

"Not the best version of you," Marissa concluded.

Isaac laughed and shrugged. "When I was in boot camp, the glasses the Marines gave to the guys who needed them looked a lot like these."

"The ol' BCs," Derek chuckled.

"BCs?" Asked Sarah.

"Birth control. There was no way anyone was getting lucky in a pair of those," Derek said, roaring with laughter.

Sarah smiled and shook her head. Selma just rolled her eyes. Marissa felt a stab of loneliness combined with a flair of jealousy. She felt like a homeless child in a snowstorm, peering through a window at a happy family on Christmas Eve.

"Why did you pick out such ugly glasses?" Derek asked, trying to catch his breath.

Nonplussed, Mike said, "They were the frames that could hold the tech I needed."

"Ok Mike, tell us what these things do," Isaac said.

"Each unit has two built-in cameras that will give me a real-time feed of what you're looking at."

"So, no more having to try and describe some electronic thingamabob," Derek said.

Mike ignored the comment and continued, "The cameras also enable object recognition."

Isaac gave a low whistle. "Facial recognition? The glasses will help you identify Zhao, and then you can tell us?"

Mike grinned. "The identification isn't limited to faces. I can train the computer to look for almost anything. Weapons, security cameras, a specific model of car. It doesn't matter. However, the more things it's looking for, the slower it will run. Right now, it's just loaded for Zhao. The really cool thing, though, is the lenses. Put them on."

Marissa put her glasses on along with everyone else. She was surprised to find the lenses acted as a heads-up display. There were three dots with a number in the center of each. The frames were still hideous, but she had to admit this was cool.

"Mike, what do those numbers mean?" Marissa asked.

"The dot is the real-time location of each member of the team. The number is the distance to that teammate. I can configure it to be in whatever unit of measure you are most comfortable using."

"I'd like my unit of measure to be Parsecs," Derek declared.

Isaac grunted. "And I'd like Mike to only communicate with you in Klingon."

Mike shook his head. "I could do that, but no. Actually, if you can tell me what a Parsec is, I'll consider it."

"I was just kidding," Derek said

Leaning over to Mike, Isaac spoke in a conspiratorial voice, a mischievous light in his eyes. "If I can tell you what a Parsec is, will you just talk to him in Klingon?"

"I'm not familiar with a Parsec. I know it's something they say in space movies and shows. Is it a real thing?" Selma asked.

Marissa was glad someone else had asked the question. She wasn't sure what they were either or how the topic was relevant. Maybe it was just part of Peregrine's process.

Mike looked like a kid coming down the stairs on Christmas Day to find Santa had not only come, but he'd needed a tractor-trailer to haul everything. "A parsec is the unit used to measure distances in space. It's equal to the distance of the radius Earth's orbit subtends an angle of one second of arc."

Derek looked like a puppy who'd just pounced on its own shadow but found nothing there. "What? Is that an actual answer? I have no clue what you just said. I've never even heard of the word subtend."

Isaac leaned forward and patted Derek on the cheek. "You're so cute when you're confused. It's a geometry term."

Derek looked like he had something to say, but before he could, Selma spoke up. Her look thoughtful. Marissa had no way of knowing the former chess protégé was, in fact, running the math in her head. "That means a parsec is larger than a light year."

"Correct. It's approximately 3.26158 times larger," Mike said. Selma nodded as though the answer made perfect sense.

"And now I'm ready for trivia night," Isaac deadpanned.

Sarah cleared her throat, a bemused expression on her face. "Let's get back to the mission. Mike, what I'm understanding is that these glasses will help us find Zhao and keep track of the other team members in real time. Is that correct?"

"Yes, but not just the team members. I can also put a beacon for the location of Zhao's phone. If you need directions, I can send arrows similar to Google Maps Live View."

This all sounded like science fiction, but Marissa wasn't about to turn down a tool that would provide unprecedented situational awareness. They'd memorized Zhao's face, and Marissa was confident she could pick him out of a crowd. Still, it was nice to have facial recognition backing her up.

"Do you have a name for these?" Sarah asked, holding up the glasses.

"I've been calling them 'The Eye of Sauron' because they see everything," Mike said.

"Except those two pesky hobbits," Isaac said. Marissa wasn't sure how she felt about being an extension of the Dark Lord. She'd made some less-than-ethical decisions in the past, but being the embodiment of evil was a bit much, even for her.

"We'll keep working on a name. In the meantime, everyone should grab some food and sleep," Sarah said. Marissa stood up and walked to the galley, not needing to be told twice.

* * *

Sham Shui Po District - Hong Kong, China

Marissa adjusted her glasses and stifled a yawn. She was thankful for the sleep she'd managed to get on the 19-hour flight. The customs check on board the aircraft had been cursory. The official in question had seemed disinterested in doing anything other than checking passports and collecting paperwork from Selma. Marissa had seen this often enough to recognize someone on the take.

She didn't know how late Selma had worked, but thus far, everything had gone smoothly. Marissa had learned a long time ago how critical logisticians were to an operation. The ability to forecast a situation's second and third-order effects gave the operators in the field a lot more flexibility.

There was no forecast for gunplay, but everyone on the team was prepared for the possibility of the situation turning dynamic. Each member carried a concealed Glock 19, two spare 15-round magazines, and a folding knife. The weapons were unsuppressed and their use would draw an immediate police response. Even though it was a card nobody wanted to play, it was nice to know that it was available.

I wonder if the CIA would bail me out if I got into trouble here? Not likely.

As they made their final descent, Mike announced that Zhao's phone was on the move. The phone had remained in the same place for nine hours, leading Mike to conclude that the location was Zhao's home. The team had walked off the plane, heading toward the target area, leaving Selma to take care of all the baggage. Walking from the tarmac through the Hong Kong

Business Aviation Center to their waiting vehicle took all of three minutes and garnered no more attention than a friendly wave from the receptionist.

Selma procured a panel van for transportation, a ubiquitous sight in Hong Kong. Derek's experience with driving larger vehicles while in the Marines earned him the position as driver.

"One is in position," Sarah said, her voice coming through a wireless earpiece in Marissa's ear. The tech made it sound like they were standing right next to each other. The team had decided to go with simple call signs. As the leader Sarah was One, Isaac Two, Marissa Three, and Derek batted cleanup. Sarah was currently strolling down the street just south of the target building. Google Maps Street View showed it to be an open-air market, providing a great cover to loiter for an extended period.

Marissa walked down the sidewalk toward her assigned location, trying to channel her inner tourist and not look like a commando with her head on a swivel. In her experience, most former Spec Ops guys were great at maintaining situational awareness, but they weren't covert. They looked like a SEAL team moving through a market, scanning for threats. This was the first time she'd conducted an operation as a member of a team since her Project Olympus days. It was an odd sensation, like the gritty mouthfeel after eating spinach.

"Two is in position. I think I'm going to try some of this roast duck," Isaac said. His position was on the eastern end of the road Marissa was approaching. The street was on the northern side of the building and the most likely point of entry.

She wondered to herself what it would be like to be walking down the street holding hands with Isaac like a wide-eyed tourist taking in Hong Kong. She imagined Isaac's hand was strong, firm, and slightly rough, fitting nicely with hers.

"All in the name of maintaining your cover, I'm sure," Derek said from the van, interrupting her daydream. He'd found a nearby lot where he could park. Now that he was in a position to support anyone who needed the help, he apparently felt the role of peanut gallery needed to be filled.

"Three is in position," Marissa called over the team net. She'd just arrived on the western end of Nam Tau Street.

Nam Tau Street wouldn't be featured on a travel brochure anytime soon. It lacked all the modern, shiny gleam of the vaunted financial center most people envisioned when thinking of Hong Kong. The road more an alley and textbook perfect for an ambush. The buildings on either side rose high enough that she had to look straight up to view the tops. Shops with graffiti-covered rollup metal doors lined either side of the street. Plastic vegetable crates were stacked high next to mountains of Styrofoam boxes, cluttering the walkway.

Then there was the smell. The stench of rotten produce mixed with frying meat and oil that had been reused too many times clawed at her nostrils. If Marissa had to guess, she'd say this was one of the places where the many restaurants around the city purchased their supplies. No tourists were coming to see the great street market of Nam Tau. The entire situation made her skin crawl.

"This looks like a bunch of warehouses. Two and Three aren't going to be able to loiter very long without raising our heat state too high." Isaac commented on the team channel.

Mike came onto the net. He'd been assigned the callsign Watchtower, but as of yet, he'd failed to use proper communication procedures. He just started talking, and whoever he was addressing needed to figure it out quickly.

"They are warehouses. The building where the phone is located is a small import-export company."

"All we need to do is positively identify Zhao. Confirm he has the phone. Mike will do the rest," Sarah said, keeping everyone focused on the mission objectives.

"So, this is interesting. The warehouse Zhao is in is owned by a shell company," Mike said.

Marissa didn't find that interesting or surprising. An import-export business was a common cover that countries, corporations, and criminals used for concealing shady dealings. She could hear the faint clicking of the Rubik's cube every time he broadcasted.

I wonder how many of those things he goes through. All that use has to wear them out.

"Pretty common for that type of business, isn't it?" Isaac asked.

"Yes, but the holding company is owned by another holding company, which is known to have ties with Cosa Nostra."

Marissa rescinded her previous opinion. That *was* interesting.

Growing up in The Bronx, she knew all about the Italian Mafia. They were thugs with delusions of honor. She'd heard plenty of stories about how they protected the neighborhood's families and ensured children were safe. But Marissa didn't believe drug trafficking, prostitution, and loan sharking were honorable professions. Killing people wasn't an honorable career either, but she'd never claimed to be particularly virtuous.

Walking around a stack of vegetable crates, Marissa froze before turning and pretending to examine the produce on the table beside her. "This is Three. We have a problem."

"Three. One. What's the issue," Sarah asked.

"I just saw another hitter, a guy I had the misfortune of working with at Banque Suisse in the past."

"The guy who just came out of the alley?"

Mike's situational perception and speed amazed Marissa. She was starting to understand why he was such a critical member of the team.

"Yes," Marissa confirmed.

"Just ran him through facial recognition. He's a bad dude. Works for Cosa Nostra and is known as The Sicilian. He's suspected of many horrific murders. There's never enough to charge him, witnesses dying or changing their stories, evidence tampering, the works."

"It's a mob warehouse. Makes sense there would be a mob guy around," Derek offered.

"This guy is a butcher. When he shows up, people die," Marissa shot back.

"Sounds like the pot calling the kettle black," Derek grumbled. Marissa had no response. He wasn't wrong.

"Three. Two. He's just entered the warehouse. I'll back your play." Isaac said. Marissa looked in his direction. Although she couldn't see him, her

HUD showed Isaac's dot closing with her.

"Copy Two. Three is on the move." Marissa started toward the entrance, thankful for the pressure of the concealed pistol at the small of her back. She'd wanted to be part of the pack and there was no better way to build bonds than in the forge of combat.

30

Isaac

Sham Shui Po District - Hong Kong, China

I waited for Marissa to join me. Her voice had held uncharacteristic concern. There were a dozen reasons a Chinese spymaster might be meeting a mafia hitter, but I felt uneasy. I was probably being paranoid, but the situation and timing just felt off. As luck would have it, the metal door had been unlocked, and no lock picking was required.

I wonder how the mob would respond to a proposal for Peregrine to evaluate their security posture. So far, they aren't doing so well.

Marissa's ability to flow through a crowd was incredible. If I hadn't been working with her or known who she was, I doubt I would have ever noticed her.

As she reached me, I transmitted over the net. "Two and Three are making entry. Four standby to provide extraction." Sarah was the team lead, but I had tactical control as the member about to make contact.

I looked at Marissa and raised my eyebrows. She nodded once, and we slipped through the doorway, pulling the metal door shut and locking it to ensure no unexpected guests came in behind us. The floor was covered in a tile mosaic that looked like it had been beautiful when it was new. Now it was dirty and chipped, with cracks running along most of the tiles.

I unholstered my pistol. Marissa already covering the hallway. I hadn't even seen her draw. We were committed, and it was stupid to pretend we were tourists. We were in a place we didn't belong and shouldn't be able to access. It was a ruse no one would believe and it would cost valuable seconds that could mean the difference between life and death.

According to our tech, Zhao's phone was 30 feet ahead and to the left. This hallway had a single door to the right and two on the left.

I pointed at my chest and then at the nearest door, telling Marissa I would be making entry through that door. I then indicated she should go to the second. With a terse nod, she moved to her assigned entry point. Holding up a hand with three fingers, I spoke in a low voice for the benefit of the rest of the team. "Breaching in three." Silently I ticked my fingers down to zero. As the count hit zero, it occurred to me Mike could see everything we were looking at.

I hope I don't get killed wearing these things. That would suck for Mike...and for me.

The door opened on a low-lit room filled with dozens of shipping containers. The container to my immediate right blocked any view of the doorway Marissa had come through. Flowing into the room, I scanned for threats, seeing nothing. The left wall was lined with locked containers, but a light source came from around the corner to the right.

I was creeping along the last container when Mike's voice boomed in my earpiece. "That's a positive ID on Zhao." Reflexively my hand tightened on the pistol grip of the Glock. I gritted my teeth in frustration.

He's gotta stop yelling in my ear while I'm trying to infiltrate evil lairs.

I scanned the room. Mike had told me there was a good chance the glasses would find Zhao in a crowd before I did, but there was no one here. Then I remembered the other team member who'd entered the warehouse with me. Marissa must have a line of sight on him.

"Two. This is Four. I'm parked out front of your location."

"Four. This is One. I'm approaching your position from the west. Be there in 30 seconds."

Derek was in place, and Sarah was moving towards a reactionary position. Now, we just needed to find Zhao and extract him.

I heard a shout. The echoes bouncing around the warehouse made it hard to pinpoint where it came from. It sounded like Marissa had made her entrance. Another yell, this one sounding decidedly panicked. Moving to the corner of the container, I peered around the edge, spotting the source of the noise.

The large man could have been a body double for Santa Claus, save the bald spot and greasy rat tail. Saint Nick's evil doppelgänger carried a wicked-looking machete and was advancing toward an elderly Chinese man. My HUD projected a green box over the Chinese man's face for a split second, confirming his identity as Zhao.

That's distracting.

I didn't see Marissa, forgetting in the moment I could have used the glasses to locate her. I hadn't seen the mafia hitman before he entered the warehouse. This must be the Sicilian. The sight of the fat, ugly man in a dirty tracksuit was a real disappointment. I had expected a guy who looked like Derek, dressed in a pinstripe suit with an interesting signature weapon. Something like a poison-tipped umbrella, a blow dart gun, or a cane sword would be memorable. The reality was a slob who made restaurants rethink their all-you-can-eat policy. Not that his apparent lack of professionalism mattered much to Zhao.

The machete arced down in a vicious swing that looked to be aimed at opening Zhao's stomach. The old spy tripped and fell flat on his back.

That's not a great place to be with a machete-wielding psychopath.

I felt like I was trying to run in the shallow end of the pool with concrete shoes. I moved out from behind the shipping container, sights lined up on the big man. Every fiber of my being wanted to open fire, but my target was out of range. I had no chance for anything resembling an accurate shot. The probability of a stray round hitting Zhao was high. I started moving forward, speaking in a low voice on the team net. "Three, I'm out of range. If you have a shot, take it."

"Two. This is One. I'm inside the building and moving to your position." I answered Sarah with a double click.

If Marissa heard me, there was no reply. The mob hitman had planted a foot on Zhao's chest and grabbed his right arm, machete raised. He was going to hack the arm off. Marissa had been right; the man was a butcher. I thought about yelling but dismissed the idea. I didn't want to throw off the swing and have him hit the jugular. You can live without an arm. Missing a throat was a bit more challenging. I'd be able to take mobster out, but it would cost the elderly Chinese spymaster at least a pound of flesh.

I heard soft footfalls behind me. A brief glance over my shoulder revealed Sarah approaching at pace.

Movement caught my attention, and I looked up in time to see a dark shadow in flight. For a split second, I could have sworn I saw a winged Valkyrie hurtling toward the ground. Marissa slammed into The Sicilian, both feet hitting him in the shoulder blades. The force of the impact drove him to the ground. A meaty thud followed by snapping sounds that could have only been bones breaking. Somehow Marissa had managed to maintain her balance and remain on the behemoth's back. The Sicilian's scream lasted mere seconds before she yanked his head back and slit his throat.

Sarah and I opened into an all-out sprint. The need for accurate shooting now gone.

Zhao vomited into the expanding crimson pool before trying to wipe away the arterial spray covering his face. Marissa released the Sicilian's head and cleaned her knife on the back of his shirt before standing. Grabbing Zhao by the collar of his shirt, she dragged him away from the mess. "Jackpot. Three has Jackpot."

Turning to Marissa, I offered her a fist bump in congratulations, which she accepted. "Nice job."

"Thanks."

Zhao lay on the floor looking bewildered. His reaction was typical of someone who'd just experienced a traumatic event. However, we didn't have time to help him process.

"Get him up," Sarah ordered.

Grabbing the front of his shirt, I hauled him to his feet. He looked at me, confused. "Who are you?"

Sarah stepped forward and slapped him hard across the face. The sudden burst of pain appeared to have its intended effect. Zhao snapped to Sarah, now focused on her. Sarah spoke softly, violence just below the surface. "We need to talk, Mr. Zhao."

31

Jimmy

Central Barracks - Hong Kong, China

Jimmy didn't know how long he'd stared out the window at Victoria Harbour. So many people out there, regular everyday folks going about their day with no idea of the horrors taking place in their midst. Maybe they did know and didn't care. Or maybe they were just thankful it wasn't them. He couldn't even begin to count the number of people who'd justified the gruesome methods the United States used on its prisoners.

It wasn't hard to fall into an Us vs. Them mindset. There was no justification for the acts of violence and terror, but often there was more to the story. Jimmy had found most people, even those with whom he disagreed, had well-thought-out reasons and justifications for their beliefs and actions. But it was easier to beat a war drum and get people behind a cause if the other side were savage barbarians or godless infidels.

Zhao had been true to his word, and no one had come in to bother Jimmy. When he'd finally returned to his cell, he'd tried to resume reading to pass the time, but without success. Sighing in frustration, he put his book down and started doing wall push-ups and sit-ups to tire himself out enough to sleep. There were no pull-up bars around, so doing handstand push-ups against the wall had to suffice.

A sudden thought brought on a bout of nearly hysterical laughter. He'd been due to take a physical fitness test after returning from the deployment to Nigeria. Obviously it had fallen off his radar of important things to worry about, being that he was dealing with captivity, torture, and whatnot. But now he was going home. The Marine Corps had a regulation for everything, and someone taking a PFT after being held captive was no exception. There would probably be some junior LT waiting to smugly inform him that according to MCO 3141.59, a Marine had 5 hours to recover from being held captive before taking a required PFT. One hour for every Navy Cross General Chesty Puller was awarded. He wasn't going to worry about it. Based on the number of wall pushups he'd just completed, he'd be fine.

The stress of the past months combined with the news that it was almost over coalesced to leave him doubled over with laughter on the floor. It was a game he and Isaac had played many times to amuse themselves: dreaming up bureaucratic idiocies so insane they just might be real. While the PFT extension idea was amusing, it wasn't the craziest thing they'd come up with to date. If they wanted to get technical, being taken captive wasn't included in Jimmy's orders, so his absence had been unauthorized. Unauthorized absences longer than 30 consecutive days were considered desertion per DoDI 1325.02. Since it was a time of war, the United States Marine Corps were well within their rights to pursue the death penalty. So, he was sure they'd tell him to be happy the staff duty NCO didn't take him out back and put a bullet in his brain pan.

Being held captive put a lot of things into perspective. Now he could truthfully say death by PowerPoint was as painful as electrocution and lasted longer. Jimmy snorted as the waves of laughter slowed and finally stopped. He wiped the tears that were streaming down his face. Man, he missed Isaac. But Jimmy was glad his friend worked with Mike and was there to be a second big brother for him. He'd have to go see them after he took his PFT and wrote a 10k-word essay about the importance of following orders and not being taken captive.

Jimmy didn't know what time it was when they shut the lights off in his cell. He didn't care. He didn't have a prayer of getting to sleep that night. How was someone supposed to sleep when in the past 24 hours, he'd gone

JIMMY

from just trying to stay alive and planning for an escape to finding out he was going home? He spent the whole night lying on the bed, staring at the ceiling, thinking about what it would feel like to see Mike. In the dark, the laughter was gone and tears of relief and the longing which he hadn't allowed himself to feel up to now rolled down his face. He couldn't wait to hug his little brother for far longer than Mike would appreciate.

The lights flipping on, followed by a sharp knock on the door, snapped Jimmy's eyes open. He'd fallen asleep somehow. For a brief panicked moment, he feared everything had just been a dream and he felt hopelessness pushing him past the breaking point. One of the guards beckoned him forward. The soldiers placed manacles on his hands and feet. He was surprised, but made no complaint when they didn't put a hood on him.

The elevator ride felt like an eternity, but when they exited the Central Barracks and stepped outside, the morning sunshine and breeze hit Jimmy like a drug. Stopping to take a couple of deep breaths earned him a nudge in the back with a baton. Four green SUVs idled next to the 10-foot rock perimeter wall. As he climbed into the second Land Rover lookalike, he caught sight of Matt Hassan being loaded into the third vehicle.

Jimmy almost didn't recognize the man. Matt had been starved, his ratty beard and hollow eyes stabbed at Jimmy. The CIA operator had clearly held out and kept the faith. Jimmy had accepted quarter and favor from the enemy and was a traitor. Looking away from Matt, he closed his eyes and tried to push down the rush of shame that threatened to overwhelm him. He hadn't betrayed America. Jimmy had only done what he needed to do to escape and return to his country. Matt was in no shape to be on the run.

The conflict tore at him. Part of Jimmy was jealous and admired Matt for having clearly resisted longer. The other side hated him. Who was he to think he could outlast a regime that had spent over 1,000 years perfecting human torture? Not putting himself in a position to return to his country was tantamount to giving up. Matt might as well have just hung himself and got it over with faster.

Jimmy had expected Colonel Zhao to travel with them. "Where is Colonel Zhao?" He asked the soldier sitting next to him as the compound gate opened and the SUVs pulled into the morning Hong Kong traffic. The soldier looked at him, perhaps considering the question or deciding whether or not to give him one last beating.

"The Colonel is in a meeting but will be at the airport to hand you over to the Americans."

The convoy crossed bridges and wove through highways flanked by the ocean and high-rise buildings of downtown Hong Kong. The sights and sounds of the city bordered on sensory overload. Jimmy was thankful when they crossed the Tsing Ma Bridge and transitioned to a tree-lined expressway. He shook his head in disbelief as they passed the Hong Kong Disney Land Resort entrance. The peace of the trees was broken by the urban and industrial buildup around the airport.

Jimmy saw the small blue Business Aviation sign as the convoy turned right into the entrance of the general aviation terminal. No one had provided details of his trip home. Unsurprisingly, the Chinese government wasn't just sticking him on a commercial flight. This exchange would be hushed and low-key. To be honest, he was surprised it wasn't taking place in the dead of night at some out-of-the-way airfield.

Jimmy didn't care how they did it. He just wanted to get home.

He assumed the Department of State would handle matters since his repatriation hadn't involved black helicopters and Delta Force. The convoy rolled past the concrete building that read Hong Kong Business Aviation Center and pulled out onto the tarmac.

The Boeing 737 parked in front of the terminal was average in size for a commercial airline, but giant for the business world. The flat gray plane towered over the neighboring Gulfstreams and Bombardiers, its engines idling and rolling staircase in place to receive passengers. Several bearded men attired in 511 tactical pants stood around the aircraft. Their suppressed long guns hung on one-point slings over plate carriers. That had to be diplomatic security. Their posture suggested they didn't expect to be here long.

The SUV doors opened, and Chinese soldiers fanned out as though protecting a VIP, their heads swiveling left and right. Their weapons were pointed muzzle down, but the rifle butt stocks were now at the shoulder. Jimmy felt a tingle at the base of his neck. These men were on high alert, and he didn't know why. This was supposed to be nothing more than a prisoner transfer.

A Chinese soldier opened the door for Jimmy to exit the SUV. Looking behind him, he saw Matt also being helped out. Their eyes met, and Matt stared at him as though seeing a ghost. Jimmy raised his chained hands in a wave, not knowing what else to do.

Matt shook off the assistance of the two soldiers escorting him as he hobbled toward Jimmy, his eyes boring into him like a pneumatic drill. His gaze was so intense Jimmy began to feel awkward, like a prize bull at a Texas auction. Jimmy accepted Matt's proffered hand before embracing the smaller man. Now was a time for hugs, not handshakes.

"It's good to see you, brother," Jimmy said, feeling his emotions swell.

Matt's voice was raspy and cracking as he spoke. "They told me you were dead. Said you hung yourself. The video. The video… was so real. How could I not believe it?" The CIA operator was crying. In all the time they'd been held by Boko Haram, Jimmy had never seen him cry. Hadn't been sure he was capable.

"I'm not dead. It's all over, and we're going home," Jimmy said. He had enough experience dealing with subordinates and post-traumatic stress to know the things they'd endured over the last few months would likely live in their dreams for the rest of their lives. Motion drew the men's attention to the plane. A middle-aged man in a navy blue pinstripe suit had appeared in the doorway of the 737 and walked purposefully down the steps flanked by two more armed men.

Stopping in front of Matt and Jimmy, he clasped each of their hands in turn. "Gunnery Sergeant Taylor, Mr. Hassan. My name is Tony Fleckman. I'm with the Department of State. I'll be escorting you gentlemen back to the United States of America." His voice compassionate and reassuring. Jimmy just nodded, unable to speak. He was going home.

Turning to one of the Chinese soldiers, Mr. Fleckman pointed at the shackles. The tone of compassion was replaced with authority. "Take those off." A soldier rushed to comply. Turning to one of his security men, Fleckman gestured toward the plane and said, "Get these heroes onto the plane. They don't need to be out here on the tarmac." Jimmy gave Matt his arm to steady him as they followed the long strides of the diplomatic security man into the aircraft.

"Grab a seat. Can I get you some water or juice? We'll have coffee, food, and perhaps something stronger available once we take off," their escort said with a wink. Jimmy smiled and leaned back into the plush seat. He might be ok if he never moved from this spot. This was possibly the most comfortable he'd ever been in his entire life. Everything was going to be ok. He was safe and going home.

Ten minutes later, Fleckman and the security team boarded, and the cabin door was closed. Fleckman took a seat near Jimmy and Matt. All but two of the security detail were seated in the middle of the aircraft, far enough away to give the men up front a token measure of privacy. The remaining two men sat in the flight attendant seats, weapons ready to engage any unwelcome guests that might want to crash the party.

"Gentlemen, we're honored to be able to bring you back home. I'm going to try to leave you alone for the flight. The suits and paper pushers are chomping at the bit to debrief you, and we all know it will be a long few days. I'll have a few admin questions after we get in the air, and then I hope you can relax."

The plane began moving, and Jimmy glanced out the window to see they were taxiing toward the runway. Across the runway, he could see a line of planes waiting in line to take off. Air Traffic Control had been instructed to expedite departure. The gray business plane was number 2 for takeoff behind an Air China 787 that had just taken position on the active runway. Moments after a Thai Airways jet touched down, they pulled into takeoff position.

The roar of the engines coming to full power was the sweetest sound Jimmy had heard in a long time. It was the sound of freedom. The aircraft rocketed down the runway before lifting skyward. He actually pinched himself to make sure he wasn't dreaming before letting out a pent-up breath

JIMMY

he hadn't realized he was holding.

It *was* over, and he *was* going home. He knew there would be an extensive debrief, but he didn't care. He'd answer whatever questions they had. Jimmy closed his eyes, truly relaxing for the first time since before he'd shipped out for Nigeria.

32

Isaac

Sham Shui Po District - Hong Kong, China

"I'm not sure how things work here in China, but in the US, when a woman says, 'We need to talk,' that usually means trouble for whatever guy she's talking to," I said, looking at Zhao. With most women, that expression was hyperbolic: they might be upset with you, but they weren't going to kill you. That was not a safe assumption to make with the two women here.

I watched Zhao glance at Marissa and shiver. She was death incarnate, with her work on full display on the floor before him. I found it hard to imagine that anyone would fail to take her seriously.

The aging spy nodded, seeming to deflate. "Would you mind if I had a chair and a glass of water? I am rather thirsty. There's an office we could go to through that door over there," Zhao said, pointing a hand toward the door behind him.

"How about my friend asks you a couple questions, and if I like your answers, we'll look into getting you a chair and drink," Marissa countered.

"I just had an old friend try to kill me. I'll tell you what I can," Zhao said with a shrug.

Sarah stuck her hands in her pockets. "We're looking for a missing American serviceman…"

ISAAC

"James Taylor or Matthew Hassan?" Zhao cut her off before she could finish her question.

Someone is eager to be helpful.

A dip of Sarah's head indicated he should continue.

"They're on their way to the airport. We're moving them to a different facility."

The frustration and futility of it hit. Jimmy had been in Hong Kong after all. We'd come so close, only to just miss him. However, there was no place they could take him that I wouldn't try and get him back.

The first step was to find out where Jimmy and this other guy were being taken. "Do you know where they're headed?" I asked.

The old Chinese spy bobbed his head. "We have a site in the United States."

My brain struggled to process what I'd just heard. They were being moved to the USA for further detention and questioning. The audacity of a foreign power having a secret prison in the US was mind-blowing. I'd heard of a lot of crazy things, but that took the cake. We had covert locations in other countries, of course, but the situation wasn't supposed to be reversed. Although I had to admit it was perfect, who would think to look for Chinese prisoners in America?

"Where in the United States?"

"A large farm near Laughlin Air Force in Texas. Taylor and Hassan believe the United States has negotiated their release, and they are being taken there to be debriefed."

Sarah pulled her phone out of her back pocket. "I need to call Naomi." Holstering her Glock she walked toward the back of the warehouse, the opposite direction from where we'd entered.

With any luck, Naomi could get the FBI Hostage Rescue Team to go pick them up from the airport when they landed. I was again thankful that the CIA agent was no longer angry about being kicked out of the meeting in Miami. I guess there's something about being saved from Russian mercenaries that helps to patch up hurt feelings.

Zhao's immediate answers had the ring of a man telling the truth. That left me to address the elephant in the room. "Why are you telling us this?"

239

I'd been confident we could wring the truth from him, but this felt too easy.

"Because none of it matters." The room suddenly felt cold, and I wouldn't have been surprised to see frost creeping along the edges of the containers. The only reason to stop caring was either a terminal diagnosis or an impending event of apocalyptic proportions.

Hopefully, it's cancer, and he's setting his affairs in order.

I'd seen enough battlefield interrogators to know *how* you asked the question was often just as important as *what* you asked. I was also self-aware enough to realize I often didn't phrase things the best way possible. I took a moment to consider my words before speaking again. Zhao had a story he wanted to tell. I just needed to provide him with an audience.

"Could you explain what you mean by that?"

Zhao accepted the invitation with a zeal most often displayed by dictators and criminal masterminds reciting their manifestos.

"Humanity is killing the planet. If allowed to run unchecked, nothing will be left for future generations. Fossil fuels will be gone in fifty years. The oceans are being fished to extinction while oxygen-giving forests are being clear-cut. Precious metals and minerals are being strip-mined without consideration for the damage left behind." Zhao paced like a caged animal, now caught up in his diatribe. I'd learned that with fanatics, it was best to let them say their piece before asking more questions.

Marissa moved close beside me and whispered in my ear, "This guy is nuts."

I wasn't so sure. He was undoubtedly dogmatic, but thus far, everything he'd said was factual and logical.

"The carbon pollution is creating a greenhouse effect that is heating the planet to never before seen levels. All of this to facilitate the convenience of life for a minority of the world's population. Globalization and technology are killing us. We fight wars and kill hundreds of thousands to maintain these lifestyles of selfishness." He looked at me with the fervor of a Sunday Morning preacher trying to reach the lost. Then, like a light switching off, it was gone. The fire in his eyes transformed to sadness or maybe pity. His shoulders slumped, leaving behind a tired old man.

"The Eden Initiative will provide a much-needed reset and help the world return to sustainable small community lifestyles. It will strike a blow and crush the technology that keeps us from being responsible caretakers of this place. Technology is a poison that must be eliminated for the host to survive." Zhao's voice was weary. This man saw the problem, but no longer believed in whatever solution he'd apparently helped to set in motion.

I shrugged. "I don't disagree with you. We certainly could make better use of the resources we have. How would this Eden Initiative fix the problem?"

"By taking down the GPS satellites and the internet."

And the award for most ambitious evil plan goes to The Eden Initiative.

The next question was easy. There wasn't any other way to ask it. "How?" There were a lot of qualifiers I could have added, but Zhao seemed to be feeling talkative right now, so I'd let him fill in the blanks.

"A missile launch against three strategic satellites. Their destruction will trigger a cascade that destroys every satellite in orbit. I believe Alexander called it the Kessler Effect."

I didn't even pretend to understand. Missiles were going to knock out satellites and somehow that would destroy the internet? I knew the world was heavily dependent on GPS. I could imagine how loss of that capability alone would have dire consequences. I didn't know enough to follow up on the technical stuff, so I continued gathering intelligence where I could.

"Where are these missiles being launched from?"

"North Korea."

That made sense. They certainly checked the requisite lunatic box.

"When is the launch?"

Probably already underway given my current luck.

"I'm not sure. I don't think they have the capabilities yet." I fought the urge to breathe a sigh of relief. It was possible, even probable that he was lying.

"Who is Alexander?"

The question seemed to confuse Zhao for a moment. As though the answer should be obvious. "Alexander. He is the one who devised this solution. Alexander Greggor." Beside me, Marissa stiffened and muttered something too softly for me to catch.

There's a name I'm familiar with.

I thought I knew the answer based on Marissa's reaction, but it wouldn't hurt to confirm. "Is he any relation to a Charles Greggor?"

"Yes, of course. Charles is his son."

"I'm going to kill him," Marissa hissed.

Alexander and Charles Greggor. I had to admit, they made quite the pair. While the son had been busy running one of the largest illegal arms networks in the world, the father was preoccupied with trying to return the planet to the Stone Age.

Marissa's hand suddenly flew behind her back, bringing her Glock out to aim at something behind me. I spun, doing the same, and searching for threats.

At the corner of a stack of containers stood what I could only assume were two warehouse workers. The men were frozen, staring. But not at us. I realized they were transfixed by the sight of the Sicilian lying slaughtered on the concrete floor.

My mind returned to that day in Iraq when I had to make the choice between killing a child or allowing the mission to be compromised. Letting the young boy live had nearly cost the lives of my entire team, and we'd only been saved because a couple of helicopter pilots disobeyed direct orders.

I reached out and pushed Marissa's gun down while lowering my own. The spell broke and the men took off running for the exit.

Marissa looked at me in disbelief.

"They're going to call the police the first chance they get," she said.

I shrugged. "We won't be here when they arrive. I'm not killing innocents." I had enough problems sleeping without adding murder to the pile.

"Four, this is Two. We need immediate evacuation; we've been compromised."

"Copy. Four is on the move. Thirty seconds out."

I nudged Zhao toward the door. Marissa fell in behind us, taking up rear security. By the time we arrived at the entrance, Sarah waited beside the open sliding door of the panel van. This was the moment of truth. Would

Zhao cooperate or attempt to make a run for it? I placed my hand on his shoulder, reminding him of the right decision.

He stepped inside the vehicle without complaint. Moments later, we were moving.

Mike's voice came over the team net. "I just intercepted a dispatch. Police are en route to your location." As if on cue, the klaxon of police sirens began to wail. I couldn't tell if they were coming from multiple directions or the sound was just bouncing off the buildings.

"Do they have a description of our vehicle?" Sarah asked.

"Not that I can find. They're just being vectored to the warehouse. The report was the discovery of a body."

"Good copy. Keep us updated. I want you and Selma to move to the safe house as soon as possible. We need to plan our next move."

I'd transported my fair share of prisoners and they were as diverse as the honorees at the International Cheese Awards. Some gave way at the slightest poke. Others were hard. Many had been rather unpleasant, while more than a couple who'd been initially declared a great prize just stank. Zhao was like a nice Monterey Jack. He was mild, holding his form while sitting quietly in his seat, but he'd melt as soon as any heat was applied.

"Already on our way," Mike said.

The thirty-minute drive felt interminable, as I waited on high alert for us to be intercepted. Several times police vehicles went screaming by on the other side of the highway. It was a matter of moments before they received a description of our van and we would be swarmed with police, the back doors ripped open, and a dozen barrels from a Hong Kong SWAT team aimed at us.

However, for some reason, the universe decided to let us have a win. Maybe it restored an equilibrium that had been upset by our just missing Jimmy. The universe, fate, or whoever pulled the strings could plan anything they wanted. I would be getting Jimmy back.

Throughout my career of providing involuntary relocation assistance, most places I'd stayed weren't getting five stars on Airbnb. Our current safe house was a different story. It was a luxury walled villa just off Golden Beach.

The front entrance of intricately carved oak double doors opened into a white marble floored atrium. I stared in disbelief at the crown molding around the top of the wall. Selma had only just closed the door behind us when Mike looked up from his laptop.

"Isaac. This place has an infinity pool."

Way to lead with the important stuff.

"Okay, so what are we going to do with Zhao?" I asked.

Sarah took Zhao by the elbow and started leading him down one of the hallways. "We're going to get Mr. Zhao something to eat and drink, then…" A loud double thump on the door interrupted Sarah.

Battering ram.

In unison Sarah, Marissa, Derek, and I drew our weapons.

"Get ready to move to the vehicles. We'll punch through," Sarah said her French accent coming on strong.

Derek turned and grabbed Mike by the shirt, hauling him off the couch. I moved to the front door as twin thuds hit it again.

Any moment the windows would shatter with flash bangs, smoke, or even teargas if the guys outside were in a nasty mood. I felt the urge to apologize to the house for the damage our presence was about to elicit.

I grabbed the handle to whip one door open so we could commence a counterattack. The force on the other side would not be prepared for the tsunami of death about to make landfall. I was under no illusion we'd all make it out alive. The amount of firepower we were facing would be overwhelming. But there was a chance at least one of us would survive.

Going down swinging was a far better choice than meekly surrendering to the Chinese authorities. A whole team of American murder suspects would be a propaganda gold mine. Our trial would be public and the outcome inevitable. The United States wouldn't be able to do anything even if they had the inclination.

Every muscle in my body tensed, ready for the hail of bullets to come. My finger moved from the slide toward the trigger, as I flung the door wide.

Instead of the stacked tactical unit I expected to see, Naomi stood on the stoop, fist raised for another thunderous knock. Her eyes widened as she took in the scene.

"Not the welcome I was expecting," she said, as though having someone almost shoot her at the door was a regular occurrence.

"Keep banging on the door like you're the SWAT team," I grumbled, holstering my pistol.

"I wasn't expecting you for another hour or so," Sarah looking relieved not to be shooting it out with the Chinese authorities.

Naomi shrugged and strolled in, an iPad in one hand and Clark following closely. They were such an odd couple. A skinny Spanish man and a powerfully built Jewish woman. Clark had always been quiet and rational, a counterbalance to Naomi's evident struggles with anger management. Mismatched pair notwithstanding, they were a welcome sight, given what I'd been expecting.

"Welcome to the party. Too bad we're all late," I said.

Naomi ignored me. Her eyes scanned the room until she found Mike. Derek still held his pistol at the low ready, standing protectively in front of the hacker.

"Mike, I have something I need you to look at for me," she said holding up the iPad. Mike tentatively stepped out from behind Derek, like a small child being offered candy by a doctor.

"You should probably sit down," Naomi said pointing to the couch. Mike complied and Naomi swiped the device and tapped an icon. A face appeared on the screen.

"Hey buddy," a deep voice I'd recognize anywhere rumbled out of the speaker. The room hung in suspended animation.

"Hello. Can you hear me?" Jimmy asked from the other side of the screen. I felt myself shudder and I was forced to blink once or twice to combat the stinging sensation at the corners of my eyes. I looked at Mike and saw he'd already lost that battle. A stream of tears ran unchecked down his face, dripping off his cheeks onto the screen.

"Jimmy? Jimmy, is that really you?" Mike whispered.

"Yeah, buddy, it's me. I'm on a plane headed home. I'm going to be real busy for the next little while, so I wanted to call you while I had the chance."

Derek and I moved behind Mike so we could get a better view of Jimmy. He looked better than he had in the proof of life video, but his eyes were still tired and haggard. The relief I felt was palpable. He was safe.

When Jimmy caught sight of us he broke into a huge smile. I gave him a quick left-handed salute and Derek waved.

"Hey man, it's great to see you. I'm going to leave you to Mike, but we'll catch up later," I said.

As much as I wanted, needed to talk to Jimmy, Mike needed him more. There would be time later. Derek and I moved away from the iPad, giving the brothers space.

I looked around and found that Clark, Marissa, and Zhao were no longer in the room. Sarah and Naomi stood together a respectful distance away.

"They moved Zhao down the hall for questioning," Naomi said in answer to my unasked question. I nodded. Clark would be able to get the necessary information from Zhao to stop the impending end of the modern world.

"So what happened? Zhao told us Jimmy was on a Chinese plane headed to a secret facility in the US," I said.

Naomi's grin was predatory. "When Sarah called to inform me of your travel plans, she provided the intel we needed to corroborate the evidence Clark and I had gathered. So, we got approval to bring a team and had a bit of luck. There was a unit I've worked with on several occasions that had just arrived back from a deployment. Once they knew the mission, they were more than happy to grab their guns and get back on a plane."

I shook my head in disbelief. "That's incredible."

Naomi nodded. "Yeah and we still almost didn't make it in time. Turns out the plane Zhao had ready to fly to the US was being operated by mercenaries posing as the Department of State. After Sarah called from the warehouse, we had a brief altercation with them that ended about 20 minutes before Jimmy's convoy arrived. We killed five mercenaries before the rest surrendered. He'll spend some time at Bethesda Naval Hospital, and there will be a few days of debriefing with various agencies, but yes, he is safe. He's back, thanks to you."

"Do I know anyone on the SAD team?" Sarah asked.

"The team leader is Tony Fleckman. I didn't know anyone else," Naomi said.

"Zhao mentioned another guy. I think his name was Matt something?"

"Matt Hassan, yes. He was also presumed dead after the raid. We have him too, but you didn't hear that from me. Officially, no one other than Jimmy is being repatriated. The Agency already had a ceremony and carved a star on the wall for Hassan," Naomi said.

I supposed they would just reassign it to the next CIA employee who died in the line of duty. It might be the first time in history that the same star had been attributed to two people. That would create a lot of exciting paperwork as it seemed unlikely there was an administrative process in place to bring someone back from the dead.

Excuse me, sir, I'm going to need you to fill out boxes 1-6, 8, and 14 on form DD-9573.13 Resurrection and Death Reversals.

Looking to Sarah I asked, "What happened to 'unsanctioned and totally illegal?'"

Sarah shrugged. "I decided Peregrine didn't have the resources to maintain a persistent surveillance presence in Hong Kong, so I called Naomi. A definite risk, but we were already on the move. There was no time for her to stop us. The possible benefits of having her in the loop could give us the little extra we needed to make this work."

It was remarkable how fast Naomi had reacted. Requisitioning a CIA paramilitary team just landing from deployment was absolute kismet. As fast as it was, it almost hadn't been fast enough. A thought I tried to ignore.

"This is all crazier than my trip to New York City," Marissa muttered. Naomi's head snapped around, eyes narrowing to stare at her former colleague.

"What did you do in New York?" Naomi asked.

I had my own suspicions, but the tension started feeling a bit thick.

"Did you take a helicopter on a joyride?"

Marissa cracked a smile. "Maybe."

"Have you visited Turks and Caicos recently?" Naomi asked with a raised eyebrow.

Marissa winked at her. "I can neither confirm nor deny."

* * *

Gulfstream G-650 - Over the Baltic Sea

Naomi lay stretched out on one of the jet's two couches. "If this is how you travel in the private sector, I'm seriously considering giving my two-week notice."

Sarah laughed and shook her head. "I wouldn't be in business for more than two weeks if this was how we traveled the whole time."

Derek glared at Naomi. "I'm glad we're convenient transportation for you. Oh yeah, thanks for your constant vigilance and tireless work to keep America safe."

Naomi flashed him a fake smile. Despite her and Sarah working out their differences, Derek and the CIA agent were still at odds.

Derek looked like he had a reply but instead stormed off.

"Why is he so mad at everyone?" Mike asked, looking up from his laptop. You could always count on Mike to say the quiet parts out loud.

I shrugged. "I don't know, buddy. What I do know is, I'm looking forward to this trip. Being in Europe will be a nice reprieve."

"Speaking of this trip," Sarah said, jumping into the conversation. "Can we review this contract again? You told me the highlights but not the details. I've had enough of operating on a wing and prayer."

Naomi sat up, swinging out her legs. "Analysts have determined that North Korea doesn't yet have the capabilities to take out critical satellites, despite the one they launched and destroyed. NASA is assessing possible constellation configurations that would make the Kessler Effect more unlikely. The fact of the matter is that it's already improbable."

"But not impossible?" I asked.

"It's hard to say anything is impossible, but it has given Space Force a new mission. Developing a plan to defend satellites," Naomi said.

"But the North Koreans could still develop the technology and shoot at these targets," Sarah said.

Naomi nodded conceding the point.

Great. Crazy Uncle Kim is still a possible threat to end the world. Then again, that's been true since they acquired nukes.

"And the rods from God?" I asked. I could only imagine the chaos that revelation had unleashed. Lots of people would be fired for failing to stop literal WMDs from being put into space. At the same time, there would be committees focused on everything from their destruction to plans for taking control of them.

Naomi shrugged. "That's not my department. My focus is elsewhere. We are confident that we have prevented the destruction of the GPS system, but we would still like to have a complete picture of the scope of the Eden Initiative. We believe only Alexander Greggor possesses that perspective and he's still in Europe. The NSA has been unable to shut down the satellites remotely. It has to be assumed that Greggor still has control of the targeting and firing mechanism. His capture is our highest priority. Unofficially, I can tell you a sizable bounty will be placed on him. The CIA would like Peregrine to join the hunt."

"So, we're bounty hunters now?" I asked, winking at Marissa.

"And this time, it's true," Marissa quipped. When I'd been a stowaway on a plane chasing the younger Greggor, I'd told Marissa I was a bounty hunter.

Sarah ignored the banter. "How would that work?"

"MerchWork has a global reach and operations in all of the major logistics hubs worldwide. We will be offering you a contract to conduct an in-depth security evaluation of our global facilities," Naomi said.

The contract was a nice touch. It would provide us with the needed cover and access to CIA resources.

"What about her?" I asked, hooking a thumb at Marissa.

Naomi looked at Marissa. "MerchWork would like to extend an employment offer. Due to the size of the contract being signed with Peregrine, we require a full-time liaison. I think you would be the best fit for the job. That would, of course, mean terminating your freelance contract with the Central Intelligence Agency."

Marissa looked like Christmas morning had come early. "I accept."

33

Isaac

Copenhagen, Denmark - Two weeks later.

The sprawling upscale neighborhood of Østerbro was trendy in all the right ways. The tree-lined streets and brick buildings gave a small-town feel to the Danish capital. Bicycles zipped by in the designated bike lanes, which helped to set Copenhagen apart as the most bike-friendly city in the world. Almost 50% of work commutes happened on bikes. They were used for everything from transporting people to cargo. The sheer number of bike types was mind-boggling. They came in just about every configuration imaginable.

The contract with the Federal Reserve was complicated, but all our contracts had an exigent circumstances clause. The provision allowed us to pause or exit a contract penalty-free if our services were engaged by the United States government in the interest of national security. The Fed had agreed to a six-month hiatus before we had to reassess and rebid the contract. That was a job I was looking forward to doing, but for now we had a fugitive to capture…for the sake of national security.

The hunt for Alexander Greggor had taken us to London, Zurich, and Vaduz, Liechtenstein. But with each lead, we arrived just a little too late. We'd learned that during his younger days, he'd worked as a Swiss intelligence operative for the Strategic Intelligence Service. With his spy craft and nearly unlimited resources, he could be anywhere in the world. The United States was working on freezing his assets, but through his work with Banque Suisse, Alexander had spent decades moving and hiding money on behalf of both governments and criminals. It was foolish to think he didn't have a fortune of his own stashed away.

The clue that brought us to Copenhagen had been a minor one at that. A detail anyone other than Mike might have missed. A third-floor apartment owned by a holding company controlled by Banque Suisse showed a sudden increase in water and power consumption.

The buildings on the street held a hybrid mix of tenants. Businesses occupied the ground floors, while the upper floors were largely residential spaces. It was a situation with ample opportunity for surveillance and minimal risk of detection.

We'd seen signs of life in the apartment. Still, we could not confirm beyond a shadow of a doubt that the person living there was Alexander Greggor. The frequent food and grocery deliveries to the surrounding buildings had given us the idea to pose as Wolt delivery drivers, who were everywhere around the city. The sight of them zipping around on their mopeds was so common that most people stopped noticing them.

"Four is in position," Derek called over the net. He was stationed two blocks down on a motorized bike with a large flat cargo space.

"Three is on the move. ETA one minute," Marissa said, the buzz of her moped coming through the comms as she spoke.

Sarah and I walked down the street, appearing to all the world to be Danish parents pushing a pram. "One and Two are approaching from the north," I called.

Marissa whipped onto the sidewalk, parking the moped in front of a bakery window next to the apartment entrance. Sarah and I were still fifty feet away, crossing in front of a Thai restaurant on the other side of the doorway.

"I'm in," Marissa said, holding the door for us. We quickly closed the gap and entered the building's ground-floor atrium. Marissa handed Sarah and me pistols and tasers retrieved from her insulated food carrier. Parking the stroller against the wall, we moved up the curved staircase toward the third floor. When we reached the door, Marissa pulled out her lock pick kit and began to work while I covered her and Sarah watched the stairs.

I had always prided myself on my lockpicking skills, but Marissa was done so fast that I would have sworn she used a key if I hadn't been watching. She swung the entry door open without a sound. I moved in, weapon up. The objective was to take Greggor, Sr. alive. Our plan was to knock him out and pack him in a container. Derek would then ride up on his bike, and we'd load up and transport him the mile and a half to the port facility.

We moved through the entryway into the dining room, our feet silent on the herringbone wood floor. Doorways opened to the left and right, and I signaled to Sarah to cover the left while I went right. Turning the corner, I saw the top of a silver head peeking over the back of an over-stuffed armchair. He seemed unaware that anyone was with him in the house. I moved left, and Marissa went right as we came around the sides of the chair.

"Alexander Greggor, I presume?" I had his face memorized, but at the moment the physical resemblance to his son Charles was uncanny.

The elder Greggor slowly folded the Wall Street Journal he was reading into a perfect rectangle. Turning his gaze on Marissa, he spoke in a calm, measured tone. "It's good to see you, my dear. It's been too long."

Marissa's face was inscrutable.

"Your resignation was unfortunate and created considerable complication," Greggor went on, still addressing Marissa as if no one else was in the room. "Your loyalty to your former Project Olympus teammate is admirable, but misguided."

Marissa stared at him as though he were a coiled snake, her hand tightening on the grip of her pistol. At that moment, I remembered her saying she would kill him if she ever saw him again.

"I never told you about Project Olympus. I never told anyone." Her voice cold.

This bomb needs to be defused. We need him alive.

Moving to her side, I placed my hand on her wrist as Alexander chuckled. "When you move in the circles I do, there are very few things that are true secrets. I knew all about Project Olympus long before you came into my employ. I was one of its strongest supporters. Your last mission led to the disbandment of the unit, but your actions were just. Still, they threw you away like a bit of rubbish. I spent considerable money and influence to cancel the termination order against you so I could hire you myself. I haven't been able to replace you, you know. No one else can fill your shoes."

Project Olympus? A Swiss Banker supporting a CIA black-ops wet work team?

The smile may have been meant to appear benevolent and grandfatherly, but what I saw was the grin of the Mako shark swimming at me. This man was a true apex predator.

I was startled by Sarah reappearing in the doorway, after having cleared the rest of the house. Her weapon was at the low ready, but she stood back, watching the scene play out.

In my experience, the devil doesn't show up in a cape with horns and a pitchfork. He's the best-looking, smoothest-talking guy around. The one who makes you feel like he's your best friend. The ultimate trap is doing what he wants, all while believing it was your idea. Alexander's manipulation was subtle, gently plucking on the strings of loyalty.

He sat up straight, body language projecting authority without being aggressive. "You didn't have to run, you know. I know there was nothing you could do to save Charles. Mr. Northe and his partner are highly skilled adversaries, and Ms. Powers is a formidable opponent. It would have been a tactical mistake to make an enemy of her by killing Mr. Northe and Mr. Russo. I wish you'd come to me right away. I was never your enemy."

This guy is smooth and I might have already lost this fight.

Alexander's verbal prowess was nothing short of awe-inspiring. His praise for the people she was working with was disarming. He seemed to have always been on Team Marissa.

He was a snake hanging from a tree lying about a piece of fruit. It was time for this to end. I was pulling the taser from my pocket when Sarah tapped her earpiece answering a phone call "Hello?"

Alexander folded his hands and watched dispassionately as I stepped toward him with the taser.

ISAAC

Something's off. He doesn't seem the least bit concerned.

"Isaac, wait." Sarah held up a hand. I stopped, my anger rising. I knew what was happening even before she finished the phone conversation. From his body language Alexander had known before we entered the apartment.

Sarah's voice carried all the emotion of addressing the pizza delivery guy. "I understand. Thanks."

She turned to address Marissa and me. "It seems Mr. Greggor has brokered a deal with the US Government and surrendered control of the satellites and their weapons. Our work here is done," she said with a twirl of her finger. Angrily I shoved the taser back into my pocket. I didn't have the words or conscious feelings to be able to properly articulate the corruption and miscarriage of justice this situation represented.

This wasn't the first time I'd experienced a target's designation change, but in every other case it was during the planning phase or while en route. Never during the takedown. I clenched my teeth and balled my fist. This abomination had tried to send the world back to the stone age and I was supposed to just let him go.

Alexander's look was smug as he flicked his hand with a shooing gesture. "I trust you can find your own way out."

I'd gone to war and watched my brothers die in dirty streets that ran with raw sewage because nineteen terrorists had hijacked four airplanes on September 11, 2001. The subsequent loss of life would seem rather pedestrian compared to what this soulless ghoul had planned.

Over the last two weeks I'd learned how intimately involved Alexander had been in the actions of the drone strike that had killed twelve Americans, as well as his role in Jimmy's imprisonment by the Chinese. He needed to pay a bigger price than just having his apocalyptic toys taken away. I was sure if I looked in a mirror I'd see a red-eyed prehistoric wolf staring back, its teeth bared in a snarl.

I was sick and tired of the wealthy and powerful doing whatever they wanted and facing no consequences. When a few dozen soldiers stole several hundred thousand dollars from the Bank in Iraq they had been prosecuted with extreme prejudice. However, when Private Military Companies and contractors siphoned off and embezzled millions, they were given more contracts and a solemn *'Thank you for serving America'*. Justice wasn't blind, she'd traded her sword for a luxury house in Malibu.

Alexander's eyes widened and his face went white. My gun was in my hand. I didn't remember drawing it.

"ISAAC!" Sarah's voice cut through the haze of rage. Her gun was out too, but instead of being pointed at Alexander, it was leveled at me. Beside me, a blur of motion told me Marissa had drawn her weapon and was now pointing it at Sarah.

"What are you doing? You'd shoot me to protect this…."

Sarah interrupted me. "No. I'll let you shoot him. He's an obscenity that deserves much worse than just being shot. I will kill you to stop you from becoming a monster." I looked into Sarah's eyes and saw the resolve. Her motives were pure and I knew if I pulled the trigger I'd be killing Alexander, Sarah and myself. The journey from life to death for three of us could be traversed with less than an inch of trigger travel.

I drew a ragged breath, nodded, and holstered my weapon.

Alexander looked relieved, and less smug than before. But my anger still needed a vent. I lashed out with a kick to Alexander's chest. The impact knocked the chair on its back. His head cracked against the floor and he lay there not moving.

"Did you just kill him?" Sarah asked. I walked about the chair and found his pulse.

"Nope."

Sarah moved from where she stood, her gaze locked on Marissa. "I've never told you this, but you did the right thing on that last mission. It didn't matter if it was sanctioned. Also, he wasn't lying to you. There was a kill order that was squashed. Naomi and I didn't know anything about it until after you disappeared."

Marissa's lower lip quivered. Her nostrils flared for a split second as she took a deep breath, and just like that she appeared to be back in control. She pointed at Alexander slumped on the floor.

"He's evil and deserves to die…"

ISAAC

"I know, but that would wreck our vacation plans," I said.

Marissa looked at me with a tentative smile. "We have vacation plans?"

"We do now," I confirmed.

Epilogue

Baros, Maldives - Three days later.

Marissa and I lay on lounge chairs basking in the sunshine on the deck of an overwater villa. The cloudless sky and clear blue waters combined to make a magic that was rarely found outside of a Disney fairy tale. Between the sun and salty breeze, I'd dried off quickly from my recent swim, but the water was calling to me again.

The bounty the CIA paid us made me feel like I was accepting blood money for the murder of my morals. I hadn't resigned from Peregrine, but I had told Sarah I needed some time to think about things. Marissa and I arrived here yesterday and were booked for the next two weeks. I wasn't sure if I'd return to Miami at the end of this trip or find another place to go. Maybe I'd go to Thailand and get some great Pho. Who knew, Marissa might even come with me.

"This is so gorgeous," Marissa gushed, cradling her camera carefully, ignoring the book in her lap. I hoped she brought enough memory cards for all the photos she was taking. I'd never seen her look so at peace.

"Lot better than being dead," I said.

"Considerably better than being dead," Marissa agreed, setting the camera aside to take a sip of the whiskey sitting on the table next to her. Ice clinked pleasantly in the crystal tumbler. Raising her glass she offered a toast. "To not becoming monsters."

I saluted her with my own drink. "To not becoming monsters."

The End

About the Author

David Scott was born in Lincoln, Nebraska, but grew up in a New Jersey suburb. He served for more than 12 years in the US military. His first four years were with the Marine Corps during which time he deployed to Japan, Afghanistan, and twice to Iraq. Leaving the Marines, he worked at the Internal Revenue Service while attending college. David then joined the US Army to become a Black Hawk helicopter pilot. After the Army, he worked as a software developer. When not writing, he works as a podcast editor. He lives in Tulsa, OK with his wife and two daughters.

You can connect with me on:
- https://davidscottbooks.net
- https://www.facebook.com/davidscottbooks
- https://www.instagram.com/davidscottbooks

Subscribe to my newsletter:
- https://davidscottbooks.net/mailing-list

Also by David Scott

"David Scott writes steady and confident as someone who has been in the writing world for a long time. His prose is elegantly crisp without meandering away from the main goal of entertaining readers with a fast-paced story."

  - Kashif Hussain, Best Thriller Books

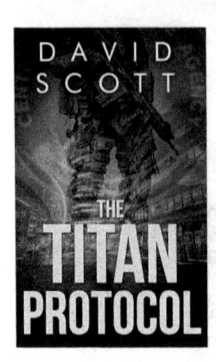

The Titan Protocol

A special ops mission in Nigeria falls apart when the raiding force sustains massive casualties from a rogue drone strike. It's another dead lead for the CIA's operation to uncover an international arms smuggling ring and prevent a cache of state-of-the-art AI weapons from ending up in terrorist hands.

The one person neither the CIA nor the smuggler counted on was Isaac Northe, recovering alcoholic and former special forces.

Isaac breaks into corporate installations for a living. A job for a defense contractor places him in the middle of the hunt. He will need all his skills to survive the assassin and army of mercenaries sent to erase the trail.

A Royal Complication

A CIA program code-named Project Olympus targets a member of the Saudi Royal family for elimination. The assassins find their attempt complicated when the butler shows up at exactly the wrong time.

CPSIA information can be obtained
at www.ICGtesting.com
Printed in the USA
BVHW051949180523
664437BV00009B/133

9 798986 323251